Praise for The Candlemaker's Woman

The Candlemaker's Woman got me at page one. This meticulously researched novel, set against a background of fifth-century upheaval, tells of Melia, a young woman sold into slavery to a brutal candlemaker. *The Candlemaker's Woman* is a story of war, of betrayal, of bigotry, and of love won and lost and won again. Charlier's skillful writing and commanding sense of history are evident in this superb novel of a woman who fights to remain unbroken by bondage and the prejudices of medieval Europe.
- Sandra Dallas, *New York Times* best-selling author

Charlier skillfully immerses you into the shadows of Europe in the early Middle Ages to tell the story of Melia, sold into slavery by her Germanic tribe. It is a story of ruthless enemies and unexpected alliances — but also of Melia's courage amidst upheaval. At its heart, this is an evocative tale of resilience, hope, and the enduring power of love during the darkest times.
- Ana Veciana-Suarez, best-selling author of *Dulcinea*

A coming-of-age story, a mother-and-daughter drama that will have readers turning pages long past bedtime ... Facing hardship and cruelty, Melia's resilience had me rooting for her, chapter after chapter. Well-imagined, dramatic, and immersive, the author's descriptions of the time and place are a marvel. Coupled with crisp pacing and vibrant prose, it's a five-star experience.
– Lynne M. Spreen, award-winning author of contemporary women's fiction

Readers' Favorite (c) Reviews

Author Marj Charlier has created a wonderful character in Melia. Her determination to survive and eventually achieve her freedom regardless of the horrific acts perpetrated on her was inspiring. That she was able to rise above the pain and suffering and maintain her positive attitude to life was wonderful. I particularly appreciated how much more difficult it was for a woman to survive in these brutal times. Not only was she considered fair game to her master, but even men from her tribe often considered women to be theirs for the taking. To be branded a whore merely because she was raped by her master was perhaps the ultimate insult. The author's corollary between the mass migrations of fifth century Europe and current world events was insightful and thought-provoking. As she so eruditely pointed out, we all came from somewhere. This is a wonderful read, an exciting adventure, and a sweet romance all rolled into one, with a telling moral twist in the tail that makes it stand out amongst its peers. I can highly recommend this read.
– Grant Leishman

Lovers of historical wars, romance, and action stories will enjoy this book. The narrative is fast-paced but the author sometimes applies a slow tempo to pile on the suspense. This novel also explores themes like loyalty, deception, love, courage, patience, and compromise. I loved the plot and development of thestory as it would make anyone think about their faith. When Fritigil's situation with the twins happened, I asked why God let bad things happen to good people. Marj Charlier wrote a movie-worthy novel. Melia was quite spirited and brave at thirteen. She also grew into a brilliant, strong, and empathetic woman. She never lost her essence. However, nothing Greta did would redeem her in my eyes. Melia's brother, Ballomar, was the only kin worthy of her loyalty. I really enjoyed this book.
–Jennifer Ibiam

... a deeply moving story that transports readers to a tumultuous period in history with resonant detail and atmosphere right from the start. The portrayal of Melia's resilience amidst adversity is accomplished, with nuanced touches to the dialogue and thought presentation that showcase the enduring power of the human spirit in the face of unimaginable challenges. The historical backdrop of mass migration and societal upheaval is well-researched and translates onto the page with all its complexity and intricacies, highlighting the emotional themes of displacement, resilience, and the quest for love and family.
– K.C. Finn

... transported me back in time to AD 405 05 in central Europe, and I lived in that era from the first page to the last. The characters, especially Melia, were so brilliantly drawn, the descriptions of her life, from the slave block in Mogantiacum to the villa in Gaul, were so vibrant that I was there with her every step of the way. The tension built again and again, leaving me quite breathless. I could not tear myself awayfrom this book. Yes, it is brutal, yet it is also a love story. Most of all, it reminded me of the harsh way of life in that period of European history. I learned so much about those times and how hard it was to survive. I loved this book and hope there might be a sequel.
– Lucinda E. Clarke,

... a compelling coming-of-age story with interesting characters ... The pace flows smoothly and the story is very well written with surprising plot twists. The history of this period of the fall of the Roman Empire is fascinating. I learned so much about the various Barbarian tribes. I did not know very much about this period in history, but Charlier's mesmerizing storytelling skills sparked my interest in the Germania tribes migrating across the lands and changing history. ... an absorbing read that will both entertain and educate readers.
– Christine Nguyen

THE CANDLEMAKER'S WOMAN

THE CANDLEMAKER'S WOMAN

MARJ CHARLIER

SUNACUMEN
PRESS

Published by Sunacumen Press
Colorado Springs, CA

ISBN: 978-1-7345643-7-2

To all of my writer friends who share my insecurities,
frustrations, doubts, rejections, and barriers, but
persevere because they have to write.

PART 1
SLAVERY

THE AUCTION

The children cling to the iron bars that surround three sides of the auction block, staring out at the crowd. Melia stands clear of them, faint from hunger, thumping her empty stomach with one fist, clutching her dirty cape to her shoulders with the other.

Weary and annoyed, she questions the necessity of the cage. Do the slavemasters think the children might jump down from the stand and escape with ropes around their ankles? That they could flee through the throng of greedy bidders that surrounds them?

Melia rubs the reddening tattoo that the auctioneer seared into her forearm that morning, marking her as a slave, and shivers in her thin dress and filthy fur. What little heat her thin body generates is sucked away by the frigid fog of the morning and the cold stone platform. If she's too tired and sore to run, too hungry to think, surely the young children are, too.

They sniffle and whine around her. She hates them all.

For weeks, they had crouched together for warmth in the open wagons, rumbling over rutted dirt roads toward the Rhine. Some like Melia were sold to slave traders in return for their tribesmen's permission to pass through Burgundian territory toward Gaul. Others were kidnapped from settlements along the way.

They had come to despise each other as much as they feared their bearded captors. With only bites of hard bread to eat and filthy water to drink, they fought and crawled over each other to grab the crusts thrown at them, clawing at each other's faces. The older children slapped the toddlers when they shat or made water in the wagons. The misery and terror forced the youngest into silence. Eventually, they all lost their voice for protest. By the time they reached the bridge over the Rhine, none retained any love for another—even those who had been friends back in their villages.

The oldest among them, Melia expects to be shoved to the front of the block for sale first—her immediate value, her ability to work, obvious—but the auctioneer reaches into the squalid group and grabs a set of twins instead. He pushes the boys forward and cracks a whip behind their backs, snarling with malice. The boys jump, cringe, and duck. The few dozen men and women gathered for bidding guffaw and snicker.

"We have here two robust ten-year-olds, ready to take on a man's work in the fields, in the bakery, in the slaughterhouse," the auctioneer calls out over the murmur of the crowd.

Ten? Melia shakes her head. They're eight if they're a year. How can these boys take on a man's work? They might have weighed forty pounds each when they were sold to the Burgundians; but they look smaller now. They will be expected to work, however. There's no pity for barbarian children.

"Can I get forty *denarii* for the pair?" the auctioneer bellows.

Over the month of their rough transport, Melia grew accustomed to the Burgundians' strange accent and words. This man sounds just as crude.

A few men shove their way to the front of the bidders below the platform and squint at the boys. One reaches up and pinches the nearest one's leg. The auctioneer flicks his whip at the trespasser. "You pay first!" he roars, to the crowd's delight.

"Thirty-five!" shouts a red-bearded man in the middle of the crowd.

"Forty!" the man next to him shouts. He's rewarded with a punch in the gut by his neighbor.

"Forty-five!" comes a cry from the back as the auctioneer teases the twins with the sting of his whip, grinning as he makes them skip. Possibly, these two boys will bring the highest price of the day. Fed well, they would be men in just a couple of years, whereas a buyer will have to feed and coddle most of the children for half a decade before they can earn their keep in Mogantiacum.

As the bids slowly rise for the two boys, Melia looks over the men gathered below. The bare-legged ones with close-cropped hair and beardless faces, dressed in white tunics with swords at their sides, are either soldiers or Gauls who have adopted Roman dress.

But most of the men look like her father, covered in trousers and long jackets, their hair tied up in a knot. A few others resemble the Burgundians who hauled them to Mogantiacum, their long red and yellow hair hanging in greasy strands around the shoulders. They wear cloaks of beaver and bear pelts and sheepskin. Long knives and axes hang off leather belts tied around ample bellies. Everyone on this side of the Rhine appears to eat well.

The women look like those of her village, too, except that decorative broaches at the neck hold their capes together over plain dresses. Only a few of the eldest women in her village have such elaborate ornaments.

If they look so much like the crowd milling around the square, what distinguishes Melia and the children as barbarians? The tattoos on her arm and on the boys' necks? Their skimpy clothing and rough cloaks? Their primitive broaches?

"Sold! Seventy *denarii*!" The auctioneer prods the boys off toward his money handler with the tip of his whip as if he were afraid to touch their filthy skin. He turns and points at Melia.

"You!" he shouts. "Woman! Step up!"

Melia hesitates, confused. Does "woman" mean something different here than it does in her village? She is thirteen, a girl, not a woman—as her mother had told men in the village who sought to take her to their huts. Her knees tremble, as she inches forward, the rope shackle chafing her legs.

"Aha! A stubborn little bitch here, huh, folks? Just waiting to be tamed!" The auctioneer laughs heartily and steps toward her, grabbing her arm, yanking her toward the front of the platform, and pulling off her cloak. He pulls a knife from his waist belt and slashes at the ropes to free her legs. With a quick flick of his wrist, he slits her tunic down the front, and it drops to the ground with her cloak.

"Look what we have here." He pinches one of her emerging breasts, still just a coin-sized pancake of a gland, and squeezes the nipple hard. Melia screams and pushes away, but he pulls her closer. She shakes involuntarily as his stench of sweat and urine fills her nostrils. She tries to cover herself with her free arm.

"I can attest that this young doe is a virgin," he calls out to the crowd, eliciting a murmur of approval from the men and hisses from the women. Melia glares at them. How can the auctioneer or anyone else know whether she has been with a man or not?

Perhaps the auctioneer saying so will raise her value, and that's all he cares about.

"Who would like to be the first lucky buck to defile this pretty little fawn?" Arms and shouts rise in the crowd.

"Twenty-five!"

"Thirty!"

"Forty!"

The auctioneer grins with pleasure at the robust bidding. He turns toward Melia and squeezes her other breast bud, this time adding a twist to the nipple with rough fingers. Her free arm flies out on its own accord and strikes him across his chest. His reaction is just as swift. In a heartbeat she is on her knees with his forearm locked under her chin.

"As I said!" He laughs, looking over her head at his audience. "A spirited little fawn!"

The audience howls.

"Bitch needs a cock!" A gruff voice from far back in the crowd.

"She's no virgin!" A woman's voice.

"Fifty *dinarii*!" A man.

"Fifty-five!" Another man.

Melia's eyes flood with tears. She can no longer see who shouts—insults or bids—but she now understands the men's interest in her, regardless what her official slave duties turn out to be.

"Sixty!" The bellow is followed by murmurs, but no more offers.

"Sold to the candlemaker!" The whip cracks behind her. "Sixty *denarii*."

WITHOUT A WORD SPOKEN BETWEEN them, Melia trails Hermann up a cobbled street, past rows of identical stucco buildings topped with red tile roofs. Near the top of the hill, he turns, grabs her freshly tattooed arm, and pushes her toward the front of a tall stone building. Tripping on a rough wood step, Melia stumbles into a tall, broad woman with heavy, sagging breasts and flabby arms. The big woman stands with her hands on her hips and scowls, blocking the door.

"How did she tear her dress? Was she trying to seduce you from the auction block?" The woman gurgles a giggle, her voice as contemptuous as the auctioneer's slurs, the dialect the same as the Burgundian. Melia keeps her head down and pulls her cloak tight over her bare chest, her teeth clattering in the cold.

"Shut up, Matildis!" Hermann roars. "You will give her one of your dresses. You have too many anyway."

"It will fall off her," the woman says, sneering. "She's not a woman yet. How much did you pay for this spindly bird?" Matildis doesn't budge from the doorway. "She's not going to be much help in the candle shop, will she?"

"She'll do just fine." Hermann steps in front of Melia and pushes Matildis back. The big woman trips over her soiled skirt and catches herself on a large vat in the middle of the room. Hermann reaches for Melia's arm again and pulls her into what looks like a candle shop and up a step into the building's living quarters, closing the door behind them.

As Hermann and Matildis argue over whether Melia was worth the sixty *dinarii* he paid for her, she takes in her surroundings. A large fire pit nestles up against the wall that separates them from the street, and a thick layer of soot blackens the stone all the way up to the vent hole in the ceiling. Three stools sit under a small, roughly hewn table; Melia wonders if there was a child in the house or if the third seat will be hers. A ladder leans against a loft that hovers low over the back half of the room. The space below it holds two low chairs, their woven willow seats stretched into deep depressions.

Two low doors on the other side of the kitchen are closed,

only loosely filling their openings. A waste pot sits next to the one that appears to lead outside to the garden behind the house. The stinging odor of urine burns in Melia's nose.

Her arguments spent and her voice now hoarse from shouting at her husband, Matildis turns to Melia. "You will fetch the water, do the cooking, the marketing, and at night, you will help with the weaving and the mending," she croaks.

"But first she will learn to make candles," Herman interjects in a tone that suggests his rule over the household is not as much a given as he wishes. He steps between the women, forcing the large one back against the hearth, and turns to Melia. "We make them for the garrison and the church and customers who come to the shop. It's hard work, but it will do no good to complain. You could ask Marta what good complaining did her. But she's no longer with us, so you will have to believe me." He laughs with a low, evil chuckle.

Marta? Melia shudders. Was that third stool under the table hers? What happened to her?

The two big Germanii stare at her, as if expecting her to ask. Melia isn't sure she wants to know.

"What? You have no questions?" Matildis asks. "Good. Silence is probably a good habit. Who knows what gibberish you speak." Abruptly, she turns and opens one of the ill-fitting doors. "I will show you the root cellar."

Hermann gives Melia a push on the back, and she follows Matildis down a couple of splintered wood stairs into the dark, musty cave. She ducks to avoid bunches of onions hanging on hooks in the ceiling as Matildis sticks her hand into a bin of straw and pulls out a carrot and a turnip.

"Here's where you keep what you get at the market." She drops the vegetables and points at a barrel in the corner. "And there's the beer we make every week. You hang hens and lamb shanks there." She points to two large hooks near the door.

Melia blinks in the semi-darkness, her eyes now crusty with drying tears. The future that flashes through her mind is as clear as her past: numbing cold, constant work, few comforts, and little sleep.

Horrible, even if she avoids the "defiling" the auctioneer incited. How is she going to do it? Can she survive until her mother comes to rescue her?

"Quit your sniffling," Matildis says, brushing past her and leading the way back into the kitchen where Hermann stands waiting.

"Get her a dress, and I will start teaching her in the shop," he says. Melia waits as Matildis pokes around in a dark trunk in the back room and returns with a smelly, rough linen shift.

"Put this on," Matildis orders. She grabs Melia's cloak from her shoulders and holds it out at arm's length, as if she were afraid of bugs that might crawl out of it. Melia glances at Hermann, who stares at her bared skin.

"I said put it on!" Matildis grabs Melia's arm and thrusts the shift into her hand. Quickly, Melia drops her torn dress onto the floor and pulls the linen over her head. It is far too big for her narrow shoulders, and the large neck opening slips down one arm.

Matildis laughs and points. She turns to Hermann. "At least that flat chest won't tempt you at night, like Marta's did!"

Hermann continues to stare and says nothing, and Melia can no longer avoid the thought of what nights hold in store. From Hermann's lurid gape, she can tell that the shape of her breasts makes no difference.

$$\underline{\hspace{8cm}}$$

THE SACRIFICE

$$\underline{\hspace{8cm}}$$

AD405 - Two months earlier, along the Danube

Greta sits back, far behind the circle of tribesmen surrounding the campfire, and watches sparks float above the crackling wood into the leafless tree branches above them.

The air is freezing, but they have found a campsite sheltered from the wind by a high bank of a sluggish stream that feeds into the Danube. It is the first calm spot they've found since leaving the village. Up to now, the dense stands of birch and chicory have failed to block the late winter gales. Even in this quiet ravine, the horses and oxen snort as the frigid air burns their nostrils.

From her cold rock perch, Greta listens to wails and recriminations of the women huddled by the fire, silhouetted by the bright flames. She prefers to suffer the cold rather than let the others see her crying. Ballomar, her husband, says she must be strong and set an example for the other women in the camp, but her tears still fall, unbidden. She hides her face, takes advantage of the dark starless night, and keeps her distance.

"The Burgundians have told us they will now allow us passage to the Rhine." The Suevi chief speaks to the gathered tribesmen over the women's cries and sobs. "We paid their price in wergild," the value of the little lives they had surrendered. He waits, perhaps for confirmation from others that this had been a wise decision, but no one raises a voice to agree. Even the men who were complicit in the decision to sell their children stay silent, anguished now by the reality of what they have done.

"We had no choice," the chief argues against the silence. "If we didn't pay, we would never get into Gaul."

"But we have sacrificed our children!" a woman shouts, her outburst letting loose a chorus of protests from the mothers.

Greta hears her cousin among them. "Why did we flee the village if we were going to give the Burgundians exactly what the Huns would have taken from us back at home? Our children?"

The chief holds up his hands, and slowly, the women quiet.

"If we did not give up the children, the Burgundians would push us back into the arms of the Huns. We cannot fight our way through; they are too many and they have the advantage of knowing these woods and marshes. We had to pay their ransom."

"Our children no more to us than ransom?" a woman shouts.

"To us, they are," says the chief, his voice rising as the women's mournful refrain resumes. "But to the Burgundians, no. We are not enemies, but they have no need to help us. They would slaughter all of us—young or old—if we gave them nothing before entering their lands."

"And now they will kill our children!"

"Not as long as they have value as slaves for the Romans," the chief answers stiffly, his patience obviously waning.

"We'll never see them again." Greta recognizes her younger

sister's voice. Vertila has no children, but she recoiled at the decision as much as any of the mothers. "We've lost them to save ourselves."

"We will buy them back or steal them once we cross the river." Ballomar joins the argument, as Greta had expected he would. "We will learn who buys them at auction. And the Burgundians brought us game and grains to feed us until we get to Mogantiacum. Do not forget that part of our agreement. It will keep us alive to retrieve those children."

Greta understands the chief's argument, however repugnant. Two hundred years have passed since the Suevi brought a Roman legion to its knees in the Marcomanni Wars. Now, their small band of tribesmen—all its men, women, horses, oxen and goats—is a pale, depleted ghost compared with the massive army that had waged those ancient battles. And they are reduced to surrendering their children because there are not enough men to fight to a win. What has happened to their tribe? To their pride?

Still no others speak up in the chief's defense, and Greta wonders how they were talked into this in the first place. Perhaps hearing their children scream in the arms of the Burgundian warriors has changed their minds. Did they think the exchange would be pleasant?

Ballomar continues, on the chief's behalf. "Without the Burgundian's help, our children would not survive the winter. Nor would we. Without their help, we would all starve."

It is preposterous, this excuse. Greta doesn't want to hate her husband for his words. But his argument is vapid: the entire tribe is doomed anyway. He had just said it: caught between the Huns behind and the Romans ahead, there is little chance they will make it into Gaul, Burgundian blessings or not. It is unlikely the Empire will let them cross the Rhine.

In their private moments, Ballomar agreed with her. The

Romans had closed the Gallic *limites* along the river to new migrants for months since their field armies left for Italy to help repel the Goth king, Radagaisus. The Roman general Stilicho had blocked the bridge at Mogantiacum to everyone except Germani merchants who supplied the soldiers with everything from comestibles to wool. Romans patrol the river with a massive river fleet and drown any migrants caught trying to swim across.

On the Germani side of the river, across from the Romans, the Burgundians have thrived by selling the residents of the Empire what they wanted—amber from the Baltics, meat and grain from the Germani farms, and slaves—at times acting as much like Roman confederates as Germani, sometimes more so.

The Suevi chief waits until the grumbling wanes to start again. "I know this is difficult," he says, "but we have some good news, too."

Greta smirks. No news will be good enough to appease the women now.

"A large cohort of Vandals from the north is travelling down the east side of Burgundian lands and will join us soon." He looks disappointed at the lack of applause, but he continues. "Alans from the steppes of Persia are also on their way from the east and will meet up with us soon. We will have plenty of allies with us when we cross the river."

History has shown such alliances to be fragile and tricky, Greta would argue, if she thought it would make any difference. Here, in these woods, the chief's word is final. Back in the village, tribal decisions had been shared with the women, but once they left on this journey, the warriors and chiefs took control of everything. With the plundering, murderous Huns on their heels, and the Roman blockade at the river, the tribe conceded the need for more efficient rule.

Greta expects the argument to continue for hours as her husband and the chief justify their decisions and the women disagree. She stands up, pulls her cloak tight around her body, and walks back through the trees to the wagons where her daughter slept the night before. She wonders how a slave owner in the Empire will treat Melia—just on the cusp of becoming a woman. Greta can only hope that Melia will be better fed and better housed in a Roman city in the Empire than she was on this slow-moving migration. Food in Gaul is plentiful, the Gallic countryside largely peaceful, the Huns far away to the east.

Melia isn't the first child Greta lost. And as with the one before, the sorrow will never leave her, but she doesn't grieve alone—her pain is the same that every woman in Germania has suffered—or suffered many times. It was something every woman knows she risks from the day she feels a new life growing in her belly.

Greta pulls herself up over the side of the wagon she and Ballomar would now share with only her sister and brother-in-law. She nestles down under the furs and blankets and gazes at the still, cold moon. She closes her eyes to concentrate, committing every curve and line of Melia's beautiful, youthful face to memory, asking the god, Wodin, to keep it there until she dies.

HERMANN

AD405 – Mogantiacum

Just hours after the humiliating trauma of the slave market and her introduction to candle making, Melia lies in the dark on a scratchy straw mattress in a corner of the candle shop, her heart pounding. Her arms and back ache from her first day as a slave, from stirring the huge tallow vat and hoisting the big wheel of wicks up and down into the smelly, melted fat. She prayed to Wodin for sleep, but instead, awake, she listens to the strange sounds of the shop, dreading what she expects: a nighttime visit from Hermann. Matildis had been wrong about his reaction to her youthful body. She'd seen it in Hermann's eyes all afternoon.

She doesn't have to wait long. The ladder to the loft creaks so loudly under Hermann's weight that she can hear him descend into the room next door. The door to the shop scrapes along the threshold. In the pale moonlight seeping in through slats in the shudders, she watches him lower his huge bulk down beside her mattress. He brushes her cheek with a rough hand. She bats it away.

"No," he says, shaking his head with a crooked smile. "You don't want to make me angry."

She spits at him, and he covers her mouth with a dirty palm. She bites and he yanks his hand away.

"Behave, strumpet. You bitch!" He hisses, spraying saliva in her face. "You will learn to do as I say." He holds her shoulder down with one filthy hand and slaps her face with the other. She slaps back. She is tiny under him, powerless to win, but she struggles anyway.

Breathing heavily, he straddles his bulk across her hips and slugs her jaw. Her head swims, the ring on his finger slicing a gash on her cheek. She feels blood trickle down onto her mattress. By the time she regains her senses, he has penetrated her, and is pounding his torso between her legs. Pain shoots up her spine and down her thighs, and she tries to pull up and away, but he leans his weight on her arms, holding her down. She holds her breath and bites her lip. Gasping for air and groaning, he finishes and flops sideways next to her. Shaking with disgust, Melia rolls away and wipes at the sticky slime of blood and semen between her legs with the torn linen shift she'd folded up next to her mattress. She had intended to mend it the next day; now she will burn it instead.

Before sunrise, Hermann rose and returned up the creaking ladder, leaving Melia exhausted and confused. Was it better to be here, suffering rape and working over the hot caldron than to lumber through the frozen forests toward the Rhine with her tribe? Never was she kidnapped and enslaved by Huns who attacked her village, and therefore Melia was spared the brutality of the barbarians of the steppes. But the miserable journey into bitter spring winds had stripped her of gratitude for her salvation.

Two weeks before they left, a Hunic raid—the second in less than a moon, the fourth already that spring—had destroyed much of their village. With little chance of surviving further attacks, the townsfolk slaughtered the pigs, smoked the hams, caged the chickens and geese, and secured everything that would fit in their wagons with rope and twine. Abandoning the settlement that perched atop a steep wooded slope by the Danube for as long as even the oldest of the villagers knew, they herded their cattle and goats before them down the muddy track heading west. For days, they slogged through mud and slush, Melia, the women, and the elderly following the oxen, the wagons, and the men on horseback, dodging steaming, pungent piles of dung in angry silence.

Two weeks into the journey, her mother woke her from a troubled sleep, shaking her shoulders and whispering in her ear. "Daughter, you must dress and follow me. It is time for you to go."

Melia covered her head and squeezed her eyelids tight.

"Go where?" she murmured, burying her face in the rough burlap bag under her head and pulling her stiff legs closer to her chest. "Are we going home?"

She pulled the rough coverings over her head and covered her ears with her hands. Exhausted, sore to the bone, Melia had nothing left but disobedience.

The wagon swayed as her mother climbed over the side of the family's wagon and leapt to the ground next to her. "Melia!" Her voice stern, it took Melia by surprise.

Slowly pulling herself upright, Melia kicked her legs loose from the tangle of skins and wool, and separated her heavy fur from the pile. She swung it over her dress, and with stiff fingers, fastened it with her broach. The cold fog of predawn seeped in between the meager layers, and she shivered as she yanked soiled leather boots over blistered toes.

"Where are we going?" Melia lifted her aching legs over the wagon side and dropped down, grimacing as the shock of the frozen ground shot through her heels and ankles to her knees. Her mother turned away, and Melia lunged for her hand, tripping over the uneven ground. "Can't we wait until we can see?"

Her mother pulled her through the dark brush toward the center of the camp where the bonfire from the night before still spat out flickering red coals. Several of the tribe's mothers and the few remaining children of the tribe had already gathered there, the women crying and clinging to their sleepy toddlers.

"What's happening, Mother?" Fear tightened Melia's throat. This gathering made no sense. She tried to shake her hand loose, but her mother's grasp was tight. "Mother, look at me!"

Greta turned toward her and grabbed Melia's other hand. "I know you cannot understand, but we have no choice." A cry burst from her lips; her wet cheeks reflected the red glow of the coals.

"No choice? What is this?"

"We are sending you ahead." Her mother choked out the words. "We will find you in Mogantiacum, the Roman city on the Rhine River. But you must be brave and work hard."

"Work? What work?" Melia shook her head and fought to free her hands, but her mother pulled her closer.

"I do not want this either," Greta whispered harshly, her impatience surfacing. "I argued against it, but the council has decided."

Melia backed away. "What are you saying? You are sending me away? To work?"

"Quiet, Melia." Her mother wiped her face with the sleeve of her cloak and waved at the shrieking children around them. "It's hard enough for you, as old as you are. It's harder for them."

"I don't care about them. What will happen to me?"

"You will go to Mogantiacum. It's the only way you can survive."

Finally, Melia understood. The Romans in Gaul keep slaves, and now she will be one. Slavery wasn't a Suevi custom, but the tribe's children, a few every year, were kidnapped—even before the Huns started their raids—in the middle of the night and sold inside the Empire. They never came back. Everyone knew what happened to them, but no one talked about it.

Melia stood in disbelief. Wasn't the idea for this migration to the river to save the rest of the children from that?

"You are selling me into slavery? Selling me so you can survive?"

"It is better than starvation or slaughter, daughter," Greta said. "And I will come and free you as soon as we cross the river. This is the only way the Burgundians will let us pass."

Melia spat into her mother's face. "You're selling me? How much *dinarii* did you get for me, Mother?"

"No, no money." Her mother grimaced. "But we'll be able to get through the Burgundian territory this way. They stand between us and Gaul. I will find you once we cross the river," she repeated. She tried again to pull Melia closer.

Melia twisted from her mother's arms and turned back toward their wagon, but Greta grabbed her cloak and held on. "I don't want this, Melia. I don't want—"

At that moment, the forest beyond the fire's embers stirred with the sound of breaking sticks and heavy footfalls. Startled, the children fell silent. Melia's father walked out of the trees from the opposite side of the campfire, followed by a dozen large men in dark, round helmets. Their long hair was like that of the men of Melia's tribe, but they wore it loose around their shoulders, instead of knotted atop their heads. Other

Germanii, clearly. But they weren't like any Melia had seen before.

"Children, come!" Melia's father roared. "Mothers, send them now." The women hesitated, their wet eyes wide with fear. Melia's father turned back to the strange men following him and waved his arm toward the children. The Germanii lunged forward for screaming toddlers, each man snaring two at a time, tearing the young ones away as their mothers fell, trying to hang on for a moment more.

Melia froze. Her mother pushed her ahead with a hand on her shoulder. Melia looked back at her in the greying morning light. "What can I do?" Her mother shrugged. "There is nothing I can do."

Melia stumbled toward her father, but his gaze was fixed on some point behind her, deep in the forest's blackness. She didn't see the hulk of a man coming at her from the side; he snatched her slim frame by the waist and hoisted her over his shoulder, his metal helmet knocking hard against her ribs.

"Father!" she yelled. "Father, stop him! Don't let him take me!"

The Germani reached up and slapped her face. Stunned, Melia felt a tickle at a crack in her lip, her tongue sensing the metallic taste of blood. She pounded the brute's leather-clad chest with her fists and writhed against his hold, but he didn't loosen his grip. He grabbed a toddler with his free arm and dragged the little boy along.

Together, they entered the darkness and left the camp behind.

Now, instead of squirming against the Burgundian, she fights Hermann for a fortnight, a losing streak that leaves her a painfully swollen wrist, a black eye, and bruises up and down her arms and on every inch of her inner thighs. The tender tissues between her legs are chafed and ache; her nipples red and sore.

Without a peaceful hour of sleep, she works with painful blisters and aching shoulders. Even then he molests her with his presence. He stands close while she cleans the table and rinses their bowls after supper, and as he teaches her candle making and escorts her to her first deliveries to the customers. He grabs her ass and pinches her breasts whenever Matildis is out of sight. The acrid odors drifting off his body make her nauseous, but when she moves away, he sidles closer.

Matildis blinks and then smirks at Melia's wounds. At first, she pretends to not notice either Hermann's daytime behavior or his nighttime absences, and Melia imagines she is relieved that she was no longer on the receiving end of his greasy sex. But Matildis doesn't show her gratitude. Instead, she hovers as Melia cooks and follows her around as she sweeps and washes, always emanating her special mix of aromas: urine, sweat, and the beer she had dribbled down the front of her dress. Melia starts to prefer the hot, slippery work in the candle shop, even with Hermann's presence, because Matildis never steps in there except to pass through to the front door.

One night, a week into her enslavement, Matildis wolfs down Melia's vegetable stew as if she has not eaten for weeks before throwing down her spoon and bellowing, "Your stew is like vomit."

Startled, Melia stands up, knocking her stool to the floor. Matildis laughs.

"You are such a weak little lamb, aren't you?" The woman stands up and slugs Hermann on the arm. "I suppose," she addresses him, "that hardens your member."

"Leave her alone, fat one." Hermann belches and takes a long swig of beer. "Why don't you cook then? Or do something more useful than fart for once?"

"I'm not the slave girl, Hermann. Your little Melia is here to do your every bidding. And for truth, I am gladdened by that."

That exchange has an effect. That night Hermann doesn't come down the ladder to visit her. Instead, through the closed door between the shop and the kitchen, Melia hears Matildis's protests and screams as Hermann takes out his anger and vents his lust on her.

Hermann returns the next night to Melia's mattress, and Matildis doesn't mention Hermann's nighttime forays again for a long time.

THE ATTACK

AD406 - East bank of the Rhine River

The Suevii's spirits start to lift as they approach the Rhine riverbank, from where they will make a formal appeal to cross into Gaul and settle their families. Even the horses and oxen seem to sense the improved prospects, and they move less reluctantly with fewer acts of defiance, although their better behavior may be due to the mostly downhill nature of the roads and the scent of water as they reach the Roman *limites*.

The warrior horsemen of the Alans have caught up with the Suevii, but their families and supply wagons are still far behind, back along the Danube River. When they first appeared, the tall, blond Persians with their huge hunting dogs and fine horses frightened the women. The men seemed intimidated by them as well. They puffed their chests out and stood tall, trying to stretch themselves to the height of the lanky Alanii.

The Persian tongue is unintelligible to the Suevi, but a few on both sides speak enough Latin to communicate, and before too many nights, the menfolk are raucously meeting and sharing what mead and beer the Suevi had left with their new allies around the campfire at night. The women begin to feel a little more secure with the dozens of additional warriors amongst them, even though grains have to be even more strictly rationed with so many additional mouths to feed. The Alans' dogs, although frightening, are welcome; fearless, strong and quick, they prove to be efficient hunters, and now squirrel, rabbits, weasels and ferrets comprise larger portions of the travelers' daily fare.

The women—about thirty have survived the trip so far—chat about retrieving their children on the other side. Even though they have no *denarii*, they plan to sell some of the remaining livestock for coin they can use to buy their girls and boys out of slavery. The tribe's scouts have reported shortages of food, especially meat and poultry, at the Mogantiacum market. It appears the livestock can be sold for a good price, and the Suevi talk of replacing the herds as they raid their way into Gaul.

No one raises the question: How will they find the children when they get there?

Greta is one of the few who knows who bought her daughter at the market. The Burgundians reported that the town candlemaker had paid a good price for Melia, and, given the hefty amount of *denarii* he'd spent, Greta prays he treats her well. Greta will find someone on the streets who knows where the candlemaker's shop is. Once she has collected her family's share of the money from the sale of the cattle, Greta will rush to her daughter's rescue.

Late in the afternoon, as the migrants and their livestock were slowing down, tired from the day's journey, shouts shoot forward from the rear of their long column. The women hold the wagons and animals as a couple of men who have been leading the way in the front rush back toward the ruckus.

The shouts and snorts of the horses rises, and Greta guesses the tribe's worst fear was unfolding. The scouts had reported that the Romans might hire mercenaries to stop the Suevi and Alans' progress and keep them from reaching the river. The Alani horsemen race back to the rear of the pack, their fierce dogs charging ahead, yelping with the excitement of potential battle, and the Suevi men follow.

From the rear, a rider returns to the women and livestock. "Leave the wagons and the animals!" he shouts. "It's the Franks! Women! Take cover in the woods. Don't come out until we come to get you!" He spins his steed around and heads back to the battle, throwing up a cloud of dust in his wake.

The women jump down from the wagons, hitch up their cloaks, and run. The forest is dark and dense, but other than the tree trunks and a few boulders, nothing promises much shelter or camouflage. Her heart pounding, Greta concentrates on lifting her feet high to clear branches and fallen logs, but several times she trips. As she picks herself up, she looks around and grimaces as she sees others also crashing to the ground. She plunges headlong through the trees again.

As they put some distance between themselves and the road, the shouts of battle and the clash of weapons on armor grow fainter, and they slow to a walk, exhausted by their clumsy flight and breathing heavily. One of the younger women who had run ahead backtracks and waves them forward.

"Over here!" she yells. "There's a cave. We can hide in there!"

Greta doesn't argue even though she knows a cave could be a trap. They could hide in it, perhaps, but if the Franks find them there, how would they escape? Too exhausted to think ahead, the women converge at the mouth of the cave and warily step back into its dark, damp depths.

The cave mutes the last sounds of the battle to near silence.

The women feel their way along the sides of the narrow cavity, cautiously moving back. As her eyes adjust to the low light, Greta points to the pile of large boulders that block passage deeper into the cave.

"We can rest here," she said.

At first, the women's chests heave as they labor to catch their breath, but as their wheezing quiets, Greta can hear the squeaks and rattles of varmints they have disturbed. She lifts her feet up and hugs her knees to her chest. Rats and squirrels will be the least of their predators. Bears and lions also live in such caves.

If the Franks don't get them, will the carnivores?

With no food or water, Greta knows the women can't stay huddled in the cave for long. If the men don't come for them soon, they will need supplies.

She says nothing for a while, letting everyone catch their breath. Finally, as the sky outside darkens, she proposes a plan.

"One or two of us should return to the wagons to gather some food," she says. "And some blankets for night. I will go. Is anyone willing to join me?"

Her sister, Vertila, speaks up immediately. "I'll go."

"Good," Greta says. "We'll go as soon as the moon is high enough to light our way. And will use it to guide us back."

"How will you know where to go?" one of the women asks.

"We'll follow the battle sounds."

"And get close enough to the battle to see what is happening," Vertila says.

"No," Greta answers quickly. "It is too dangerous. We'll hear all we need to know from the wagons."

"I want to know what's happening to Milo."

Greta worries; perhaps her impulsive sister is not the best one to take with her. But would anyone else be more sensible?

"We all want to know what is happening to our husbands," one of Greta's cousins says, answering Greta's unspoken question.

Perhaps they would all be foolish enough to approach the battle. "But don't be ridiculous, Vertila," the cousin continues. "You could be caught or you might lead the Franks right back to us."

"She's right," Greta says, jumping on the opportunity to second that sentiment. "We'll stick together, get what we need and come right back."

As soon as they leave the cave, Greta suspects that Vertila is going to ignore her cousin's advice. In Vertila's eager steps, she senses the mischief that has defined her younger sister from childhood. As if the treacherous trail they've been on over the past months hasn't provided enough excitement, Vertila seems energized by the proximity of battle.

"Don't be a fool, Vertila," Greta whispers as they pick their way through the dense forest. "If you are thinking of going near that fighting, I will kill you myself now."

"How, sister? How are you going to do that?"

"Vertila, please listen! We are needed. We have to get back with the food and blankets."

Shaking off her trepidation, Greta forges ahead toward the waning battle sounds. Perhaps, the battle is being hampered by darkness. Or perhaps it is nearly over. Soon, they will know the fate of the men, whether Vertila misbehaved or not.

The journey is treacherous, and Greta and Vertila trip and stumble in the moonlight, their attempt to hurry easily sabotaged by the rough terrain. Fleeing over downed tree trunks and around rocks and boulders in the daytime, they had covered more ground than Greta had remembered. Their flight to the cave in daylight had taken half as much time as their return to the wagons.

"Stop there!" A voice startles Greta as they finally approach the road.

Greta's heart leaps into her throat, but then she realizes the man speaks Suevi. An older man, he is guarding their possessions while the warriors fight behind them.

"It's me, Greta," she answers. "We've come to get some blankets and food."

The man steps out into the moonlight.

"What's happening back there?" she asks.

"The Franks," the man says. "They were sent by the Romans, of course. I'm afraid we have many dead."

Greta feels sick. Ballomar could be one of them. Her heart pounds, and she walks up to the first wagon and leans against it. "How much worse can it get?" she moans. "After all of this misery, are we to die here in these wretched woods?"

The man approaches and puts his hand on Greta's shoulder. She looks into his face and recognizes him as one of Ballomar's old uncles. "Uncle, what will become of us?" she repeats.

"You are brave to come back, Greta, but you must gather what you need and leave. There's no telling who will be coming for these wagons. It could be our people, but it could be the Franks."

"But we have so little left," Greta says.

"The livestock, the wagons. They'll take it all."

"Okay, we will hurry." Greta nods and pushes herself free of the wagon side.

"We?" the uncle asks.

Greta turns around to look for Vertila. She isn't there.

"Curse her!" Greta exclaims in a harsh whisper. "I knew I shouldn't trust her. Did you see where she went?"

"Who?"

"Vertila!"

"I didn't see her, Greta. But you must hurry. I'll send her back when I see her."

"I'm sure she went toward the fighting," Greta says. "I should never have brought her."

The old man helps Greta climb into one of the wagons, and she collects an armful of blankets. "Wrap up some dried meat in a satchel for me, will you?" she asks the old man.

With her arms full and her heart heavy, Greta trudges back toward the cave alone, keeping the moon at her side as a guide. It is foolish to walk through strange forests in the dark, especially alone, but if she gets lost, at least she has blankets to keep her warm and some food to sustain her until she relocates the cave in the daylight. Only as she starts back through the dark woods does she accept how likely it is that she will get lost. It had seemed less risky when there were two of them travelling, although now Greta can't fathom why.

Stopping frequently to rest her arms and back, Greta calculates how far the moon would have moved through the sky during her journey so as keep her trajectory correct. Again, she wishes she weren't alone. She steps quietly, but with every footstep, she knows she was calling attention to herself. The bears and lions that live in these woods will make quick work of separating her muscles from her bones, if they decide to. She could toss her dried meat to distract them for a moment, but even then she would have little chance of fending off their greedy teeth.

Scanning the woods ahead and around her, she catches fleeting glimpses of moonlight reflected in tiny eyes. Probably shrews, lemurs, rats, squirrels, or possums, she tells herself. They'll be more afraid of her than she of them, she rationalizes, but still her heart pounds in her ears. The real danger is back at the rear of the wagons, where the most lethal of all creatures are—the men doing Rome's dirty work.

For two nights after Greta returned to the cave, she prays to Wodin for Vertila's return. She considers going back to the wagons to look for her, but she recognizes how futile it would be. Whatever has happened to her sister would likely happen to her. If Vertila was captured, she would not survive. On the other hand, if she hadn't been taken, she would have found her way back by now.

On their third day in the cave, the women have shed all the tears they have for themselves and for the husbands, sons, and fathers they fear they have lost. But as they huddle in tight knots wrapped in the blankets Greta delivered, they hear men shouting in Suevi, coming toward them through the woods.

The women untangle themselves and jump up. "We're here!" they shout back in unison, pour through the cave's mouth, and wave the men toward them.

Greta stands back at the mouth of their shelter and scans the approaching party for Ballomar. He isn't with them. Perhaps he is needed back at the wagons, she tells herself.

"What happened?" the women plead. "Are we safe?"

Bits of stories of the brutal attack are passed around as some of the women embrace the very men they had been expecting to grieve. It was a narrow and costly victory. The battle had raged, nearly one-sided in favor of the attackers, for most of the first day. All had appeared to be lost when on the second day, the anticipated arrival of the large migration of Vandals caught up with the attacking Franks and overwhelmed them. The Suevi and Alans were saved, but many from both armies had fallen.

Following behind the rescue party, Ballomar's old uncle walks slowly toward Greta, his eyes tortured with pain.

She shakes her head and falls to her knees. "No!" she screams into her hands as she covers her face.

"I'm sorry," the old uncle says. He kneels beside her and puts an arm over her shoulders. "We haven't seen him. The men are looking now, but there are many dead in the woods. Some may never be found."

Greta tries to quiet her sobs but can only spit out two more words. "And Vertila?"

"Her body has not been found either," he says, softly. "But only her husband has been looking for her."

GRETA HAS ONLY A SHORT time to search for Ballomar's body before she will have to join the slow progression toward the Rhine without him. Not knowing when the Franks might re-group and attack again, the tribes have formed a line of defense on the east side of their camp. Only those bodies found the first half-day will be carried forward and committed to funeral pyres. The rest must be abandoned to the wolves and bears, as the tribes trudge on.

Greta stumbles recklessly over dead horses and bodies splayed along the road that their wagons had traversed three days before. She avoids looking in the wide, dead eyes of those who are not her husband, swatting at the flies buzzing around her legs, feasting on the quickly rotting flesh. Of the forty Suevi men, thirty have survived; there were more deaths among the Alans, but there were many more of them.

Knowing that Vertila is likely a victim of the Franks, Milo has set out in search of her while others trek into the woods to retrieve the women. After the men and women return, Milo delivers the bad news: he has found her body, ravaged and naked, her throat sliced, far down the road behind the wagon train in the direction of the retreating Franks. Her death has been particularly brutal, preceded by the worst persecution a woman could suffer. Milo chose to bury her in the woods close to where he found her rather than bring her naked body back to camp to suffer the final indignity of a public display.

Now he precedes Greta through the mass of severed heads and limbs in search of Ballomar.

"Greta," he says softly, stopping a few yards in front of her and holding out a palm. "Greta, stop. I have found him, but there is no need for you to see."

Greta ignores him and rushes forward, tripping over a broken hand axe still held tight in the stiff arm of a fallen Frank. Milo steps back and grabs her arm to lift her off her knees.

"Greta, you shouldn't see him like this," Milo says, holding her shoulders at arm's length. "You must remember him as the strong, brave warrior he was."

Greta twists loose and plunges around her brother-in-law. She looks down into Ballomar's face, the square jaw, the bright yellow hair, propped up by the still-heaving torso of his horse. His eyes are closed, and his chin rests deep against his chest. The sword had sliced his body just below his chest, and his dark viscera had spilled out over his wide-spread legs. The horse's front legs are broken, twisted at sharp angles, and its eyes dart back and forth in anguish, as he lay dying under his master.

"Please, Milo," Greta cries, pointing to the miserable animal. "Help him die."

Milo nods and steps forward, quickly slicing through the horse's muscular neck with his sword. A final shutter, and the animal lies quiet.

"Now go back to the wagons," Milo says quietly. "I'll bring Ballomar. You have been brave. But that is enough. Go back."

CANDLEMAKING

AD406 - Mogantiacum, early September

A hot, gray fog rises from the river and creeps into town as a malodorous haze, coating everything in tacky, sticky wetness. By mid-morning, the merchants manning their stalls in the market sit with their backs hunched and their heads bowed, nodding and fighting off drowsiness in the unusual autumn heat and humidity.

Melia and her friend Fritigil pass the meat stalls. Flies swarm crazily around the hanging carcasses of goats and chickens, and hover over the tubs of sweetbreads. Only insects can be animated by such weather. Even the feral dogs that trail after them through the market maze on most days, their jowls barely clearing the ground, hang back in the shade. The curs raise their eyes as the young women pass but leave their heads lolling on filthy paws.

The sultry weather thickens the melancholy that has infested Mogantiacum ever since Stilicho pulled most of the Roman soldiers away from the fort and sent them to fight the Goths in Pannonia and Noricum. As Melia wanders, groggy herself, through the stalls, she realizes it was the first time she has passed through without spying a single soldier in the center of the market.

"Do you think the Romans will eventually send the legions back?" Melia asks. She turned to wait for Fritigil to complete her purchase of a few soft plums. "Or are we all going to speak only German from now on? Other than the priest, no one has spoken Latin to me for weeks."

"German is fine with me." Fritigil lays the overripe fruit on top of the cheese and bread in her basket. "I don't care if I ever speak Rome's language again."

Melia laughs. "Me either. Any love for Rome I ever had has worn off. But look how many still wait to get into the Empire." She points across the river, where the flickering lights of Germani bonfires have glowed at night for months. Every now and then winds carry voices across the river, the only thing that the Romans allow to cross, other than the wagons of Burgundian merchants.

"That's because they don't know how miserable it is here." Fritigil stops and rubs her belly, swollen with child, and wipes the sweat off her forehead.

"Perhaps. But I wish they'd let them come over. I've only had two customers at the shop all week. The fort isn't buying many candles these days, and I wonder what will happen to me if I have no work."

"I suppose you still believe your mother will come and save you." Fritigil has heard Melia's story about her mother's promise dozens of times, at first cheerfully, but lately with a roll of her eyes. "Don't you think it's about time you gave up on that?"

"No. Never." How could she? "I will not live the rest of my life as Hermann's slave."

Fritigil reaches out and squeezes Melia's arm. "I know. I'm sorry. But I will miss you."

Finished shopping, the young women turn west and up the slight hill toward the residential section of the city, pulling themselves slowly above the sticky riverine fog. They fall silent, Fritigil unable to climb into the neighborhood and talk at the same time.

Just beyond the market, they pass the Christian church and, as usual, they wave a greeting to the priest who stands on the front step with his hands clasped behind his back. He nods without a word and returns to whatever big thoughts demand his attention. The presbyter is one of Melia's regular customers—lately nearly the only one. Weakly, she pulls her two-wheeled delivery cart down to restock his candle and votive supply.

When she first arrived in the city and had settled into her routine in the candlemaker's shop, she found the city both wonderous and frightening. Although she couldn't go inside them, the grand bathhouses and theatre made her feel part of the rich, Roman, civilized world, so different from the simple village back on the Danube. There were so many Roman officials, so much orderliness, so many taverns and shops. Someone in the city is responsible for picking up the horse manure and dog feces off the streets, and a night watchman lights the lanterns along the main streets at dusk.

The constant rattle of carts up and down the cobblestones kept her on edge at first, and she was wary of the hundreds of strangers around her. But as she learned to walk quickly and nod at men and women on the street with confidence, she felt more Gallic, less Suevi.

Danger still lurks around every blind corner—thieves in the guise of beggars, soldiers hungry for the pleasures of the flesh unavailable in the garrison, and racoons and feral dogs so accustomed to men's kicks and children's stones that her small feet cause them no trepidation. Still, those streets are her refuge from Hermann's attentions and Matildis's scorn. As she waits for her mother to cross the river and rescue her, Melia takes on any errand that would allow her to leave the shop and the house, her way of coping with abuse and loneliness.

Halfway up the hill, Melia reaches over and takes Fritigil's basket.

"Let me," she says. "You have enough to carry these days."

Breathing heavily, Fritigil nods her thanks. The baby growing in Fritigil's frame is her master's, not unusual for slaves in Mogantiacum. Their owners have the right to use a slave's body in whatever way pleases them, and although many girls visit the wicce market for the silphium powders thought to prevent pregnancy, the seeds are getting harder to find and more expensive all the time. Fewer supplies are coming from the countryside or across the *limites* into the Empire.

"Is Julius being kind to you?" Melia asks. "Is he still happy about the baby?"

"Yes." Fritigil stops to talk and lets out a little huff of a laugh. "He's much gentler now. He hasn't punched me since I told him I was with child. And since this happened"—she circles the growing girth of her stomach with her hand—"he quit entering me. He still fondles my breasts and pleases himself, but I have to do little." She huffs to catch her breath. "Despite my sicknesses, I'm starting to think this has its advantages."

Melia grimaces. Yes, a respite from nightly rape would be wonderful, but she doesn't want to earn it that way.

"Are you getting enough to eat?"

"Oh, yes. My allotment of wine is bigger now, too. It helps with the pain, and it helps me fall asleep while he does his things next to me."

Only a few weeks after Hermann bought her at the slave market and dragged her home, Melia met Fritigil. Fritigil had come to Mogantiacum from northern Gaul, sent by a Frankish warrior-king to Julius as a bribe for Roman tax forgiveness. Julius collects taxes for the diocese, and at first, he had little interest in his female slave beyond what she cooked him for dinner and how willingly she spread her legs for him at night.

That had changed with Fritigil's pregnancy. As dangerous as childbirth was, perhaps in Fritigil's case, it is worth the risk.

Months before, when Fritigil learned she was pregnant, she was more embarrassed than worried, even though it would be months before anyone would notice her swelling belly. Before her pregnancy, Fritigil had been a large girl—with broad hips and generous breasts. No one would have mistaken her and the short, skinny Melia as sisters.

As soon as she recognized her condition, Fritigil came to the candle shop to find Melia—her only friend—and confide in her. Melia sat with her on the step to the street.

"I will look like a fool," Fritigil said. "Everyone will laugh at me like I didn't know how to prevent this."

"No one in town knows you but me and our friend Dodi," Melia said and immediately regretted it. No slaves needed to be reminded of how little notice they attracted from free people, how few people would help them.

Fritigil wept noisily. Melia took her hand and squeezed it. "Do you want to get rid of it?" she asked.

"No," Fritigil admitted through her sniffles, and Melia waited for her to continue. "I may not have planned for this, but Julius will have to be good to me now. I will be the mother of his child."

"So, you will stay here with him?" Melia asked. Since the beginning, they had talked about their wish to escape their slavery.

Fritigil nodded. "I won't have a choice now."

"I still plan to go," Melia whispered.

Fritigil lowered her voice, too. "I know you do. But I will need you here. And we've talked about what happens to runaway slaves!"

Melia knew: whipping, dismemberment. For many, death.

"My mother…," Melia started, but Fritigil's rolling eyes stopped her.

As they resume their climb through town now, the narrow, cobbled streets are quiet. Melia has walked these same blocks, past rows of identical white-plastered rectangle houses with red-tile roofs, along the same route every day but Sunday for nearly two years. But in the past few months, the streets have emptied. Few legionnaires linger on corners, and many of the merchants' shops are closed.

A plodding mule pulls a cart up the hill behind them, the clack of his hoofs on stone echoing off the buildings in the stillness of the day. As it passes, Melia recognizes the wagon driver as Claude, the man who regularly delivers animal fat to the candlemaker's shop from the garrison's butcher. Among Melia's duties is overseeing the deliveries, although she and Claude never exchange much more than a single word and a nod.

Its echo fades as the cart continues up the hill, and Melia wonders if the unsettled feeling she has been waking up with the past few days is due to the unseasonable weather, the growing horde across the river, or the eerie, nearly abandoned streets. An uneasy sensation has been crawling over her skin, an imbalance of her body's humors perhaps, as if her own tissues know something big is going to happen, something unpleasant, maybe worse.

Melia and Fritigil reach Fritigil's corner, stop, and share a quick hug. Fritigil takes her basket from Melia's arm and turns down the alley toward Julius's house. Farther up the street, Melia lifts the latch at the candle shop and steps through to the rooms behind. She sets her basket down.

"Every day you are slower, whore! Where have you been? What were you doing?"

Melia spins around to face the candlemaker's wife, who stands with her hands on her wide, flabby hips. Melia guesses that resting on those hips was the only thing those hands have done all morning. The woman drinks beer, eats, complains, gossips with the neighbors, and scolds. The only domestic duty she still undertakes is malting the barley and making the household's beer once a week, and an occasional mend to Hermann's ever-stretched trousers. The brew Matildis cooks up is awful—barely drinkable—but Melia is happy to let Matildis make it. The rest of the housekeeping, cooking, and laundry is all Melia's to do, as well as the candlemaking.

Melia, now practiced at ignoring the wife's outbursts, stares back at her. Matildis doesn't deserve an answer to her insults. At first, the wife's tirades had frightened Melia, and she tried to reason with her. But Matildis never stopped yelling, and Melia learned that the quickest way to end the vocal battle was to remain mute, and so they've settled into a much more efficient, if no friendlier, routine. Matildis screams insults, Melia ignores her, Matildis repeats herself, Melia waits. Eventually Matildis abandons her crude Burgundian and reverts to her strange Gothic tongue, which neither Melia nor Hermann understands, until she's run out of words, and the house goes quiet again.

This hot, humid day, the tirade ends more quickly than usual. Fidgeting in the awkward silence, the older woman scowls, and shuffles in her worn slippers to the rear of the house, below the sleeping loft that she and Hermann share. The woman plops down heavily with a grunt, and the cane seat responds with squeaky protest.

Melia turns back to her basket and sniffs the hen the butcher has wrapped in a burlap bag to determine how long it has been dead, and how soon she'll need to cook it. She takes the basket to the root cellar on the side of the room and steps down into its dark, damp coolness. She hangs the chicken on a hook, shoves the carrots, beets, and turnips she purchased deep into the straw-filled bin, and strings the onions and shallots on the ceiling.

She stops and pulls in a deep breath of the cellar's air. She takes her time choosing what ingredients she will use for the evening meal, giving Matildis time to doze off.

Melia can count the times she and Matildis have had a quiet, sustained conversation on the thumb of one hand. It happened shortly after Melia arrived. Matildis asked where Melia had come from. Melia thought at first that the wife was genuinely concerned about her welfare, or her family, or her fate as a slave. But soon after that brief exchange, she addressed Melia only with insults and commands informed by the information she had drawn from Melia.

"Whore" is her most common invective. But her slurs include "slave," "bitch," "slut," "pig," and "mule." She calls Melia a filthy, disgusting, vile peasant. Worthless. She reminds Melia her mother sold her into slavery, and not knowing anything about the particulars of the exchange, Matilda opines that her mother "got much more for you than you are worth."

Melia knows what the candlemaker's wife hates most about her, but it isn't something she has any control over, and it isn't something she'll debase herself to apologize for.

As soon as she thinks Matildis will be dozing, Melia climbs out of the cellar, and tiptoes back to the candle shop, closing the door behind her. The light coming in from the windows lining the stone walls along the ceiling is best at midday. It illuminates the high wooden worktable where she fills votives and sorts tapers, the vat where she cooks the tallow and dips the wicks, and the shelves where she stores beeswax, dyes, herbs, and other aromatic ingredients she adds to the more expensive candles. The mattress where she sleeps at night lies in the dark corner farthest from the living quarters. Behind it sits a small cupboard that is Melia's only private space in the world. There she keeps her spare dress, her bearskin cloak, and undergarments; and the broach that secures her cloak in the winter. There too is the tiny tin box that holds the few coins she has risked skimming off the candlemaker's sales.

She pulls her leather apron off the peg by the door and, even though the shop is too warm for comfort, she ties it tight around her neck and behind her back. If she leaves it loose, it catches the end of the big wooden paddle she uses to stir the tallow and knocks it out of her hand. If the paddle sinks into the tallow, she has to douse the fire and wait for the pot to cool enough to pull the paddle out, clean it, squeeze the bellows to stoke the fire, and bring the tallow back up to a boil. It wastes time, and she won't be allowed to eat dinner as punishment for not keeping up her production.

Melia pulls the paddle down off the wall and stirs the fat she started cooking earlier that morning. She is pleased to see very little detritus floating on top, which means it had been trimmed well. It will take less time than usual to skim off bone chips and hair, and the higher quality will make candles worthy of the church.

She secures the paddle on a hook on the side of the pot and reaches for the rope to lower the wheel-shaped wood frame hanging high over it. The day before, she cut a few dozen lengths of the cotton she braided for wicks, and now she strings them through the holes in the spokes of the wood wheel, each length forming two wicks connected by the length of string that loops over the top of the wooden spoke. On the bottom of each wick she ties a heavy lead pellet to weigh the wick down and keep it straight through the first couple of dips in the tallow. The threading takes a couple of hours, and although her back usually hurts from the long reach, Melia enjoys this step in the process. The anticipation of pretty, fluted candles cheer her. As she works, the strings hang, dancing cheerfully in the breeze wafting through the open door.

When the tallow has cooked to the right consistency, Melia opens the large transom over the door with a long pole. She dowses the flames under the vat, watching the steamy smoke obediently fly up and out the window. As it rushes out, it pulls a cool draft in under the doors of the living quarters all the way from root cellar. She closes her eyes with her back toward its path and pulls the loose hairs from her hair knot off her neck. She only rests a moment before turning to reach for a can of beeswax and ladles some into the vat. The priest wants candles that burn hotter; the more beeswax she adds, the harder the candles are and the less smoke they emit.

Hermann showed her the basics of candle making in her first week or so, but over the past two years, Melia experimented with her tallow mixtures and figured out just how much beeswax she needs to meet the church's demanding criteria—and not one spoonful more. From time to time, when she can afford to add them to her market basket, she spices up the tallow with ground nuts, herbs, or dyes to change its color or aroma. The almond and rosemary candles are a favorite of the Praetorian Prefect's wife, but it has been some time since the woman, dressed in fine clothes and riding in a pretty little coach, has come to the shop to buy them. Melia wonders if she has joined the exodus from the province with other military men and their wives.

As dusk falls, Hermann stumbles over the threshold into the house, his cheeks and jowls dripping with sweat, a low grumble emanating from somewhere between his ugly Adam's apple and his crotch. As usual, he has kept himself busy all day—drinking at the guesthouse down the street or the tavern near the market, playing dice at a public table down by the river, or discussing the Empire's military and political errors with other know-it-all merchants at the guild hall. He makes sure he doesn't return until the daylight is low enough that he won't need to do anything to justify the moniker of candlemaker.

All he does in the candle shop now is count the tapers and votives Melia makes each week and count the money she collects for them. He usually does that on Sunday morning when most other merchants are in church. Melia guesses that he worships those coins with the same fervor his Christian friends worship their God. He drops his heavy, lidded, leather tankard on the table.

Every afternoon, before Hermann starts his trek up the hill toward home, his friend who owns the guesthouse fills it with ale or mead. Melia imagines the host's generosity is less a gesture of friendship than a desire to chase him away and give his guests a rest from Hermann's bombast. He deems Matilda's ale drinkable only when preceded by a significant amount of brew from someone who buys his beer from someone knows what they're doing.

By the time he arrives home, Melia has stopped working in the shop, tended to the stew over the firepit in the corner of the kitchen, and set bowls on the table for supper. Only when she hears his heavy feet on the doorstep does the wife stand up and run to stir the pot, as if she's been doing so all afternoon.

"Bring in some more wood for the stove," she shouts over her shoulder, as if she'd been sweating over the fire long enough to know whether it needed refueling or not.

"Melia! Get it." Hermann scowls. "I've had a hard day." Melia can only wish he has. If only it has been long and hard enough to grant her some peace at night.

DUTIES

On the floor in the corner of the shop, the fresh straw in Melia's mattress pokes at her back. She wiggles and brushes at the needle-sharp points. If the summer heat continues to linger, it won't take long for her sweat and the humidity to penetrate the thin ticking and turn the rough sticks into a stinky sponge and then a hard mass, just like the smelly, moldy clump she threw out earlier that day.

Melia waits and listens for the creak of the ladder rungs that signal Hermann's descent from the sleeping loft. Melia figures he waits until Matildis slips into an ale-induced coma before climbing down and falling heavily onto the mattress beside Melia. Some nights he never comes—nights after he manages to carry his big tankard home without spilling much ale along the way and succeeds at pouring most of it down his gullet. But even then, Melia is unable to fall asleep until the church bells down the street strike four or five times, and she is certain he won't be bothering her that night.

As she lies, coverless, her skin glistening with sweat under her slim nightshirt, she fingers the scar that runs along her jawline. In two years, it has healed well. Fritigil assured her it was barely noticeable, even up close, but Melia can still feel its ridge and remember its initial sting.

A wave of nausea hits as it always does when she remembers the day she stumbled up the cobbled street in tears, clutching her cloak and holding her ruined shift together at the neck as she tried to keep up with the burly Burgundian immigrant who, starting that day, ruled her life—day and night.

Over time, Melia has adjusted how and when she fights back against Hermann or his wife. Her pride tamped down, she now knows what battles she can win and what ones she will always lose. She ignores Matildis' complaints, knowing it makes no difference how she cooks, cleans or sews. Despite her criticisms, Matildis never teaches her a better way to do anything.

And when it comes to Hermann, Melia has learned something else; his pleasure comes from the violence he commits in her bed and power he holds over her. He wants her to give him a reason to strike her. He wants her to resist his penetration so that he can force himself on her. If she doesn't, if she lies still and spreads her legs willingly, he will pester her, lingering on her mattress all night, his erection weak and wilting. It is better put up a bit of resistance, let him huff putrid breath into her nostrils and drip sweat into her face. That's how he is quickly sated. After, he will fall heavily on his side, snoring for a couple of hours. Then he is gone, back up the ladder to his marital bed.

Over the first few months in Mogantiacum, her injuries subsided, and Herman visited her mattress less often. But he still creeps down the ladder more nights than not. She wonders if he wants her to bear him a child. If so, he never mentions it.

She has expected it might happen despite her efforts to prevent it, but after two years of his nightly visits, when she still hasn't conceived, she has decided his seed is probably bad. After all, Matildis is childless as well.

Melia has never learned what had happened to Marta. The only time her name was spoken in the house was the first day Melia arrived, and although she is curious, Melia didn't want to ask. Had she borne a child? Was that child lost? Had Marta died as many women did in childbirth?

Waiting that night for his descent from the loft, Melia hears a cat in heat screech outside the shop, and she turns toward the window. Some unfortunate feline will suffer the same fate as she: an attack by a male unconstrained—perhaps even excited— by her disinclination to mate. She wishes the female a speedy escape.

Melia stares out the transom at the pale moonlit sky and wonders how different humans are from cats. A female cat can't possibly connect the male attack with kittens that come weeks later—she is just a dumb animal, after all. And even if she shuns the tom's advance, the heat and musk of her body betray her. Are most humans conceived the same way: through violence and violation?

She shakes her head. That can't be true. That wasn't how young couples looked at the campfires back in the village at the approach of nightfall. She saw her parents embrace and heard them tangling at night on the mattress next to hers. In the village, no one hid what happened between men and women from the children. Even youngsters knew what begat their siblings. There was no place in the longhouses to hide.

In her last year or so at home, she, too, had felt amorous stirrings in her body at dusk, an intense and deep energy that swelled in the presence of men—especially the muscular warriors who strutted back to the village after a hunt or after a scouting mission, bringing news of dangerous Huns and benign but strange alien tribes. The feelings hadn't surprised her even as she feared their power. But now, Melia wonders if she'll ever feel the desire again. Has her life as a slave precluded such willing pairing? Will she always cringe at the approach of a man?

Melia's body tenses as she hears the loft ladder protest Hermann's heavy load. In a way, she is relieved to hear him coming. It is earlier than usual—perhaps the heat has lulled the wife to sleep quickly. This night's visit will be over soon, and she might get to sleep earlier as well.

"Hello, little whore," Hermann whispers as he kneels on the edge of her bed. "What special pleasure do you have in store for me tonight?"

Melia stares at the ceiling and says nothing.

He stretches his bulk out alongside her, crowding her to the edge of the thin mattress, and cups his hand on her breast. He squeezes it roughly; his touch is not meant for her pleasure, but to remind her how much he can hurt her.

"Well, these lovely teats are forming nicely, little one," he says, pulling his body up on an elbow and licking her nipple. She wills it not to respond, and silently denounces it for stiffening despite her revulsion. She thinks again of the poor cat in heat outside.

Hermann leans back and stares at the fleshy breast in the low glow of the moonlight. "They were so small when you came to me. I believe they have enjoyed my attention."

She turns her face toward the window, expecting her display of resistance to add to his urgency, encouraging him to finish his violence more quickly. If she gets more sleep that night, she can accomplish more the next day—her workday won't be as strenuous. All she can ask for in her enslavement is some sleep and time to complete her tasks, including this one.

"Well, little slut, it's not your pretty little breasts I'm here for though, is it?" He pushes himself up with a grunt and twists his fat frame on top of her. He reaches for her hand and pushes it between their bodies to his erection. She pretends to refuse at first, and then clenches her teeth and takes ahold of him. As his greedy hand instructs, she moves her grip up and down. She doesn't mind this part so much, if it brings him pleasure faster. The harder he gets, the quicker he climaxes, and the sooner he leaves her bed and lets her sleep.

Only a few strokes are enough to harden him. With a grunt, he flexes his knees between hers, pushing her legs apart, and enters.

She keeps her face turned toward the window. He slaps her to turn her gaze toward him, and she closes her eyes. As she expected, her small acts of resistance please him, and his thrusts grow harder and closer together, and soon he arches his back and moans. She feels his hot liquid spill inside her.

He collapses heavily with another moan, and she pushes his spent bulk off. The night's violation has been easier than most. He didn't demand she put her mouth on his erection. He didn't turn her over to assault her like a dog. She chuckles at the thought: if it were always this easy, she'd be much more rested in the day. Perhaps then she could make more candles, which would mean he could buy more ale, which would mean he could get drunk and fall unconscious longer, and his nighttime assaults would happen less often.

She imagines what the pattern could look like: she'll sleep more, he'll make more money, he'll spend it on more ale, he'll drink more, she'll sleep more. She can't stop the convulsion of silent giggles that erupt as she turns her back to his snore.

COLLECTING WATER FROM THE COMMUNITY well and hauling it up the hill is one of the tasks that fell to Melia ever since Matildis abdicated responsibility for household chores. It's one that Melia enjoys. After only a month of carrying full buckets of water at the ends of a yoke balanced on her shoulders, her legs and back have grown strong and the strain of the task eased.

By then she had memorized the faces of the other women who meet at the well at about the same time in the morning, before she heads back down the hill again for the market.

One morning she finishes her turn at the well, pulling her second bucket back up, when she is startled by someone calling her name. She turns quickly, letting her bucket fall back down with a wasteful splash.

"Canuto!" she greets the young boy standing behind her. "You are still here, too?"

Canuto is one of the older boys—maybe now ten or eleven years old—sold to the Burgundians with her and auctioned off while she was being led away by Hermann. The last time she saw him, he was a skinny little lad, barely big enough to carry an empty bucket, let alone two full ones. Yet here he is, waiting his turn for water with a yoke across his shoulders.

"You look…," Melia stops. She is about to say "miserable," but that is not going to help him. His feet are filthy, bare, and calloused, and a whiff of manure blows off his tattered and dirty tunic and mass of unruly hair. But his body has grown as strong as hers had. Clearly, he has been working hard, and not just fetching water.

"…strong!" she finishes. "Are you treated well? Where are you living?"

"Hurry up!" a woman behind her yells. "We need water, too."

Melia turns back to the well and pulls her bucket up again. She hauls it over the side of the well and away from the crowd. Canuto follows her, giving up his turn in line and setting his buckets and yoke down between them.

"Where are you working in Mogantiacum? I hope you have a gentle master."

"Hello, Melia," Canuto answers, nearly smiling, and then

lowers his eyes. He is still the shy boy she remembers, the one who took much abuse in that miserable trip from the Danube to the auction block. "I'm in the stables."

"Ah, so you are working with the horses."

"Mostly mucking."

"Yes, I suppose," Melia says. She pities the boy. Her work at the candle vat is hot and her nightly rapes are horrific, but Canuto's days—and they are probably as long as hers—are spent in horse manure. No wonder he smells.

"Where are you?" he asks, still too shy to lift his eyes to hers.

"I'm making candles for the candlemaker," she says. No reason to burden him with stories about her duties or abuse. "It is hard, but I am learning."

"I wish I could make candles," he says. He rocks from one foot to the other and looks away, toward the hills above town. Then he sighs and lifts the yoke back onto his shoulders. "I had better go now, though."

"Well, I pray I will see you again, soon," Melia calls after him.

He turns and gazes over her shoulder toward the river. "Do you think they are coming?"

It takes Melia a moment to realize what he is asking. "Yes!" she says. "I am sure they are. I am sure your mother will find you, Canuto. Soon."

The boy nods slightly and walks back to get in line at the well.

She is not sure she believes it anymore, either.

THE ANTICIPATION OF SUNDAY MAKES Saturday evening Melia's favorite of the week, although it, too, poses its challenges.

Melia has half of Sunday free, which makes it her favorite day. Even the expectation of another disgusting visit from Hermann on Saturday night doesn't quell her cheer at Saturday supper.

But every now and then, Matildis invokes an emergency and demands that Melia stay in the house all Sunday, waiting with her for some imaginary threat to pass. Lately, Matildis has professed concern over the threat of invasion by the horde of Germanii camped on the east bank of the river. In Matildis's imagination, any minute, the warriors will lead the charge across the bridge, pass by the market and the gold objects in the church and the treasures in the Praetorian Prefect's mansion, and head straight for her front door—or so she pretends to believe.

"You will be kidnapped and raped," Matildis declares, pointing a grimy finger at Melia. "The barbarians won't even let you cry for help."

Raped? Matildis knows that happens to Melia right here in the shop, in Melia's own bed. Why does she think that rape by an invader would be any different? But bringing up her husband's misdeeds won't help get Melia out of the house any sooner.

Instead, she appeals to logic, even while knowing it won't make a difference either. "Why do you think such an invasion will only happen on a Sunday, and not when I'm walking to the market the other days of the week? Or delivering candles? Or carrying water? Why aren't you worried for me then? They will only cross on Sundays?"

Melia figures the wife proclaims these emergencies because she doesn't want to be the only one held prisoner in her house with Hermann all day. Most days, Hermann is out with his friends, but on Sundays, the taverns are closed to regular customers, and he will subject Matildis to his bad humor all day. He hasn't let Matildis venture far since Melia arrived. He forbids her to leave the house. Now that Melia runs the errands, gets water, does the marketing, and makes candle deliveries, Matildis has no excuse to escape the walls of the house and candle shop. Her only daytime escapes, in Hermann's absence, are to visit her friend Ingoberga next door.

Melia isn't sure why Hermann doesn't want Matildis outside, but perhaps the unsightly figure cut by his wife embarrasses him.

He may be proud that Matildis is fat—well provided for by her husband—but her indifferent grooming reflects poorly on him, especially as he compares her with the more elegant wives of Roman bureaucrats and priests he sees on the streets.

"I don't think Melia should leave tomorrow," she tells Hermann again that Saturday night, her voice squeaky with fake concern. "It's not safe. Everyone knows it's only a matter of time…"

"Shut up," Hermann says, cutting her off. He is in a particularly ugly mood that day. "You don't know anything about an invasion, and neither does anyone else."

"But what if…"

Hermann slaps his palm on the table, knocking his spoon with a clang onto the stone floor. Unable to bend over for it himself, he points at it for Melia to retrieve, and then shakes it at his wife.

"No more! No more words from you. Not tonight. Not ever."

An idle command, Melia thinks. She has occasionally come close to feeling sorry for Matildis, for being treated like a child by the brute. But wouldn't it be nice if Matildis were silenced? No more scolding and complaints? Even if for only one night? She smiles into the beet and onion stew in her bowl and lets them argue. She has Sunday to think about.

Melia clears the breakfast soup bowls, stores the remains of a loaf of bread in the metal breadbox, and sweeps up the crumbs Hermann knocked onto the floor. She hums a melody she learned as a child—one the children sang as they ran around the village playing tricks on their parents and chasing the village curs with sticks.

Finished with her morning tasks, Melia pulls off her apron, hooks her small coin bag on her belt, and strides out of the shop a few minutes earlier than usual. As she steps into the street, she hears Matildis calling after her to come back, but emboldened by her own good cheer, Melia ignores her.

Two blocks away, she waits for Fritigil at her corner, and arm and arm they let gravity pull them down the street toward the guesthouse where their friend Chrododild manages a tavern for her father. Although the boarding rooms of the guesthouse are open to travelers on Sunday, the ale room is closed to guests by a recent edict from the bishop, a strict cleric to whom all pleasure is dubious and drinking for entertainment, in particular, is sinful and wasteful. The declaration frees Chrododild from a day of demanding guests, and it gives the three young women a safe place to sit, drink the best ale in town, and talk. At a knock, they let other friends in the door as well, and beer flows free for all until curfew sends them scrambling indoors.

"There they are," cries Chrododield, unlocking the side door to the tavern and embracing them. "The loveliest women in all of Gaul!"

They follow her inside and sit at the thick wooden slab of a bar while Dodi, as they call the young barmaid, pulls them each a tall beverage. Thick stone walls dating back to the first arrival of Romans on the Rhine keep the hot air outside, making the tavern a favorite of travelers passing through Mogantiacum, men of the garrison, and merchants from the market. This day, it feels like heaven to Melia, and she breathes a deep lungful of the ale-scented, cool air.

Dodi leans across the bar with the heavy mugs, showing off well-tuned arms accustomed to hoisting tankards and mugs across the room. The muscles remind Melia of her mother's, although Dodi wasn't an immigrant from across the Rhine. Her narrow face, dark brown eyes and nearly black hair make that obvious. Her mother is the daughter of a Roman senator who has served in the Army in central Gaul for a decade. The senator has returned to the Roman forum, and his married daughter followed him, leaving behind Dodi and her Gallic father, whose ancestors lived in this part of the Empire since the days of Tacitus.

"How were your horrendous masters this week? Any worse than my father?" Dodi asks.

"Does your father squeeze your teats and make you spread your legs for him?" Melia asks. It is only with these two women she can complain of Hermann's disgusting nighttime groping.

"Oh, my dear. Why don't you kick him in the balls some night? Cause some real pain?" She points to Fritigil's stomach. "At least you haven't ended up like this one."

"Yet," Fritigil interjects, not looking a bit insulted by her friend's joke.

"Now that you say that," Melia says, turning serious, "don't you think it's curious, what, with the way Hermann has his way with me all the time, that neither me nor his wife has ever been pregnant?"

"Maybe she has, but the baby's been afraid to come out and see what her mama and papa look like," Dodi quips. She chuckles heartily at her joke, takes a big swallow of ale, and brushes the liquid mustache off with her sleeve. She is certainly in a jolly mood, and Melia wonders why. She is generally the cheeriest of the three of them—that is understandable, of course, since she is the only free woman of the trio. But this afternoon, she seems particularly bright.

It doesn't take long for the answer to come knocking. Literally.

"That could be Theo!" Dodi exclaims, a bit theatrically, jumping up and heading for the door. "I didn't know he was coming."

"Which means that she actually did," Melia says under her breath just loud enough for Fritigil to hear. Fritigil rewards her joke with a broad smile.

Dodi has told them about her new man, Theo, a high-ranking official in the *limitanei*—one of the few soldiers still garrisoned at the fort in Mogantiacum. He would be an impossible match for Melia or Fritigil, but Dodi's grandfather's status is undoubtedly attractive to Dodi's ambitious boyfriend. She has bragged about Theo's recent promotion at the fort, and if the camps on the other side of the Rhine stay put, it won't be long before he could be elevated to Legate, second in command at the fort.

Dodi opens the door and stands on her toes to accept a quick kiss on the cheek from her handsome officer. Alongside stands another young man, a blond and well-built Germani. Perhaps Suevi?

"Close the door!" Fritigil shouts at their friend. "You're letting all that heat in. I'm sweating as it is!"

A trio of young men follow on the heels of Theo and his blond sidekick, and three young women file in behind them. Soon the tavern is filled with young people and the quiet stillness of a Sunday afternoon replaced by the hub of boisterous, off-duty slave girls and a mix of Germani and Gallo-Roman soldiers, bored with the "sit and wait" stalemate at the fort.

"These are Theo's soldiers?" Melia's eyes stick on Theo's blond friend as Dodi slides behind the bar to pour the new arrivals mugs of beer.

"Not all of them. They all know Theo," the barmaid answers. "But I only know Ruggie, his best friend. The blond." She smiles at Melia as if she were reading her friend's mind. "Interested a little?" she teased.

"In what?" Melia protests, but her eyes are glued to the young Germani. He seems at ease among the boisterous group of Romans and Germanii alike, but across the room with his back toward her, she can't see his face.

"Ruggie, perhaps?" Dodie suggests, setting more mugs of beer on the bar. "Why don't you do the man a favor and take him one of these."

"Ruggie? What kind of a name is that?" Melia says, frozen in her seat.

"Ruggenius. Some Latin bastardization of a Germani name. I have no idea what." She pushes a mug toward Melia. "Go find out."

"Aren't proper introductions required?" Melia whispers. "I shouldn't walk up to him like a common prostitute." That isn't the only thing holding her back. Melia still struggles with some of the more difficult nuances of Rome's language, and she is afraid the young Germani will expect her to converse in Latin.

Dodi leans over the bar and takes Melia's face in her hands. "Melia. We may be facing the end of times with those barbarians across the river. If you're ever going to find love, you can't waste time waiting for a proper introduction."

Melia laughs and frees herself from her friend's grasp. "Hand me that platter." She points to the pewter platter propped up behind the bar—the girls often admire their reflections in its shiny surface. Melia searches her face for smudges left from her morning kitchen chores and sticks a loose tendril of hair back behind her ear. She grabs a freshly poured mug by the handle and slips off the stool.

"Whoa! Where are you going with that beer, woman?"

Ruggie has quietly moved in behind her, and Melia stops abruptly, the ale sloshing out of the mug in her hand and splashing on his tunic. But most startling: She realizes he speaks in the dialect she knows best. Suevi.

"I beg your pardon," she stammers, brushing at the foamy mess on his chest. "I— I—"

"You have spilled good beer for no good purpose," he says gruffly, but the grin in his eyes betray him. He watches her swipe at the wasted ale on his chest.

She shoves the mug into his hands and turns away. She pulls herself back onto the stool and takes a deep breath to calm herself. Dodi's laugh is loud, and Fritigil's even louder. What is so hilarious?

"Hey! I was only doing what I was told!" She frowns, leans forward, and lowers her voice to a whisper. "I will get my revenge on you two."

"Well, *Fräulein*," Ruggie speaks over her back, "my thought is you were careless, but you meant well. May I introduce myself?"

"See, a proper introduction! And in a proper tongue." Melia spits the words at Dodi before turning around to face him.

"Yes, you may. But I already guess that you are Theo's frie—." Melia slaps her mouth shut before finishing the word. A tattoo on his neck stops her. It is identical to the one on her forearm. He is a Suevi slave? A slave brought over by the Burgundians?

Ruggie's eyes register her stare at the mark, and he touches it with his free hand. It has stretched and faded. It must have been burned into his skin many years before.

"Yes," he says, answering her unspoken question "Suevi. But now I am Roman." He reaches over and pushes the sleeve of her dress back to reveal her mark. "I see you also have the mark of a Burgundian slave. And given your ease with my words, should I assume you are Suevi also?"

Melia feels her face grow hot, and her eyes swim over his face. His blue eyes remind her of her father's, and his cheekbones are of the same shape as hers.

"Perhaps kinsmen," she says quietly, nearly choking on her words. She turns quickly to take a sip of beer to wet her dry tongue.

"And you are called what?" he asks, his palm resting on her mark. She pulls her arm away.

"Melia. Slave to the candlemaker. Daughter of Ballomar and Hildegreta." She holds his eyes as if challenging him to turn from her now. "My parents are in one of the camps across the river. If they've made it that far."

A flash of surprise crosses his face. "You said Ballomar?"

"Yes. My father's name. Why?"

He takes a swig of beer, his eyes locked on hers, and answers: "I've heard it before. But not for many years." He pauses, as if considering saying more about that, but changes the subject instead. "What is your story? How did you lose your freedom?"

"My mother thrust me into the arms of a Burgundian on the

orders of our tribal council," she says. "But I expect her to come across the bridge any day now and buy my freedom back."

Ruggie's expression changes to amused. "Are you always this forthcoming when you meet men who find you interesting?"

"You think I find you interesting?" she answers. "Yes, I am a slave, but only temporarily." She is gaining confidence, perhaps bolstered by the ale she continues to sip. She waits for his reaction, but he stands before her, mute, his eyebrows knitted in puzzlement.

He takes another long swig of his beer and leans toward her to whisper. "You should probably be careful what you say. It could get back to your master."

Melia blanches. He is right. She doesn't know most of the people in the room. Even if they are young, they might know Hermann. He owns the only candle shop in town.

"And what is your story?" she asks.

"I really don't know," Ruggie answers. He squints, as if puzzled about something, but continues. "It happened a long time ago. I was too young to remember. But I am not unhappy about where I am."

Melia doesn't know what to say to that. How can anyone be sanguine about their own bondage? Her disbelief must show, as Ruggie shrugs, swallows more beer, and turns away without another word. Melia looks at Dodi and tries to hide her disappointment with a smile.

"What did you say to send him away?" Dodi hisses.

"Nothing." Melia watches Ruggie disappear into the swarm of afternoon revelers. She turns back to her friend. "I don't think I said anything. But something strange seemed to happen there between us."

"Attraction?"

"I don't think that's all. Something else. But who knows?" Melia shakes off her confusion and focuses on her ale.

THAT NIGHT, LYING IN THE steamy candle shop, waiting for Hermann to creep down to her or not, she wonders, too, what had happened between her and Ruggie.

Why did he turn away so quickly? Was she supposed to agree that being a slave wasn't a bad thing? Did he embarrass himself admitting that? Ruggie likely doesn't have to lie on a mattress on the floor every night, waiting to be molested by his owner. His life in the garrison has to be better than hers. She is doomed, however, to a lifetime of abuse. Unless her mother crosses that river and buys her freedom. Unless Hermann is willing to accept *solidi* in exchange for her body.

Perhaps Ruggie wanted her to be coy and flirtatious. He will have to find that elsewhere. Melia doubts she'd ever melt and giggle in the face of a young man, regardless how attractive, regardless of how much he reminds her of home. Not after what she endures with Hermann.

Suddenly Hermann is looking down at her from his knees. How has she missed the sound of his heavy steps on the ladder?

"Hello, my little whore," he snarls. "I think it's a good night for a favor." He throws her over onto her stomach, grabs her hips and lifts them until she's on her knees.

It hurts like hell, but at least she won't get pregnant this way.

RUGGIE

With the door open to air out the shop, Melia can hear Claude urge his draft horse up the hill toward her. She looks out as the beast stops in front of the shop, snorts a complaint and braces itself to hold the lorry against the steep incline of the street.

Melia hangs the tallow paddle on its hook and shoos away the village dog who had followed her home from the market that morning. He's been sleeping on her step ever since. She hasn't minded his company, but he is in Claude's way.

"Claude," she addresses him through the doorway. "You are just in time. I started the fire and was waiting for your delivery."

Claude secures the reins and jumps down from his perch.

"Good morning, Melia," he says. Usually those are the only words he ever speaks to her, but this morning, he continues. "And this is Ruggie." Theo's blond friend from Dodi's bar jumps down after Claude and grins at her, mischief in his eyes.

Melia feels the blood sink to her feet and reaches out to steady herself on the frame of the door.

"Oh!" she exclaims, not able to look away as Ruggie steps forward. "Where's Armanius?"

Armanius, one of the garrisoned soldiers from the fort, usually accompanies Claude and helps him hoist the huge slabs of fat from the wagon into the tallow vat. For the past year, Claude hasn't been able to manage the task on his own; Melia imagines that anyone's back would eventually wear out under the grueling load. And Claude's graying temples and sloping back indicate he is aging under its weight.

"Armanius is missing. Probably defected," Ruggie answers for Claude in Suevi. "It's happening a lot these days, now that pay from the Praetorian Prefect arrives late, when it arrives at all. And pleased to meet you, young woman."

"We have met, and you know it," she snaps. She doesn't mean to respond stiffly. Is she angry at him? He showed her no disrespect at the tavern. He'd simply turned away to rejoin his friends.

"Yes, we have," he says, with a nod that seems like an apology. "Come on, Claude, let's get this smelly lard unloaded."

Standing back to allow room for the men to pass, Melia takes advantage of the opportunity to look Ruggie over in a way she couldn't in the dark tavern. He is taller than Claude or Hermann, lean, and muscular. His white-blond hair is short, unlike the Suevi men's hair she was accustomed to, but, like her father's, it is nearly white in the sunlight and darkens when he walks inside. Clean-shaven, he is dressed in a white tunic with a thick leather belt and high leather boots. It appears he is one of those Germans who have embraced *Romanitas*—all things Roman—at least in his choice of clothing and hairstyle. Or perhaps as a slave in a Roman fort, he has no choice.

Melia watches the men make trips back and forth from the

wagon, tipping slabs of fat into the tallow pot. Something about how Ruggie moves reminds her of her father as well. Did all Suevi men move with the same fluid efficiency, and she'd been too young to notice until now?

As they finished unloading, Claude wipes his hands on his leather apron, nods to Melia, and steps outside. He walks around the horse and busies himself with the wagon rigging.

Ruggie looks out the door after him but leans back toward Melia and whispers. "I do hope Armanius doesn't return. Maybe we will have a little more time next week to talk. Maybe you can tell me about your Suevi village back on the Danube."

"Perhaps," Melia says, surprised at his invitation. She pauses. She needs to know something: "Did you come here on purpose today?"

He ignores her question. "I walked away from you at the tavern on Sunday. I was confused and prideful. I wanted to tell you what's happening with the Suevi, but I was afraid to."

"What's happening? What's happening where?"

"On the east bank of the river," Ruggie pauses and leans out the door, his eyes scanning for Claude. The driver is still fussing with the reins, and Ruggie turns back. "The Franks killed many Alans and Suevi in a raid before they reached the river. There are rumors of hundreds of bodies littering the forests beyond their camps. Only the sudden arrival of the Vandals finally backed the Franks away. Some Suevi were killed, too."

"So now, I am so informed," Melia says stiffly, tears stinging her eyes. She heard rumors of the raid, and now she knows it to be true. "Why are you telling me this?"

"You said you are waiting for your mother to buy your freedom. It may be your parents are not alive," he says. "They may not come for you."

Melia frowns and angrily wipes at the tears that fall down her cheeks. Did he ask to get assigned to this delivery so he could tell her that her rescue is probably unlikely? Something that she already knows? It is not only rude, it is painful.

"I have already heard about the Franks," she says, pulling the paddle off its hook and pushing the fat slabs around so they line the bottom of the vat. "But I must hold hope in my heart. Anyway, as a soldier isn't it your job to keep my parents on the other side? To make sure they don't come over?"

"I'm not a soldier."

"What?" Melia hasn't considered the possibility that a friend of Theo's might not be garrisoned with him. "So what are you?"

"I'm a brewer, not a legionnaire," he says. "I live at the fort, but I'm there to make their beer and mead. I work in the kitchen with the butcher. That's why I knew I could help Claude today. I thought it was a sign, a coincidence. I didn't know for sure you'd be here."

"I'm here always, except for Sunday afternoons." Melia hangs the paddle back on the hook and follows Ruggie out the door to the wagon. Already, just knowing he was a brewer and not a soldier, she feels differently about him. Whatever happened across the river, at least Ruggie won't face her father with a sword in his hand. "Maybe I'll see you next Sunday, or next time Claude comes."

Ruggie nods, touches his fingers to his head in a kind of salute, and hops lightly up to the seat. Claude snaps the reins, and the creaks and groans of the old wagon are lost in the clatter of hooves.

In two years of coming and going from the market and making candle deliveries to the church, the fort, the Praetorian Prefect's wife, and merchants along the streets, Melia has never taken a detour from her official duties to do something for herself.

Now, however, she knows of no other way to find out more about Ruggie.

"You go ahead," she tells Fritigil the next morning after their marketing. "I've got to run an errand. You should go home and get some rest."

Fritigil, more than seven months into her pregnancy, shows no interest in Melia's "errand." She is sweating and breathing heavily; getting back to the inspector's house looks like the only thing on her mind. She trudges ahead without a word. Melia watches her climb the next few steps, worried but distracted by her own concern: who is Ruggie and should she trust him with her secrets?

Dodi's father's tavern is cool and quiet when Melia pushes through the front door. It is the first time she's ever come in by the regular customer entrance, and the perspective it gives her is new enough to distract her for a moment. The tavern is more spacious than she'd realized. The bar where Dodi stands, washing mugs and tankards, is in the back of the room by the side door where Melia and Fritigil have always entered. At mid-morning, most of the dozen or so tables between the front entry and the bar are empty; only a couple of traveling men in colorful robes sit together in a corner, their heads close together. Melia passes close enough by them to see they are studying a scroll of parchment covered with Arabic numerals.

"Well, Melia!" Dodi throws her bar rag over her shoulder and runs around to greet her friend with a warm hug. "What a surprise. It's a bit early for a beer, though, isn't it?"

Melia kisses her cheek and points to a stool. "Do you mind if I sit? I'm not here to drink anything. I want to ask you something."

Dodi looks surprised but waves Melia toward a stool at the bar. "No. Fine. Just fine. My father's down at the market until mid-day, getting meat for supper. I'm alone, but as you can see"—she waves at the nearly empty room—"I'm not exactly busy."

Melia puts her market basket on the floor and pulls herself

onto a stool. "Who are the travelers?" she asks, nodding toward the men in the corner.

"Amber traders," Dodi says. "Goths, I think, from their bad accents. They've been coming through on their way to Lutetia and Londinium for as long as I can remember. West in the spring, and back east to the mouth of the Elbe in the fall."

Melia sees Dodi flash a wistful glance in the men's direction.

"Why the frown?" Melia asks.

Dodi sighs, her eyes focused far beyond the men's table as if in a trance. "I have always wanted to go to those places," she answers, her hands resting on the counter, wrapped in the drying rag as if she's forgotten what to do with them.

"Is that true?" Melia pauses to think. Has she ever wanted to explore Brittania or more of Gaul? No. That is not something she wants to do. What she wishes for most at night, waiting for her disgusting master to come and go, is to return to the village on the Danube. The place she will describe to Ruggie next time they meet—if they do.

Dodi's spell breaks, and she returns to the dirty herd of mugs on the bar. "Theo has told me the fine things he's seen in Britannia, Rome, and Milan. I would love to walk over the Alps and cross the North Sea. Don't you want to have those adventures, Melia? Don't you want to see more of Gaul than this nasty fort?"

"I've already seen more of Gaul than I want to." Melia shakes her head. "I've already walked and been hauled in wagons as far as I want to go. Maybe Theo hasn't told you how hard it is. Walking the rain, trudging through mud. The snows on the Alps? The rough—"

"Oh, stop!" Dodi holds her hand up to interrupt and laughs. "I suppose you are right. But if Theo goes back to Milan, or gets sent to Britannia, I will suffer anything if I can be with him."

"And he's asked you to come along with him?"

"No, but then he hasn't been transferred yet. I'm hoping, though." Now Dodi's faraway expression betrays something else: she is smitten.

The men at the corner table hail her, and Dodi skips toward them as if walking on air. She returns with their empty mugs, fills them with beer, and carries them back.

"I have to get back to the shop soon," Melia says when her friend returns. "I bought barley at the market and slurry from the yeast maker that Matildis needs for her beer. It's the only thing she does all week, and I don't want to give her an excuse to give me that job too."

"What did you want to ask me, then?"

"I came to ask you about Ruggie." Melia feels her face flush.

"Ah! Of course! What makes you think of him today?"

"He helped Claude deliver the tallow yesterday, and he said he wants to know more about my people, the Suevi. He was one of us."

"Yes. You do look alike," Dodi observes. "But you know that he is a slave, too."

Melia sniffs. "Of course. We have the same mark." She pulls up her sleeve to show it to her friend again.

Dodi nods. "And he's not a soldier. He's the beer maker."

"I know that too. He told me."

"What do you think I can tell you that you don't already know?"

"Does he have a wife? Is he a good man? What does Theo know about him?"

"I know he does not have a wife. But other than that? I guess you will have to ask Theo. When we're together, we don't talk about Ruggie." Dodi dips her head and smiles crookedly. "Actually, we don't talk much at all."

Melia pretends not to catch her innuendo. "But maybe you can ask him," she suggests.

"This much I can tell you," Dodi says. "He makes the best beer in the diocese. He's supposed to only brew for the fort, but my father has convinced him to bring us barrels once a week. He spices the beer with heather and sweet gale, which makes it last longer, especially in this warm weather. Haven't you ever noticed how different it is?"

"Well, anything would be better than Matildis' rotten brew!" Melia laughs. "I guess I've noticed it is more bitter, tastier."

Dodi shrugs. "A lot more people must think it's good, because business has picked up since we started to sell Ruggie's beer instead of our own.

"By the way," she adds, leaning over the bar to whisper, "did you hear that the Praetorian Prefect is going to draft townsmen to replace the legions if it looks like the barbarians are coming?"

MELIA REGRETS HER ERRAND. SHE learned little from Dodi, except for the news about the draft of townsmen. The barmaid's thoughts were occupied with her own sweetheart and dreams. And the trip to her bar has taken Melia too much time. She runs up the hill to the candle shop with her heavy basket. Matildis will be waiting at the door, ready to chastise her for tardiness, whenever she returns. But today, Melia is later than usual, and she'll have to scramble in the afternoon to catch up in the shop.

As she steps through the door into the house, she hears the familiar voice of Matildis' only friend, their neighbor Ingoberga.

"…and I think we should all be afraid," the woman says before looking up and giving Melia a desultory wave. Whatever she finds frightening, seated at the table with a mug of beer, Ingaberga looks more drunk than scared. So does Matildis.

"Melia is probably happy," Matildis says. "Her barbarian cousins are sitting over the river, imagining the sodomy and thievery that awaits them." She snorts and pretends she doesn't see Melia come in. "They will rape us all."

Rape? Melia doesn't have to wait for 'barbarians" to suffer that. She hangs the leg of lamb in the cellar, puts the barley in a pot of water to soak, and escapes to the shop, closing the door between herself and the sotted women. But now she is curious. All the talk about an invasion by the people camped across the river makes little sense. The Romans cut off passage over the bridge early that summer, and with the river patrol for the upper Rhine based just below the fort, its boats coming and going all hours of the day and night, only a rare, solo swimmer ever manages to sneak across the swift current and stagger ashore. How can an entire tribe—accompanied by women, children, wagons, and livestock—get through?

But it seems that is all the town can talk about these days. Is there something she doesn't understand about invasions? With the exodus of so many Roman legions and their families, most of the people who remain in Mogantiacum came from Germania or the Gothic provinces south of the Danube already. How will these new migrants be so different from the people who are already there? Are they so much more dangerous, more barbarous? She can't imagine the men from her village raping women and burning buildings.

When she talks with Ruggie, perhaps she can ask him. He works at the fort; he will know as much as anyone in town about what might happen. But then, maybe she'll never have a chance to find out. Maybe Armanius will come back, and Claude won't need Ruggie to help with the deliveries. And if Theo gets that transfer to Britannia or Milan, maybe Ruggie will go, too. It is better, she decides, dejected, if she doesn't expect too much from either Ruggie or Theo—on any account.

PREGNANCY

Fritigil doesn't meet Melia at their usual corner the next day. It is drizzling and the cobblestones were slick, but at least the unseasonable heat has broken. Perhaps the slippery streets have slowed her friend down.

But after waiting for a quarter hour, Melia worries Fritigil is having a problem with the baby. She hitches up her skirt and runs up the alley. She pulls the chain to ring the bell at the door of Julius's house and is surprised when he answers.

"Hurry," he says, recognizing Melia. "I think she needs help."

Melia follows him up a steep flight of stairs to a small room at the back of the house. Fritigil lies on a narrow, iron-framed bed, thrashing about in sweat-soaked sheets, moaning through dry, cracked lips.

"Dear friend!" Melia drops her basket and kneels by the low bed. "What's wrong? Is the baby coming?" Melia does some quick math in her head. It is October, and the baby isn't supposed to come until late December. If it comes now, it won't live more than a few hours, if at all.

Fritigil twists her torso toward Melia and reaches for her hand. "I don't know what happened," she whispers between heavy, labored breaths. "I was getting ready to come and meet you." She pauses and shutters, pointing to a spot in her swollen belly. "Right here," she says simply. She grimaces.

"Pain?"

Fritigil nods, her eyes squeezed shut.

"Lie still," Melia says. She looks up at Julius, who stands over them, his face white—is it fear or squeamishness? "I'm going to get the midwife. She'll know what to do. Don't leave her."

Melia shoots down the stairs and out the door. Stumbling over the slippery stones, she half-slides and half-runs down the hill, and turns up a narrow street behind the church toward the midwife's house. All the slave girls know Helga, the midwife: it is she to whom they go to get advice about preventing pregnancy or ridding themselves of unwanted ones. Prostitutes, noble women, and merchant girls like Dodi all visit her shortly after their first monthly bleeding to learn their lessons. Helga is discrete, and she knows all about potions, seeds, powders, rubs, and liquids.

As soon as Melia confided her nightly rapes to Fritigil, her friend brought her to Helga for silphium seeds, which Melia grinds into a powder she adds to her beer. Helga showed her how to make the sticky mixture of cedar oil and honey, which Melia keeps hidden by her bed and inserts as soon as she lies down. It is supposed to keep Hermann's seed from penetrating her womb. So far, it appears one or the other of these remedies has worked.

Pushing wet, loose hair away from her face, Melia bangs on Helga's door. Her small fist hardly makes a sound. Her eyes swimming with panic, she searches for something hard to rap on the wood. Nothing. She can find nothing. She takes a deep breath and shouts at the upstairs window. "Help! Helga, help!"

A few moments later, the shutter flies open, banging heavily against the stucco.

The midwife sticks her head out the window, blinking sleepily at the daylight.

"What is it?" she says through a yawn. She shields her eyes with her hand and peers out. "Oh, it's you, Melia. I have just gone to bed. Magritte had her baby at midnight."

"It's Fritigil!" Melia shouts. "She's having pains. She needs help. You have to come now."

Without another word, Helga closes the shutter. In a matter of seconds, she appears at the front door, pulling a hooded cloak over a thin linen nightshirt. As they scamper back up the street toward the house, Melia tells Helga what she knows about Fritigil's pregnancy.

"I have been warning her," Melia says. "She isn't even close to time, but she's already carrying it so low." Girls in her village had learned all about pregnancy at a young age; like sex, matters of childbirth were open affairs. By the time Melia was old enough to understand that babies were made in a woman's belly, she knew what the stages of pregnancy looked like. Fritigil's bulge looked too big for six months, and it was riding too low on her frame.

Melia leads Helga up the narrow steps to Fritigil's room and pulls the comatose Julius out of the way to give the midwife room to work. "Cool water!" Helga orders. "And cloths. Several clean cloths."

Julius stands, scared and confused. Melia pushes him out the door. "Go! Do as she says."

Julius stumbles over his lead feet, finally making his way down the stairs.

"What do you feel?"

Helga kneels by Fritigil's bed and puts her hand on her mound of baby.

"Pain. Like a knife," Fritigil grunts. She pulls in a big breath and holds it.

"Breathe!" Helga tells her. "The baby needs air. Don't hold your breath."

Helga rises taller on her knees and puts her ear to Fritigil's belly. Fritigil moans.

"Quiet," Helga says. "Just breathe easy. I want to listen."

The room seems to spin, and Melia leans against the wall to steady herself. She hadn't realized she, too, has been holding her breath. The room is quiet as Helga moves her ear from one section of Fritigil's bulge to another.

"I'm quite sure," she says, finally, sitting up and putting a comforting hand on Fritigil's forehead, "that everything is fine with both of them."

"You mean Fritigil and the baby?" Melia asks.

"No," Helga looks back over her shoulder and smiles. "I mean with both babies." She turns back to Fritigil. "You've been blessed with twins, my dear girl."

Fritigil doesn't appear to hear her. Helga turns to Melia. "Now help me with those clean cloths. Let's wash her off. It's important she be clean and dry."

After tending to Fritigil's hygiene, Melia and Helga leave Julius to administer cool compresses to the patient's forehead—if he will. Helga waits in the drizzle on the front step as Melia finds Fritigil's market basket. Together they head down the street, no longer in a hurry, stepping carefully on the wet stones.

"She needs to stop moving around until the babies come," Helga says. "And you should make sure she gets plenty of meat and milk. A little beer will be good for the babies, but not too much."

"Do you mean stay in bed until the birth?" Melia asks.

"Yes, and no sitting in a bath. Julius should leave her alone, too. No nightly visits. It's too dangerous at this stage."

Melia considers assuring Helga that the nightly visits she alluded to had ended weeks before, but she simply nods. Even with Helga, there are some things better left private. "I will lecture them both," she says.

They reach the church, and Helga puts her hand on Melia's shoulder before turning down her alley. "She needs you most of all now," she says. "Julius won't understand much of this. It's only a woman who can help her get through this."

"Is everything going to be fine?"

Helga looks away, and Melia wonders if she going to answer. Finally: "I don't want to say. I think it's going to be difficult. We can pray and keep her calm. That's all we can do."

SLIPPING DOWN THE WET STREET to the market, Melia pulls the hood of her cloak over her hair. The tunnel vision suits her. She doesn't want any distractions. She needs to figure out how she can tend to Julius's meals and housekeeping while doing her own work for Hermann and Matildis. She will have to get up earlier and get more candles made before she goes to the market.

Perhaps on the way back from shopping for herself and for Fritigil, she can start the evening meal at Julius's house, and leave it to cook slowly over a few coals all day. It will be better if she can convince Julius to eat his meals at the tavern for the next three months. His salary is certainly no restraint. While he eats, Melia could stay with Fritigil, giving them time to talk and plan for Fritigil's imminent and scary work of caring for two babies at once.

Whatever solution she comes to, Melia can imagine how much Matildis is going to complain about Melia's absences. Not having Melia to lord over and curse will rob her of her greatest pleasure. And what will she do with her extra time alone? Cook more? Sew more? Perhaps she could spin some of the wick that Melia needs for the candles.

Melia snorts at her own silliness. The only thing that will change at the shop will be the amount of sleep she gets between Hermann's sweaty nighttime visits and the time she rises to get started on her work.

"Melia?"

Startled, Melia slides to a stop and pushes the hood back from her eyes.

"Theo?" How has he recognized her, covered from head to toe as she is?

"You should watch where you walk. You could hurt someone." Dodi's sweetheart laughs and addresses her in Latin. Dodi has said he knew Germani in many of its dialects, but Melia has never heard him speak anything but Rome's tongue.

"I'm sorry. I am in a hurry," she apologizes, her heart pounding at the surprise of running into him.

"What's so urgent?" he says, laughing at her. "Someone's candle has burned all the way down?"

Melia stiffens. Why make light of her work? As many candles as the fort burned through, she would have thought he would have more respect for it.

"I'm going to the market. I have to shop for Fritigil now, too. She's… well, she's…," she stutters. Latin is still difficult for her, and although she is comfortable with women's bodies and pregnancy, it is strange to talk about such things with men— especially one as powerful as Theo.

"Is it the baby?" Theo reached out and rests his long fingers on her shoulder. Such familiarity is surprising. Melia swings her head around to see if anyone witnesses his touch.

"Well, yes." No one is watching them, and she relaxes a bit. "But she has babies, not baby."

Theo knits his eyebrows and cocks his head. It reminds

Melia of the way the neighborhood curs look at her, apparently confused when she talks to them, and it makes her laugh.

"Yes, twins," she says, more comfortable now. "She is to be blessed with twins. If it is a blessing." She stops. She has just repeated the midwife's comment—that twins are a blessing—without even considering if it were true. Perhaps it is said that twins are a blessing because Rome was founded by the twins Romulus and Remus. And men boast that fathering twins proves the abundance and robustness of their seed and their manhood. But for the women—especially a slave woman without her own slaves or servants to help—the one who truly bears this "blessing"—it delivers more work and double the worry.

"It is a blessing," Theo says, definitively. Does he sense her ambivalence and feels the right to declare a judgment? He tips his hat. "I must be heading back to the fort, Melia. It was a pleasure to see you."

"Wait!" Melia reaches out to stop him, catching a bit of his sleeve. Theo looks down at her grasp with a frown.

Melia lets go. "I'm sorry, but I have no one else to ask."

"What is it you need to know?" Theo's face is stern, but his voice softens.

"What is happening over there?" Melia points toward the river. "On the other side? Will they be allowed to cross? Or will they be sent back? What's going to happen?"

"Ah," Theo says. "Of course. The Germanii. Your people, I know. Yes, your kings have asked for settlement in Gaul. They want Stilicho to accept them as he has the Franks in Austrasia and the Alamanni in the Agri Decumates."

Melia nods. She is familiar with the regions of Gaul: Neustria and Austrasia in the north and the Decumates nestled next to the Rhine to the south—territories that the Empire once defended against the people thought of as barbarians. More Germanii than Gallo-Romans live there now, and the Empire depend on

German troops to man the garrisons along the *limites.*

"And what does Stilicho say?"

"So far he is refusing. Gaul is already enfeebled by the drain of legions to the Danube," Theo says. "But... ." He leans in as if to share a secret. "He is a barbarian himself. Who knows what his intentions are?"

Melia frowns at his smirk. Where do Theo's loyalties lie? He could easily be tried for treason for what he has just said.

But Theo continues. "He'll probably invite them over the river when he returns from Illyricum. We'll all be speaking German then."

Melia isn't surprised that Theo would mock Stilicho. As the commander in chief of the armies he is the most powerful man in the Empire, even more powerful than the emperor Honorius. And Stilicho is only half barbarian—his father was a Vandal who had served as a federated soldier in the Roman legion—and many Romans, like Theo perhaps, distrust his allegiance to the Empire. But she is surprised Theo would share his opinion with her. Why trust her to not report his indiscretions?

She says nothing for a moment, turning this over in her mind. Perhaps he feels a slave woman—Germani, as well—wouldn't be believed. It is one more insult. She is starting to dislike the man.

"But if he allows no settlement, what then?" she asks. "Does the Empire push them back into the swords and axes of the Huns?"

Theo shakes his head. At first, she thinks that meant he doesn't know. But then she realizes he is once again—what three times in one short conversation?—mocking her.

"Woman, you ask too many questions," he says. "You are a slave, and"—he points to her basket—"you have shopping to do. Go take care of your friend Fritigil and her two babies."

Melia watches him turn on a heel and march away. She wonders what Dodi sees in him. Of course, as a Gallo-Roman, Dodi won't suffer nearly the condescension Melia does. But still. The arrogance!

She pulls the hood of her cloak back over her wet hair and heads for the market square. She learned little from Theo, except for one thing: he'd said "your kings." Kings? The Suevi have tribal chiefs, and believe that leadership runs in some families, but they have never called anyone a "king." Does Theo confuse the idea of a chief with a king? Certainly, Stilicho wouldn't. His barbarian roots are too recent for that kind of misunderstanding.

But she has no more time to think about it. She steps quickly around a pack of dogs arguing noisily over a bloody, mangled squirrel and heads for the baker's stall. With the trip to Fritigil's bedside, her detour to fetch the midwife, and now the conversation with Theo, she is going to be much later than usual. Again! Matildis will be furious. No doubt she will revel in this latest excuse to curse Melia. It could last for hours.

JULIUS

As expected, Matildis hollers, clenches her fists, and stomps around the room as Melia unloads her market basket.

"Fritigil has been sent to bed to rest," Melia says, explaining her tardiness. She slides the bread into its tin box, ducks to avoid the wife's swinging arm, and steps into the cellar to hang the duck carcass on a hook. "She is having twins, and she's not well. I did her shopping for her."

"That slut!" Matildis shouts. "That's her reward for her lust. All you slave girls are whores!"

…and cooks, and candlemakers, and housekeepers, and bakers, and butchers, and beer brewers, Melia thinks. And not by choice. This town could not function without slaves. Nearly a third of the soldiers, townsfolk, laborers, farmers, and all the wet nurses in Mogantiacum are not free persons. Or so the priest told her the first time she delivered candles to him, and he recognized her tattoo.

"You need not hang your head in my presence," he said. "God does not care what your status is here on earth. We are all his children."

Saving her breath by ignoring Matildis's rant, Melia hangs the iron kettle over the firepit in the corner and pours a couple of tankards of water into it. Quickly, she chops turnips, onions, carrots, and cabbage for the stew, and slides them into the pot along with the chicken bones she saved from supper the night before.

Matildis is still ranting in her unintelligible Gothic language as Melia dries her hands on her apron and steps over the sill into the shop and closes the door. When the sun dips below the roofline next door, blocking the rays from lighting the shop, she will stop making candles and return to the kitchen to stoke the fire under the pot and add the duck.

The tallow in the vat has been cooling all morning. Melia holds her hand over the top of the mixture to test its temperature, and then swings the wheel threaded with wicks over the pot. She pulls the windows and the shop door closed against the draft and waits for the wicks to hang still.

With no fresh air coming in, the room heats up quickly. Melia wipes her forehead to keep the sweat out of her eyes, unties the rope that keeps the wheel elevated above the tallow, and lowers the wicks, watching the lead weights sink slowly through the thick fat and beeswax mixture. She raises the wheel back over the vat and pulling a second rope, slowly swings the wheel from above the vat to a large tub of water. She lowers the wicks, cooling the tapers, and pulls the wheel up again.

When Hermann taught Melia the candlemaking process, he told her to count to one thousand between the dip in the water and the next dip in the tallow. But if Melia does that, she can't concentrate on anything else. So, she devised a different way to measure time. She sets a candle marked with horizontal lines in a holder, each line representing the right amount of burn time, and sets the holder on the metal worktable in the back of the room. She sticks a nail in the first line of the marked candle and lights the wick. When the candle burns down to the mark, the nail falls onto the metal letting her know it is time to dip the wicks into the tallow again.

When she explained her timing method to Hermann, he scoffed at her. It was obvious, though, that he was only feigning disinterest. He'd never thought of it.

"Yes, I know you can do that," he said. "But my count is more accurate." It didn't matter. Since he spends no time working in the shop anymore, she ignores him and does it her way.

While she waits for the nail to fall, she sprinkles sulfur crystals in a few dozen ceramic jars. Later she'll fill these with tallow and wicks and sell them to the garrison as fumigators to rid the horse stables and the barracks of bedbugs, fleas, and wasps.

Working through the afternoon, Melia recalls Theo's news. Who are these kings he talked about? The stories that the elders told around the village fires at night had been of kings who had led the people across the Danube to meet the Romans in the Marcomanni Wars in a long-ago time. The tribes north of the river had been starving after months of poor weather and could see no other options than to tap into the wealth of Pannonia, the Roman territory south of the river. The Romans required the tribes to vest one man with the power to negotiate with their emperor, and that man became king. But after the war, kings became chiefs again, and power was redistributed. Now, perhaps negotiating with the Romans has again required the Suevi to name kings.

More troubling, it seems unlikely the Suevi can come over the Rhine if the legions don't want them to. What chance, then, does her mother have of making it over? All the soldiers in the fort have to do is line up on the west end of the bridge and shoot arrows at anyone who tries. She can't see how an alliance with the Vandals and Alans will make the crossing much easier unless it means the Romans will eventually run out of arrows.

She had heard nothing from Greta since she pushed Melia into the arms of the Burgundian. Does her mother have any idea where she is? Maybe she hasn't even made it to the river. As Ruggie had confirmed, the Romans recruited Franks from the north to attack the "barbarians" well east of the river.

For the first time in the two years since she arrived, Melia begins to consider the likelihood she'll spend the rest of her life as a slave. When Hermann and Matildis die, she'll be sold to another master, and then perhaps to another, until she is old and worn out and no good to anyone anymore. And for the first time since she stood naked on the platform of the slave auction, Melia feels the burning tears of self-pity.

THE SHOP TURNS DARK AS the sun ducks behind the house next door, and Melia hangs up her apron and steps back into the kitchen. Usually, she and Matildis sit in the back of the house, Melia busy with needlework, and wait for Hermann to stumble into the house from his afternoon of gambling and drinking. But Fritigil needs her help. She puts the duck in the pot, scrapes the ash off the coals in the hearth, and blows on some kindling. Once the flame rises, she piles on larger pieces of wood, and waits until the pot boils.

"You will need to tend this, Matildis," she advises the wife. "I need to go to Fritigil now. Don't let it boil over. If Hermann isn't home before the sun sets, let the flame burn down or you'll overcook the duck."

"You tell me what to do?" Matildis crows. "You are the slave in this house. I will be the one to give orders, little mule."

"Fine. You can do that when I get back. Right now, I need to help my friend."

"No, you won't!" Matildis pushes herself up from her chair and charges across the room at Melia. She trips over her dirty shift and lands in a pile halfway across the room, and Melia laughs. "You'll have to come up with a better strategy than that," she says, surprised by her own new-found hubris. Where has that come from?

Melia pulls her cloak off the hook by the door, passes through the shop, and steps out to the street. Once again, Matildis reverts to her Gothic tongue, and whatever she is yelling at Melia through two doors is a waste of breath.

Low rainclouds shroud the damp street in premature darkness. The streetlamps won't be lighted by the night watchmen for another hour, and Melia picks her way down the cobblestones carefully. A broken arm or knee would render her unable to do her work, let alone take on the new double duty she faces. Hermann still can prevent her from helping her friend once he finds out about it, but if that happens, Melia had a plan. It would be a gamble, but one she is willing to make for Fritigil's sake.

Julius lets Melia into his house. He answered the door only a moment after her knock; she imagines he must have worried that she wouldn't come.

"How is she?" Melia asks, stepping in out of the drizzle and shaking off her cloak.

"Sleeping." Julius leads Melia upstairs, steps aside, and lets her tiptoe into Fritigil's bedroom first.

"Melia." Fritigil opens her eyes and smiles. She raises an arm from the elbow, seeking Melia's touch. "You came."

Melia takes the hand her friend offers. "How is the pain?"

"Gone. I'm feeling better, but weak. I don't want to get up. Can I just rest?"

"Oh, yes. You have to. The midwife said bedrest until the babies come. I'm here to take care of Julius. Your only job right now is to take care of those babies." Melia wipes the hair from Fritigil's forehead, surprised to feel how cool and damp it is.

"Thank you," Fritigil says and closes her eyes.

Melia looks up into Julius's worried face. "We should let her sleep," she whispers.

They tip-toe down the stairs, and Julius leads Melia through the downstairs rooms to the kitchen. It is the first time Melia has gone deep into the splendid house. She takes in its extravagance as they pass through. In the formal reception room, several fine chairs surround a large fire pit, the setting almost dreamlike in its tranquility. A dining room with a long table covered with a fine silk cloth is large enough to seat a dozen, and off a wide hallway, a large, cushioned chair nestles below a stack of shelves, lighted this late in the day with six or seven lanterns. On the shelves lie several leather-bound volumes—Melia has never seen so many in one place. Since she can decipher no more than her name, she can't imagine being able to read one, let alone all of them. It would take a lifetime!

Fritigil never told her about these luxurious surroundings,. How did she manage it all? Melia vaguely recalls a housekeeper— one who doesn't live in the mansion. Melia realizes that taking care of Julius while Fritigil rests will be possible only if the housekeeper still manages the cleaning.

The kitchen itself is a wonder as well. Over the big firepit at one end of the spacious room hangs three pots of varied sizes. The rock backdrop to the pit reaches all the way to the top of the high-ceiling, and against it lean huge billows, long iron tongs, a thin ash shovel and a thick iron poker. An oven built into a stone-faced wall looks like it can acccommodate a dozen loaves of bread at a time. A long metal table in the middle of the room is too tall for dining, and Melia realizes it is a working table, not an eating space. The cellar door is off on one side, and a shiny, smooth stone floor underlies the entire room.

Melia catches her breath as her eyes stop on the greatest luxury of all: a water pump that rests inside a large slate sink next to a door leading to the garden behind the house. Imagine not having to haul water from the community pump down the street!

"What a beautiful space!" she cries. She turns to Julius behind her. "I can't imagine how wonderful it must be to cook in here. You could feed an army."

Julius smiles crookedly. "I suppose you could," he says. "If we still had one."

He reaches into the small suede purse that hangs on his belt and hands her a few *denarii*.

"For the market tomorrow," he says, as if Melia wouldn't have understood. "Take her basket with you tonight."

He starts to leave the room, but Melia stops him.

"I am only able to be here a couple of hours in the evening," she says.

He turns back to her. He frowns but nodded as if he has figured that out for himself. "I will see if I can find a cook to help until she is better."

Melia wonders if he thinks Fritigil will be better soon. If he does, he is wrong. It will be at least two months before the delivery, and Fritigil will need help for some time after that, with two babies in hand. But what do men like him know of a slave's work? Of childbirth? Of infants?

She picks up the large poker and stirs the coals in the firepit. "Perhaps you could carry some water to this pot," she says, pointing to the smallest one hanging on a hook above the center.

Julius doesn't answer. She turns to see he has retreated to the room with his books. How silly of her to think he would want to help. Kitchen work is women's work, and a noble bureaucrat will never consider pumping water for a slave who is cooking his meals. The luxury of the house and the concern he showed for

Fritigil has misled her into thinking he is somehow different from Hermann.

In many ways, he is. Her friend has described what happened regularly, and apparently quite effectively, in Fritigil's narrow bed as fun. It wasn't anything like what Melia experiences on her mattress in the candle shop. And Fritigil claimed he has hinted at freeing her from slavery, and they might even marry. All of that is possible and legal. But helping in the kitchen? What had she been thinking?

The items Melia had handed to Julius on the doorstep when she came back from the market that morning still lie on the metal table, and Melia shoos a trio of flies off the small wheat loaves and rabbit carcasses. Julius will never be able to take care of himself if he doesn't even know enough to put food in the root cellar instead of leaving it out for flies and who-knew-what other critters to nibble on. But then he doesn't have to know: he has had Fritigil at his disposal.

An hour later, Julius has devoured an entire loaf of bread, the meat of both rabbits, and most of the vegetables she laid out in front of him at the big dining table. As soon as he is finished, he pushes back and returns to the library. Melia carries a bowl of broth and half of one of the small loaves of bread up the stairs for her friend.

"I'm not hungry," Fritigil says, her eyes barely open.

Melia sets the tray down on a low chest and motions for Fritigil to sit up. Her friend shakes her head and looks away. Stepping quietly down the hall to another bedroom, Melia steals a pillow and returns. Lifting Fritigil's shoulders, she shoves the pillow behind her back.

"You must eat. Your babies are hungry even if you aren't," she says, laying the tray across Fritigil's lap. She sits down at the foot of the bed.

"You know I can't lie here forever," Fritigil says, picking up the spoon. "I have work to do. Julius is good to me, but I am still a slave. I must do his work."

"We will worry about that tomorrow," Melia says. "Tell me something, though. Who helps you keep this house? And when does she come to work?"

"Clodia," Fritigil answers after swallowing a few spoonsful of broth. She is hungrier than she said. "She comes four days a week. She should be here tomorrow. She doesn't care for me much, and I try to stay out of her way." She stops to slurp some broth. "She manages the household except for the kitchen. She has dark hairs sticking out of her chin."

Melia laughs at that last detail. "Dark hairs? Like a beard?"

"Not exactly. Just like random hairs."

"Why doesn't she pull them out?"

"I think she doesn't even know they're there." Fritigil giggles. Melia is relieved to see her friend retain some humor.

"Why don't you tell her?"

"I think that would be an excuse for her to kill me."

It is meant to be a joke, but Melia frowns. Was there real enmity between them—the young, beautiful slave who has won her master's affection and the elder housekeeper who resents the passing of her youth and beauty? What danger might Fritigil be in, lying here day after day, doing nothing to earn her keep except for incubating Julius's babies?

Walking home in the damp darkness, Melia is exhausted. Maybe she won't be able to manage both her own work and Fritigil's. Julius seems to think Fritigil will be up and cooking again soon. Perhaps Fritigil's cooking pleases him as much as her lovemaking did. He sure seems capable of polishing off a big meal. She has to convince him to hire a cook at least until the babies come.

BARBARIANS

After Hermann leaves her mattress about midnight, Melia lights the candle she prepared earlier in the afternoon with a nail that will drop an hour or so before sunrise. She plans to begin work then so she can finish dipping the candles she started the day before, and then she can head out to pull water and go to the market. She is eager to get back to the shop early so she'll be there when Claude—and, she hopes, Ruggie—comes with the weekly delivery of tallow.

Lying back down, she wipes herself clean, the third thing—after taking silphium and inserting the honeyed cedar oil in her vagina—that she does to prevent conceiving. Hermann barely produces much semen anymore, which is a relief for Melia, but that doesn't mean he has stopped trying.

She pulls a thin sheet over her legs to keep flies from bothering her the rest of the night and tries to quiet down. But an image of Ruggie pops into her mind, crowding out sleep. She imagines him lying on this thin mattress next to her instead of Hermann. How can she even consider that after Hermann's demands and abuse?

She shakes her head to dispel the thought and tries to focus on how she will describe her village to Ruggie instead. What can she tell him? The differences between a Suevi village and a Roman fort city are so vast it will be hard for him to grasp, especially since he's been in Mogantiacum most of his life. She will describe the low-slung, grass-roofed huts with sheep, goats, chickens, and geese housed underneath. Will he understand how comfortable it is to sleep on the floor over the livestock? How the heat from the animals keeps them warm? Will he be able to imagine the communal nighttime bonfires and ritual offerings to Wodin?

An image of her village crowds out her thoughts of Ruggie. It is summer, and around her, the younger children chase each other and wrestle, tumbling noisily, shouting and teasing. The young village curs try to join the scrums while the always-pregnant bitches lie panting off to the side in the shade. Tree branches in the corners reach toward each other to form a cool, green canopy across the open center of the small village.

Women sit with their looms in the shade, and talk about nothing and everything, weaving linen and wool as they watch the antics of their young sons and daughters. The men and older boys are out with the livestock, and the older girls sit near their mothers, pulling on strands of sheered wool and twisting them into the warp and weft their mothers will dye, dry, and weave.

The sun is sinking down toward the horizon, filtered by the quaking leaves of the huge oak trees around the camp, and the men laugh and shout as they return from the herds. The scene is so sweetly bucolic, and Melia wonders if it is more nostalgia than memory.

As if answering, she remembers a different day. A horde of

strangers on horseback charge into the village while the men are away with the livestock. Their dark hair and slanted eyes are those of Huns, men of the steppes to the east, men with little sympathy for the villages they raid, or for the women they rape. But that day, they seek only one thing: young girls and boys to sell as slaves in the Empire south of the Danube. Their raids on the Suevi have increased as they were repelled in the south by the Romans and Goths and on the north by the Vandals.

Women jump up from their looms and grab their toddlers, pulling them inside the huts and barring the doors. They know that if the Huns want to, they will burn down the houses, force everyone out, and take anything they can carry, including the women. If they hadn't been able to grab enough slave booty, they would have. But that day, their appetites are small. They snatch up a half-dozen frightened young women, and congratulating themselves with shouts and whoops, they leave as quickly as they had come.

Melia, returning from a trip into the woods to gather nuts, watches with horror from behind a large oak tree. Her friends fight with their fists and teeth, but they are tiny and weak compared with the brutes who snatch them, leaping back onto their saddles as if carrying bags of feathers, not writhing, biting humans.

When the Suevi men return to the village that evening, they find a circle of weeping women, some lying prone in the center of the village, beating themselves with switches torn from the willows on the riverbank.

Melia remembers the discussion around the fire that night— sober and fraught with anger and argument. It isn't the first time the Huns have taken children to sell as slaves. This time, though, will be the last. The Suevi's only escape is to the west, across the lands of the Alamanni and Burgundians, and over the Rhine into the wealthy empire of the Romans.

There, it is decided, they will settle and farm, safe from the Hunic horde.

FRIGHTENED TO A SWEAT BY dreams of marauding Huns, Melia wakes long before the candle's nail falls onto the metal table. Shaking, she considers her relative fortune: Whatever rape and disgrace she suffered at the hands of Hermann and Matildis, she is safer in Mogantiacum than she would have been strapped to the saddle of a Hun's steed.

Wiping the moisture from the back of her neck, she rises, throws her cloak over her shoulders, and walks out the side door of the shop to the outhouse behind the building. The drizzle of the day before continues, and musty, rotting leaves cushion her path. A couple of houses away, a dog hears her shuffle and barks.

"Shh!" she hisses and closes the outhouse door behind her. She wipes the surface around the hole in the bench to chase away the insects and critters that might interfere with her business and sits. The acrid smell of urine and decomposing human waste rises as she lets her water fall. She wonders what life is like for her mother—if she still lives—across the river. Do they build outhouses in those camps? Do they erect houses of any sort, or have they been sleeping in open wagons since they left the Suevi village more than two years before?

The cold shocks her fully awake, and once back inside, Melia moves quietly to dress, light a couple of oil lamps, and get to work. The tallow has cooled too much overnight to continue dipping her tapers. She stirs the coals and adds some small logs to raise the temperature in the vat.

Her empty, growling stomach surprises her. She has forgotten that in the evening before, she cooked for Hermann and Matildis, and cooked for Julius and fed Fritigil, but she neglected to feed herself. If she doesn't eat something soon, she might faint. It won't be the first time. Back when she first came to the shop with Hermann, and fought viciously against his nighttime assaults, she'd been too miserable and sick to eat. Only after she fainted in the kitchen one day, and Matildis slapped her back to consciousness, did she realize she'd have to eat to live, and she'd rather live than die dizzy and hungry.

Sneaking quietly into the house for something to tide her over until the midmorning meal, Melia hears loud snores in the sleeping loft above. She opens the breadbox, grimacing at its squeak, and tears a piece off the dry bread from the loaf she purchased the day before. Back in the shop, she investigates it for any sign of green mold. Although some merchants claim their moldy loaves helps fight off the plague and dysentery, among other things, its furry presence disgusts her.

On the other hand, it is said that old bread can be used in place of sprouted barley to make beer. As she chews the dry crumbles, Melia decides it is another thing to talk to Ruggie about. Perhaps she can come up with more things to ask him, more than they can cover in one visit to the shop. That will mean she'll have an excuse to seek him out at the tavern the next Sunday as well.

Finished eating, Melia stirs the tallow. Quickly it reaches the right consistency, and she swings the wick wheel back over the vat and lowers it. It will take three more dips before the candles reach the diameter she needs, and she can start a second batch. She is determined to use up most of the tallow by the time Ruggie and Claude visit that afternoon.

Dip, cool, dip, cool, dip, cool. The hours pass quickly, and by the time the candles are fat enough to move onto the high racks to harden, the sun is burning off the drizzling clouds. Hermann and Matildis have yet to arise from their bed when Melia slips out the door into the misty light and heads toward the well with the buckets, and then to the market with two baskets on her arms.

Fewer merchants have been manning their booths in the market every week. They, too, are following the legions south to Pannonia or returning to Genua, Roma, or Treverorum in search of more robust sales. And at each stop in her shopping, Melia hears more talk of invasion—of barbarians forcing their way across the bridge and pillaging town. Surely, that is scaring some tradesmen away as well.

"Aren't you Germani, too?" she interrupts the baker speaking with alarm about barbarians with the girl who counts coins for him. From his accent, she can tell what tribe he is from. "Don't you want your fellow Burgundians to cross, too?"

"I am Roman, not barbarian!" the baker howls at her. His words are Latin, but his tongue still speaks Germani. "I have nothing in common with those creatures on the other side. Their bread is unleavened—they don't even take the time for the dough to rise before they gobble down their dry crusts." He leans forward and adds in a harsh whisper: "They eat dog, even their own children!"

Melia has heard soldiers in the tavern say the same things, but she has no time to argue. She thanks the baker for the warning, hands his girl two coins, and places a loaf of nicely leavened bread in each basket.

As she climbs back up the hill, Melia reasons that no horde of barbarians can cross the Rhine and overwhelm even the small legion that remained in the fort. The bridge is no more than ten meters wide. A mass of humans, whether warriors or families in wagons, will have a better chance of falling into the river and drowning than getting across to the other side.

But that is another thing to ask Ruggie about.

"This is not an illness that will pass in a week," Melia tells Julius, finding the bureaucrat at home when she arrives with Fritigil's market basket. "You will need someone to cook for at least two months until the babies arrive. And given her weak condition and how hard it is to handle two babies, perhaps for a few months beyond that."

"But that will cost me too much!" Julius's protest is far more vociferous than Melia had expected. Isn't Fritigil's life more important to him than a few dozen *denarii*? Glancing around at the splendor of the house, Melia is certain he can easily afford it. His father had been a bureaucrat before him, and it is well known that tax collectors skim *dinarii* from the levy and collect bribes from citizens in return for assessing lower duties.

"The cost of not doing this could be Fritigil's life," Melia says quietly. She doesn't want her friend upstairs to hear their discussion through the floor. "Are you willing to lose her?

Julius looks at her through narrow eyes. "You don't speak like a slave girl," he says. It is not a compliment.

"I have been a slave only two years now," she says. "I have spent most of my life as a free woman, and I intend to be one again, soon."

"Should I report that to Hermann?" he asks. His eyes stay narrow and his lip hints at a snarl.

Melia shakes her head. "I don't care if you do," she lies. "But if you do, he will know I'm coming to help you, and he'll forbid it. He won't share me with you."

"And how are you going to free yourself?" Julius seems genuinely interested in her plan to escape slavery. Perhaps he worries that Fritigil also has such intentions.

"My mother will arrive to buy back my freedom one day. I have told Hermann about that often," she lies again. "He can use the money he gets for me to buy another slave. The auction block never runs out of human chattel."

Julius looks confused for a moment. Has he forgotten about the slave auction? Then his face brightens.

"Yes!" he says, as if he's just had an epiphany. "I shall get another cook tomorrow morning at the auction. I will need someone when I set up my household in Treverorum at the end of the year anyway."

"Treverorum?"

"Yes, I am accepting a promotion, managing tax collections for the diocese in both cities," he says.

"Does Fritigil know this?"

"No." His expression adds: why should she?

Melia shouldn't be surprised at his arrogance, although Fritigil seems to be blind to it. In two years, Melia has seen that no matter how many Germanii they rely upon to fill military ranks, butcher their meat, brew their beer, and make their candles—all matters that their comfortable, Roman life depends on—the Gallo-Roman inhabitants of Mogantiacum hold themselves above the relative newcomers—even the Franks like Fritigil who've been Roman federates for decades.

And it isn't the occupations that provoke their disdain; Roman butchers snub Suevi butchers, Roman legionnaires grumble about Burgundian legionnaires, and Roman mid-wives belittle Frankish ones. And that is true even though the Romans, who had pushed first the Celts and then many Gauls west to islands beyond the sea, were invaders themselves.

Walking back to the chandler's shop, Melia considers all she's learned from Julius. First, it is clear that he does not see his relationship with Fritigil as special as she does; perhaps it is always this way. Masters are more important to a slave than a slave is to a master. The slave can be replaced at will; not so the master.

Second, his threat to expose Melia's desire for freedom underscores his contempt for her. Does he think people choose to not be free? Are happy with their lot?

She has threatened him as well: "Expose my plan and I'll not help you." It is a safe threat. A bureaucrat of Julius's standing would rarely run into, let alone speak to a tradesman of Germani descent like Hermann. Hermann pays taxes to one of Julius's subordinates. Her plan would likely never be relayed.

What bothers her most, though, is Julius's plan to move his primary residence to Treverorum, and that Fritigil knows nothing of it. What will become of her friend and the twins? She is tempted to share the news with Fritigil, but she doubts it would make things better.

Fritigil's condition is already too fragile.

THE VOTIVE

Claude's cart rattles up to the door of the candle shop mid-afternoon. Melia, who has been listening for it since she returned from the market and Julius's house, is giddy. She pulls off her grease-spattered work apron and skips out to the street.

"Claude." She nods at the driver as he jumps down from the wagon. "Ruggie," she says next, straining to use the same cool tone of voice. "I ran out of tallow this morning. It's good to see you have some rendering for me."

"As always, Melia." Claude grabs the first slab of fat and throws it over his shoulder.

Ruggie pulls a slab off the wagon and follows Claude to the vat, avoiding Melia's eyes. Perhaps her anticipation was wasted; maybe they won't talk that afternoon.

The unloading proceeds quickly, and Claude hops back up and picks up the reins. "Come on, Ruggie," he barks. "I need to get back. I'm grinding sausage this afternoon."

"No. Go without me," Ruggie stands at the door and waves Claude on. "I'm going to walk back. I need to stop at the church to give the priest a message from Theo and check on the tavern's beer supply."

He watches Claude turn the cart around in the street and head back down the hill before he steps back inside the shop.

"Oh, is that true?" Melia asks. "The priest? For Theo?"

"Claude doesn't need to know what I'm doing. I work for the baker, not for him." Ruggie sounds defensive. "But it's true. Theo asked me to talk to the priest about his plans with Dodi."

So, Dodi was right. She is likely to marry disagreeable Theo.

"Well, thank you for stopping in," Melia says, her cheeks burning.

"You were going to tell me about the village you came from," he says, watching as she pokes at the coals under the vat and throws some kindling on them. "I suppose we didn't come from the same village, but I'm certain I'm Suevi, as you are."

"When did you leave?" she asks, pushing the kindling onto the hottest coals.

"Leave?" Ruggie snorts, but not unkindly. "I didn't leave as much as was stolen. I was only two, they tell me, and I was taken by Burgundians, as you were." He touches the stamp on his neck; perhaps a tic triggered by thoughts of his past.

Melia remembers the day in the tavern when she told him she'd been sold by her parents. He had listened and then turned away without a response.

"You were stolen? Or sold by your parents?" she asks.

"I will never know," he says. "I was too young to remember. But all of that is past. I don't remember any of the village life, nothing about being Suevi."

"But you still speak the language," Melia says.

"There are plenty of Suevi at the garrison. I've never stopped speaking it."

"And your Latin is perfect. I wish I could—"

"Not perfect. Just ask Theo!" Ruggie laughs.

Melia hangs the fire poker up on a hook on the wall and walks around the vat to the metal table to resume wrapping the candles she finished two days before. "I must continue to work, but I am happy to have your company. I don't want to forget my native tongue. I expect my mother to arrive any day, and she doesn't speak Latin."

"So you told me," he says. "You hope she is one of the barbarians on the far bank."

"Yes, but I don't call them barbarians. They are refugees from the Huns. No more barbaric than you or I."

"And your village?" Ruggie leans crookedly against her table, resting his weight on an elbow. Melia wonders why he is intent on learning about Suevi life. Perhaps the Romanized Germanii have the same yearning for their tribe that she has.

"If you've always lived here, it's probably hard for you to understand how different it is, living in the village, in the woods." Melia starts, obliging his curiosity. She tells him about their longhouses, children playing in the dirt courtyard, nightly bonfires and conversation, village dogs and the herds of livestock.

"Women were different there," she adds at the end. It was something she hasn't thought much about back in the village, but now, it seems important. It is certainly different in the Empire. "They spoke at the village meetings. Our work was our own, but we were part of the tribe just like the men."

"We?" Ruggie smiles crookedly. "You were hardly a woman then, were you?"

"Why do you say that?"

"And you are still young and naïve besides," he answers. She isn't sure if he meant it as an insult or simply an observation.

"Naïve? In what way?"

"You still expect your mother to rescue you. You still want to be her child."

It's unexpected, but Melia gets his point. He is right; she is too old to think like a child who needs her mother. But he is wrong in another way: he likely doesn't know what kind of a woman she is forced to be here in the shop at night. He can't know why getting away from Hermann is so important to her—and she doesn't want him to know.

"My desire is to be free of slavery," she says, tautly. "It isn't to return to my mother's hearth."

Ruggie stands still, observing her as she continues to pack her wagon with her merchandise.

"What do you think about my village?" Melia says. "Does it bring back memories for you?"

Ruggie nods, his eyes glaze over as if they are focused on the past. "I remember little except for two things: the big fire, perhaps like the one you described in the middle of the village. And the dogs. I remember running with the dogs." He pauses and frowns. "No one plays with the curs in Mogantiacum. Not even the children."

Melia laughs. "You are right," she says, the tension between them broken. "Sometimes I see them look at me like they want to play. It's almost like they talk to me."

"And I remember my mother's face. At least I think I do. Sometimes I see it in my dreams." He pauses, as if struck with nostalgia. "Do you want to go back?" he finally asks.

She hadn't expected that question; indeed, she hadn't thought much lately about where she wanted to go.

"I don't think that's possible," she says. "The Huns are still raiding along the Danube, I'm told. And I'm afraid there are things I've gotten used to here, too. Civilized things. But I would like to leave Mogantiacum," and Hermann, she adds silently. "Why? Do you want to go back?"

Ruggie stands away from the table, leans back against the wall, and takes his time to answer. Does he care what she thinks of his response? Does it matter to him somehow?

"I am now Roman," he says, but without the arrogance of Julius or Theo. "I am a slave, but I have accepted Roman ways. I don't know that I could go back either, even if it were possible. I know little of village life in Germania. I know nothing about raising livestock or building houses. But…" He stops.

"But?"

"I would like to go to Castra Regina to become a master brewer."

He smiles, and his story gains momentum. "You must come see my little brewery at the fort some time. I make wonderful beer." The words are boastful, but they don't sound that way. "In Regina there is a brewery, a large one that supplies the entire town. They're making malt from different grains. If I went there, I could try some new ideas, try herbs beyond sweet gale and heather. I understand they are adding hops to some of their beers. I can't get hops here, but I'd like to see how that tastes." He pauses again, his eyebrows furled. "I'd go, but…"

"But? Why not?"

"But, Melia," he says with a wry smile. "I am a slave in the Roman legion. The camp prefect decides what I do. I don't control my life any more than you."

That isn't true. Yes, he is a slave, but he has much more freedom than Melia. Ruggie can't know how much her life is controlled by Hermann and Matildis—especially Hermann.

Ruggie looks like he wants to say something else, and Melia encourages him. "Tell me what you are thinking."

"You must keep what I tell you a secret," he says.

Melia nods. Who would she tell?

"I am saving money to buy my freedom. Theo allows me to keep the money for beer I sell to taverns and diocese officials. No one else knows that I have saved it all, but I have nearly enough to free myself. Theo has said he will accept my manumission. Then I will be free to go."

"Theo is a good friend, not just your master, though."

Ruggie accepts that qualification with a nod. "Yes, and now I need to go and talk to the priest for him," Ruggie says, pushing himself away from the wall. "Theo and Dodi are planning to bond themselves, one to the other, and he wants to see if the priest will give them his blessing, even though Dodi is a Frank."

"But she's a Christian," Melia says. "What difference will being Germani make?"

"I don't know," Ruggie says. "And neither does Theo. That's why I am sent to ask."

He hesitates as he steps out the shop door, as if he doesn't want to leave yet. He pauses on the step and gives a little wave. Melia thinks it looks like something Dodi would do.

Shortly after Ruggie leaves, Melia's wagon is ready for the trip down the hill, but she waits and works the fresh fat around in the vat with the paddle instead. It would be better if Ruggie were gone before she gets to the church. She doesn't want to interrupt him, and she wants to light a candle for Fritigil's health. It would be difficult to explain that to Ruggie, given that she isn't a Christian. He knows by now she only prays to Wodin and worships the Valkyries.

Turning Ruggie's question over in her head, she considers where she will go once her mother buys her freedom. At one time, not long ago, she had thought she would want to return to her old village on the Danube. But now, she accepts the likelihood that it is either deserted or settled by Huns from the east or Goths from south of the river. She might be willing stay in Mogantiacum, which has come to feel like home over time, but only if she can get away from Hermann and be free.

It has been only a couple of days since Dodi had talked about going to Lutetia—the city on the Seine, on an island in the middle of the river. Melia had disavowed any interest in the rest of Gaul, but with its Roman baths and fine amphitheater, Lutetia would be like Mogantiacum, only better. What about Genua? Or Rome? She laughs. Rome won't likely welcome another Germani like her. Or will she go wherever her mother goes?

Why has she not thought ahead and made plans? That's what Ruggie is doing. Perhaps women don't do that: female slaves follow their masters; and her mother, like most women, follows her husband. But if Melia has neither master nor husband, she could decide for herself. On the other hand, Ruggie dreams of going to Castra Regina on the Danube, and if she could go with him, she could start her own candle shop. Could she follow him and still feel like she was deciding for herself? Would he want her to?

Melia lets the fire burn down to a low flame before she shakes off her daydreams and heads down the hill toward the church with her wagon of tapers.

"I'm glad you're here," the priest says as he opens the big front door for Melia and her wagon. "Our votive supply is getting low." He closes the door after her and follows her into the nave. "Many are worried about a raid from across the river. They've been burning more votives than ever."

"When I'm done here, I'd like to light one for Fritigil," Melia says, as she begins unloading her merchandise into the bins that holds candles for offerings. "She is with twins. I am concerned for her."

"Yes, I heard she isn't well." The priest stands with his idle hands clasped in front of his long tunic. She wishes he'd help her finish her unload, but he never does.

"I'm helping Julius, but only until he hires another cook."

"That is generous of you and especially of Hermann."

Melia doesn't argue. It surprises her that everyone assumes Hermann ran the household or condones her helping Fritigil, when, in fact, he knows little of what goes on in the shop or the household unless it comes to counting his precious coins. If he knew she is helping Julius, he would order her to stop.

"But you recognize her sin, too, Melia?" the priest adds.

Melia stops unloading, surprised. Does the priest think what he calls her "sin" is Fritigil's idea? Does he think she had any choice when Julius first pushes her legs apart? Does he think Hermann's abuse was Melia's fault? Perhaps he does. That allows him to blame the bastard children on the very women who need his prayers, not on the men who force themselves on young slaves and provide funds for his church.

Melia wants the conversation to be over. "Yes, Father," she says through clenched teeth, hoping that will be enough to bring it to a close.

It doesn't work. "How about you, Melia?" he continues. "Have you left your worship of the pagan gods behind you? I do not see you in confession or at Mass. You are Christian?"

"Yes, Father," she lies. She knows she doesn't sound sincere. But she has little free time in her week, and she isn't going to spend it on her knees worshipping the Roman's God. Yes, the Suevi had nominally accepted the Christian faith before she was born. But it was a strategic acceptance, not heart-felt—necessary to keep on the right side of the Empire after Theodosius outlawed their pagan observances and prayers to the deities of Germania.

But she has no interest in being a Roman or a Christian. To her, the Christian faith is the religion of the Empire, not the religion of a proud Germani.

Why then, she wonders, does she want to burn a votive for Fritigil? Maybe it simply feels like the only thing she can do.

And since her friend is a Christian, maybe it will help her. Melia shakes her head and laughs at herself as she finishes unloading the wagon. She seems to have more questions than answers these days—about many things, and it seems she had no one to help her figure them out but herself.

After she stacks her candles in the bins, the priest mumbles a benediction over them, and Melia gathers up the spent votives for cleaning and refilling. She pulls her wagon back to the door of the church, places a coin in the collection box, and chooses a small votive. Pulling the hood of her cloak over her head, she kneels on the bench before the bye-altar at the side of the nave. Melia knows little about praying to the Christian God, but with her eyes closed and her fingers intertwined in front of her, she whispers pleas for Fritigil's health and the birth of healthy twins. When she rises to her feet, she is relieved the priest is nowhere in sight.

Later that evening, after completing her duties for Matildis and Hermann, and visiting Julius and Fritigil, she lies exhausted on her mattress. She pleads with Wodin to keep Hermann away for the night and tries again to imagine her future. If she follows her mother, will it be farther into Gaul? Down into Hispania? Across into Britannia? But what if Ruggie is her destiny? Could she find herself in Castra Regina?

She has forgotten to ask Ruggie about the invasion, about how anyone could think a horde—however large or armed— could get across the bridge without being knocked down with Roman arrows and swords. She will ask him at Dodi's tavern on Sunday.

DRAFTED

After two more days of Melia's double duty, Julius meets her at the door with the news that he has acquired a cook who will start that evening. Melia won't have to return to cook. Relieved, she hands him the market basket and climbs the stairs to visit Fritigil.

"I'll miss going with you to the tavern on Sunday." Fritigil whines, but she looks happier and healthier than she has in days. "I can't stay here for two months. I'll go mad."

"Perhaps you can move a little," Melia suggests. "I'll ask Helga what she thinks."

"What does Helga know?"

"More than you and me," Melia answers. "I've never delivered a baby before. Have you?"

"No, but delivering a baby and carrying one in your gut are two different things. How many has Helga had?"

"I'm not arguing this with you, Fritigil. And you'll stay there until Helga visits again. I'll ask her to come tomorrow."

Fritigil sticks her tongue through her lips and blows a spray of saliva at Melia.

Melia waves the mist away and sits back to avoid another attack.

"The good news is Julius has found another cook, though," she says. "I can still come to visit you, but I won't have to cook for him."

Fritigil looks confused. "He found another cook? What are you talking about, Melia?"

"You didn't know?" Melia frowns. "He told me he acquired another cook today. I'd suggested it a few days ago. Hermann will not like it if I keep up this double duty."

"He didn't tell me about a new cook," Fritigil says. Her expression blackens, and she turns her face toward the window. "He isn't telling me anything, Melia."

"You mean he's not talking with you?"

"Not since we found out that I have twins. He sends the housekeeper up with my food and beer. And she hardly says a word. She hates me."

"Why would she hate you?"

Fritigil shrugs and keeps her eyes on some distant point out the window.

Melia doesn't want to believe what she is hearing. Men often grow chilly toward their slaves—even toward their wives—once they find out about an imminent baby. Some men don't like the celibacy the church orders for nursing mothers. Others simply aren't happy about supporting another slave baby who could take years to become a useful asset.

But Julius had been happy about Fritigil's condition—at least at first. Maybe all that has changed with the twins, but Melia doubts it. It probably has more to do with his impending move to Treverorum.

If Fritigil doesn't know anything about that, Melia doesn't want to be the one to break the news to her. She searches her brain for something else to talk about. She chooses Ruggie.

"Ruggie came to the shop yesterday," she says, trying to sound vaguely disinterested in her own topic. "He says he'd like to move to Castra Regina to be a brewer for the town."

"Hmmm." Fritigil's stare doesn't shift from the window.

"Until he told me that, I didn't know there was such a thing."

"Such what thing?"

"As a brewery that could fill an entire town's tankards," Melia says.

"Hmmmm."

"What are you thinking, Fritigil? You're not even listening, are you?"

"Do you think he'll abandon me?"

Perhaps Fritigil knows more than she lets on.

"Why would you think that?"

Fritigil turns and catches Melia's eyes.

"I don't know. But I'm afraid he'll leave me. I think I've always known he would. A rich man can simply buy another slave. He'll sell me and the babies and be done with us." She turns back to the window. "A new cook, huh? That makes sense."

Melia sits with Fritigil in silence until shouts rise from the street below. For the moment, she doesn't care what the noise was about—it isn't enough of a ruckus to represent an invasion. Apparently, even with all her attention focused on some point out the window, Fritigil doesn't care either.

Melia leaves Fritigil staring into space and walks back to the shop and her work. Whatever excitement had filled the streets while she sat upstairs is over. No evidence of carnage or pillaging. Apparently, the tribes haven't made an assault on the bridge yet.

She is relieved to be through with her extra duty at Julius's house, but has she been wrong in suggesting he hire a new cook?

Fritigil is bedridden and can't fulfill her duties. Now Julius will simply wait for the babies to come, and then arrange to put Fritigil and the infants on the auction block as soon as she can walk and carry them.

Her head down with worry, Melia trudges back up the street. She looks up just as she reaches the shop door and is surprised to see Matildis and her noisy neighbor Ingoberga sitting on the front step, weeping and slobbering with their arms wrapped around each other.

Worn out by Fritigil's sorrows, Melia has little sympathy or energy left for the women's troubles, whatever they are.

"What's this?" she asks brusquely.

Matildis wails, untangles herself from Ingoberga's flabby arms, rises, and slouches through the shop and into the kitchen.

Ingoberga wipes her wet face with the sleeve of her dress and answers Melia. "They've called the men to the fort." Slobber sprays out with her words.

"What do you mean?"

Ingoberga takes a deep, stuttering breath and pushes herself up, wringing her hands in her apron. She follows Melia into the shop.

"They ordered all the men to report to the garrison," Ingoberga says. "They're being drafted to defend us from the barbarians."

Melia stops and considers the news. Her first thought is to wonder how Hermann could possibly help the fort defend Gaul against anyone. What weapon would he carry? A beer tankard to hit warriors over the head? She stifles the urge to laugh at the image and wonders next why Julius is still in his home. Perhaps bureaucrats assigned the essential task of collecting taxes are exempt from the draft.

Entering the house, Melia feels an unexpected and thrilling sense of relief. Hermann will not be visiting her at night again for a while—at least until the tribes across the river move away or make their desperate plunge across the bridge. She considers her calculation: she is more repulsed by fat Hermann than the horde of barbarians that has everyone else cringing in fear.

"Is he gone already?" Melia tries to keep the joy out of her voice. She doesn't fully succeed.

Ingoberga follows Melia into the living quarters, takes a stool, and answers for her. "You don't care! You and your filthy tribesmen. Why didn't you stay where you belong? What are you doing in the Empire? We don't need you. We don't want you."

"Well, I'm not here by choice," Melia answers tersely. "And, yes, you do need us. You and your lazy friend here need us very much." Ingoberga lifts her heavy torso off the stool and reaches out to slap Melia across the face. Melia steps back to avoid her. Ingoberga shrieks at her incoherently and hobbles out of the house on her stiff, flabby legs. Melia closes the door after her, steps back into the house, and puts her market purchases away. She doesn't look at Matildis, who is sitting in the back of the room, sobbing and sniffling.

What an act! What a display of self-pity! The woman couldn't stand her husband when he is there. They barely talk except to complain about each other and to discuss Melia's shortcomings. Melia imagines Matildis hasn't welcomed Hermann's amorous groping in years. And yet now she slobbers all over herself about his disappearance. Is it fear of facing an invasion alone?

Melia closes the door between the house and the shop and starts her work. If the fort is going to be full again—however fat and unfit Hermann and many others are—they are going to need more candles. And with Hermann gone, Melia will be able to collect the payments for them, and she'll be able to skim a little more off the top for herself—at least that portion that had gone to pay for Hermann's gambling and afternoon drinking. She skips a little hop of joy.

How odd. Just when everyone else in Mogantiacum seems to be sinking into misery, Melia feels liberated.

That evening, with Hermann away and Matildis frozen in her ersatz grief in the back of the room, Melia roasts two tiny game hens and some turnips, eats alone, leaves Matildis's portion on the table, and retreats to the shop.

She sets the spent votives from the church on a narrow metal tray and balances it over the edge of the vat to heat. It is essential to save the residual waxy mixture, mixed with expensive beeswax. With votives, it is even more important that worshippers who buy them won't be repulsed by the smoke of pure beef tallow. As soon as the residual wax melts, she scrapes out the little glass vessels, and saves the liquid. She tosses the burned cotton wicks out and wipes the votives clean to be refilled.

She strips some rosemary leaves off the bunches she picked from the garden earlier in the afternoon and crushes them with a pestle. She adds some almonds to the mortar and mashes them with the rosemary until the oily paste is smooth and fragrant. The idea to make scented votives had occurred to her as she knelt at the church. The priest had never asked for scented votives, but he hadn't prohibited them either.

Stopping to rest while the wax turned to liquid, Melia feels different. Her entire body seems to sink onto her work stool, her muscles softening at the same time as the wax melts in the votives. It is odd for that time of the day. Usually she starts bracing for Hermann's approach hours before it happens. Now she doesn't have to. Is this what she used to feel like, before she became his unwilling concubine?

THE NEXT MORNING, MELIA MAKES a detour to Julius's house on the way to the market. She plans to use the excuse of offering to help the new cook navigate the stalls to cover for her real mission: to see what he knows about townsmen's draft into the fort.

Overnight, once she convinced herself that Hermann would not be coming into the shop—that he would not somehow be relieved of military duty for his lack of ability—she slept the best she ever had in Mogantiacum. How long could she expect that to last?

To Melia's surprise, Fritigil answers her knock at Julius's door.

"What are you doing down here?" Melia nearly shouts. "You are supposed to be in bed."

"I couldn't anymore. I just couldn't lie there any longer," Fritigil answers, leading Melia down the long hallway to the kitchen. A tall, yellow-haired woman sits on a stool, her back toward them, slicing beets. She turns and smiles, showing a rare perfect row of straight, white teeth. Her eyes are a brilliant light blue, like the noon-day sky.

"This is Briggeta," Fritigil says. "And Melia," she tells the tall woman in her Frankish dialect, "is my friend. She's been helping me before you came. But she is the candlemaker's slave, not ours."

Judging from her mood, it seems unlikely that Fritigil has yet to discover Julius's plans to move to Treverorum.

Melia pushes her worry aside. At least Fritigil has help now. "Are you going to the market?" she asks Briggeta in Latin. "I'll show you around." Briggeta furls her brow.

"She only speaks a Frankish dialect," Fritigil tells Melia in Latin. "I'm glad. I have missed the ease of a language that slips off your tongue." Fritigil translates Melia's question for the new cook.

"Ja," Briggeta says, adding something that Melia takes to mean an eagerness for an escort.

With baskets in hand, they head down the hill. Melia doesn't try to make conversation, given their language hurdle, but enjoys the quiet of the morning and a wonderful energetic lilt in her step that she credits to a great night's sleep.

The market is quieter than ever. More than half the stalls are empty, and the butcher's offerings have dwindled to a few geese and rabbits, a couple of overpriced legs of lamb, and a vat of bloody sweet breads. It is a good thing the city is being abandoned by so many; there isn't enough food to feed them. And now Melia doesn't have to feed Hermann. That has become the fort's concern, and she wonders where the garrison will find the meat to feed all the recruits the camp prefect has drafted.

From the shortage of meat, grains and vegetables in the market, Melia guesses that the inhabitants of the farming villas in the countryside are avoiding Mogantiacum and the dangerous tribes gathering across the river. Are they all going to Lugdunum? Or north to Belgiaca? Into Aquitania? Or all the way to Milan? Will they come back?

Melia wishes she could talk with Ruggie about it all. If the merchants in town are recruited to fight off the barbarians, Ruggie might be drafted too. As she and Briggeta walk out of the market and back up the hill, Melia feels the energy from her good night's sleep drain away, sunk by new worries and uncertainty.

For the first time in two years, she begins to wonder if the tribes on the other side of the river deserve the name "barbarians." If they represent danger rather than salvation—even for her— perhaps they do.

THE BREWERY

Matildis sits on the front step as Melia walks up from the market. It is so unusual to see her out of the house, Melia is startled. Usually, the wife hangs around the kitchen, waiting to scold Melia for tardiness, and then she retires to the back corner to avoid any possibility of being in the path of some household duty, like starting the mid-morning meal.

"Did you hear any news?" Matildis asks. "What is everyone saying?"

Melia shakes her head and walks past her into the kitchen. "I heard nothing." Matildis follows her inside, her hands wringing sweaty wrinkles into her dress. Melia puts her basket on the table and pulls out a bunch of carrots and a small hen that will constitute both of the day's meals, and a dozen apples she plans to cook and mix with honey to make a soft cake.

"The streets are nearly empty," Melia says. It feels odd to talk with Matildis instead of listening mutely to her tirade. The wife has yelled and shrieked at her for two years; only for one day at the very beginning had they carried on any exchange in a normal tone of voice.

Melia walks around Matildis's generous frame and goes about her usual business: setting an iron pot on a hook over the firepit and starting the fire. She brushes the dirt off the carrots and cuts off the green tops, which she will later chop into a fine, fresh garnish for the finished stew. With the chicken and the vegetables in the pot, she steps into the candle shop to start filling the votives.

"You sleep with him." Melia is surprised at Matildis's voice—not so much by what she said, but by the fact that the wife has followed her into the shop. Usually, Matildis comes into the shop only to pass from the living space to the street and back. In how many ways will she surprise Melia that day?

Melia considers Matildis's comment and whether to answer it. Slowly she turns to face Matildis.

"I don't sleep with him," she says, forcing her voice to stay calm and neutral. "I don't sleep until he leaves me alone. Until then, I bite my tongue and pray for it to be over." She turns to tie on her apron.

"You are a whore."

Melia spins around to face Matildis again.

"A whore?" she shouts. "You think I want his attention?"

Matildis looks too miserable to answer. She stands, her arms at her side, and her back hunched under a ratty shawl.

"I fought him with my teeth and my nails. Don't you remember my bruises? My black eyes? My swollen wrists?"

Matildis averts her eyes but doesn't move.

"If you don't, it's because you wanted to believe it was my idea."

Melia turns to pull the paddle down from the wall. She doesn't care whether Matildis responded to that or not. For several minutes, she didn't, but Melia could feel her stiff presence behind her.

"I despise him." The words are spoken so softly, Melia thinks maybe they have come out of Matildis's eyes instead of her mouth.

Melia blinks and faces her. "You hate him?"

"Yes."

"Why?"

"Because he leaves me to go to you in the middle of the night."

"Why did you let him do that? Why didn't you stop him?"

"I was tired of him doing it to me."

At that, Matildis turns and steps back up into the house, and closes the door behind her.

In her two years as a slave, Melia has never thought much about what Matildis's life might be like. How could she? Melia has been miserable; she has been abused physically by Hermann and verbally by Matildis. She works eighteen hours a day and has nothing but a few skimmed coins to her name. She has little sympathy for a loud, crude woman who does nothing but eat, drink, and complain, and who lets her husband leave their bed and rape Melia any time he wants.

But Matildis's face has just told Melia something she's not considered: that Matildis is profoundly sad. Many people are, of course. Gaul is no paradise. Poverty and hard work are more common than her tribe had thought. And for women, it is even more harsh. There is more than one kind of slavery in this Empire—an Empire of men. There is more than one way they imprison women, turn them into property and kill their dreams—those who are foolish enough to have them. Melia is a prisoner by way of ownership; Matildis is one by marriage.

Perhaps Hermann's absence is as much of a blessing to Matildis as it is to Melia. Maybe yesterday's tears and sobs were as much from relief as concern for his safety. It is silly to hope that Melia will not only enjoy good nights' sleep now, but that Matildis will quit screaming at her as well. But Melia can't help it.

MELIA DOESN'T EXPECT THE TRUCE with Matildis to last. She expects that as soon as she spills some broth or overcooks a turnip morsel, insults and contempt will rain down on her as usual.

She works until shortly before mid-day, spicing the votive glasses with a little almond-rosemary oil, and ladling in a beeswax and tallow mixture around their short, braided wicks. It is more tedious and time consuming than dipping tapers. She has to hold the wicks upright until the wax solidifies around them. It wasn't the first time she wishes she could improve the process, but the only solution she has devised required too many slivers of wood that she couldn't spare from the fire.

She stops before the sun reaches its zenith and goes into the kitchen to dish up bowls of broth and vegetables for herself and Matildis. As she tears off chunks of bread from the loaf in the breadbox, Matildis helps by setting spoons on the table and pouring two mugs of beer. Melia doesn't know how to react to her help. She says nothing, worried that if she does, it will be the wrong thing.

As they slurp up the soup, Matildis' sniffling starts again. Melia looks up at the woman's red eyes. What does she really feel about her husband?

Matildis answers before Melia asks the question. "I don't want him to die."

Melia has trouble imagining Hermann in the midst of any skirmish. He doesn't move fast enough to fight or to run. If he were thrown into battle, he'd be one of the first casualties. His greatest contribution would be falling heavily on his face, his body blocking the enemy's advance. Maybe that's what the commanders want men like Hermann to do: succumb quickly and provide a human barrier between the real soldiers and the onslaught of invaders.

"You want him back, even if you hate him?" Melia asks. "Don't worry. He will return if for no other reason than to prolong our misery."

Matildis drops her spoon with a clatter.

"You disgusting pig!" Matildis screams. "He is my husband! He has to come home!"

Melia stammers. "You said you hate him." How quickly Matildis' attitude changed. Maybe she regrets her earlier confession. Realizing he could die fighting may have softened her heart toward him. But Melia is having trouble keeping up with her vacillations.

Matildis looks more confused than angry. Is this the first time the woman has tried to reconcile her conflicting feelings about her husband? How has she fooled herself for years—wallowing in hate that knew no soft edges—only to realize she can't live without him?

"I'm going to the barracks to find him," Matildis announces, standing up and knocking her wide hips against the table. Melia steadies her wobbling bowl.

"They won't let you near the fort," Melia says. "You are wasting your time."

"I will find him. I will bring him home." She shuffles around the table toward the door and pulls a cloak over her shoulders.

"You can't go," Melia says. "This is folly. Stay."

Matildis hesitates for a moment, and Melia leaps up to block the door. She has no love for Matildis, but she doesn't want to have to go out to rescue her from whatever trouble she gets herself into.

"I'll go out later and see what I can find out," Melia offers. "Dodi's betrothed is an officer. He'll know where Hermann is. But you can't go down there. You know that!"

Matildis surrenders, and shuffles back to the rear of the house, dropping heavily into her chair. She mumbles incoherently, and Melia doesn't know if she is praying or just talking to herself in her Gothic language.

Instead of going back to work immediately on the votives, Melia takes off her work apron and dons her coat. While Matildis would not be received at the fort, Melia knows she can get in. Ruggie had invited her to his little brewery and, even with all else on her mind, she is curious about it.

THE MAN AT THE GATE to the fort is larger than any human being she's ever seen. It is easy to see why he was chosen to be the first guard any intruder will encounter. The dark and bulky bear coat he wears almost casually over his shoulders make him even more intimidating. The only thing he is missing is a huge set of incisors or he could pass for the animal itself.

Melia stands tall, takes a deep breath, and approaches him. "I'm here to see the brewer, Ruggenius," she says.

"You don't have to yell at me, Fraulein," the big man answers. He smiles down at her with an almost toothless grin. "I'm way up here, and you're way down there, but I can still hear."

His humor surprises Melia, and she relaxes a bit.

"Well, thank you for establishing that," she says. She grins at him broadly. "I wasn't certain that a man of your stature would even see me, let alone hear my little voice."

"And you want to see Ruggie for what purpose?"

"Does it matter?" Melia maintains her smile.

"No, I guess it doesn't. But that will be up to him. Who is asking for him?"

"Melia. Candlemaker's assistant." Melia's description of herself is meant to improve upon her status, but as soon as she says it, she realizes the man doesn't care.

"I will send a guard to fetch him for you, woman." The big

man gestures toward a large, flat stone at the gate, which she takes as a suggestion to sit to wait, and so she does.

A minute later, Ruggie approaches the gate, nearly hidden by the guard's bulk. He wears a cook's cap and tips it toward her. "Fraulein, please follow me. You are here to inspect our brewing facility, I assume."

Ruggie puts a hand behind her elbow to escort her through the gate, nodding at the guard as they pass. Melia notes his wink but acts as if she doesn't.

Once inside the fort, Melia looks around. The barracks look much like the houses that lined her own street—a white wattle and daub finish on the exterior walls and red tile roofs. They are low and long; it looks like each one could house a hundred men or more. And there are dozens of them. The fort has at one time housed an entire legion, she knows—about 5,000 men— but she's never thought about the amount of space they need to stay there.

In the distance, men shout, stomp, and grunt in what she imagines are military exercises intended to get the town's men ready for an invasion. Ruggie leads her between the rows of long buildings to a stone structure in the middle.

"The dining hall," he says. "The kitchens, the ovens, and the brewery are in the back." He holds the door open. Inside, a room as big as the nave in the church is furnished with row after row of long tables and benches. She imagines how noisy it is when it is full of legionnaires, laughing and cursing at each other over their bread and stew.

Pillars and half-walls cordon off the back quarter of the space, behind which are long worktables and firepits. Ovens faced with bricks, interrupted here and there with metal oven doors, line one wall. Melia wonders how much bread one could make, how much meat one could roast there. Above three firepits hang huge iron pots with handles on two sides. It must take two men to lift each one—even when they're empty. A man wearing the same kind of hat as Ruggie is tipping a dark broth out of one of them into a large ceramic vessel.

"What is he doing?" Melia asks.

"He's pouring off finished broth for this evening's meal," Ruggie says. "He's making room for another batch. He has to make several now that we have all the town's merchants and tradesmen to feed."

Ruggie opens a door in the back of the kitchen and waves Melia through to a narrow room that runs the width of the kitchen, open to the air. Only a lattice of wood hangs above them, and the room is enclosed by the same half-walls that separate the dining hall from the kitchen. A mesh of fine copper wire fills the space between the top of the half walls and the ceiling, and Melia guesses that keeps birds from flying in and varmints from crawling over.

Long wooden tables line either side of the narrow room. On one, Melia recognizes a thin layer of sprouted barley, drying in the frigid air. Atop another is a series of shallow pans as wide as the table, filled with water and grains of barley. A millstone and several vats sit at the end of the room.

"Do you recognize all of this?" Ruggie asks.

"Yes," Melia says, "but tell me about it anyway." She isn't trying to be coy; she thinks perhaps she could pick up some pointers that might improve Matildis's brew if she pays attention.

"We soak the barley in these big tubs," Ruggie says, pointing to the watery ponds. "You can see this grain here is sprouting, while that in the next pan has just been started." Melia nods. "And over here, the sprouted grain is drying. Once it's dry, we grind it in the mill, and then place it in hot water to ferment. It ferments as the water cools."

"But don't you have to add yeast from the yeast grower?"

"No, we let the yeast from each batch fertilize the next

batch," Ruggie says. "And the open air brings free yeasts that float in the air. I would prefer not to do that, as it makes the beer unpredictable, but that's one of the things I haven't been able to change."

Melia smiles and nods, feigning great interest, even though he isn't telling her much new. The entire process is similar to the way Matildis made her beer. Only the pans and the drying table are much cleaner, and the vats much larger. Maybe if Matildis pays more attention to cleanliness, her beer will improve.

Ruggie opens a door to the outside and points to a row of vats lined up against the half-wall. "In the winter, we store the covered beer outside, which makes it taste better, and keeps it fresh longer."

"When do you add the sweet gale and heather?" she asks.

Ruggie looks at her and grins. "You remembered! You remembered that I told you about them." Melia doesn't correct him, even though it was Dodi who told her about his secret ingredients.

He leads her back inside to the mill and shows her several cotton bags filled with herbs. "I put them in the vats along with the hot water. I let them steep for a day or so, and then I remove them with a sieve, so they don't stick in the legionnaire's teeth."

Melia laughs. "But the beer gets the flavor?"

"Yes," he says. He lowers his voice and steps closer. "That's another thing I'd like to know—how they are using hops for flavor and preserving in Castra Regina. There's still so much to learn."

"I hope you find a way," Melia whispers. She looks up into his face, just a few inches from hers, surprised to find herself so close to him. She moves back and catches a quick flash of a frown on his face.

"I also came here to see you today for another reason," she says, wishing she could relax and not sound so formal.

"What?"

"I came to see if I could calm Matildis down with some information. Do you know anything about Hermann?" As she says his name, Melia feels a shudder. His absence has been so profound that she's nearly forgotten the repulsion with which she beholds him.

"I would guess that he's been training with the other town recruits in the field on the other side of the barracks," Ruggie says. "But I don't know anything specific. I suppose she's worried about him."

"Of course. Is there anything you can tell me that could help her?"

Ruggie shakes his head. "I can check, but I doubt anyone knows him from all the other worthless townsfolk out here. Their training is pretty basic: march in front and give the real soldiers cover."

Ruggie has confirmed her suspicions; Hermann and other town draftees will be sent out to take the arrows and blows first, blunting whatever charge the barbarians make as they rush into Mogantiacum.

"But if no one knows him, what's to keep him from escaping? Disappearing from the ranks?"

"No one gets into or out of this fort without passing Reginald out there," Ruggie says. He pointed up to the tall wall in the distance that surrounds the compound. "Once the barbarians come across the bridge, the gates close, and even they won't be able to breach these walls."

"I'm glad to hear that," Melia says, thinking now of Ruggie staying safely inside and forgetting she is supposed to be concerned for Hermann or thinking of her mother.

Hours later, after finishing refilling and wicking her votives, Melia sets out the evening meal. Matildis has accepted Melia's advice and stays in the back of the room all afternoon. She stops sniffling and sobbing and falls asleep in her chair. Melia imagines she did not sleep much the night before. While Melia had slept better in Hermann's absence, Matildis is probably frightened to sleep without Hermann in the house to protect her.

Melia huffs a derisive snort. As if Hermann could or would keep anyone from anything other than his tankard of ale!

A COUPLE OF WEEKS PASS, and Hermann doesn't return. Melia assures Matildis—when she is in a good enough mood to listen—that the fort is well protected, and he is certainly safe.

Melia has survived two years of enslavement, kept sane only by anticipating her mother's arrival. But even as a barbarian crossing starts to feel imminent, Melia is losing faith in her mother's promise to find her. An invasion might bring her nothing more than it brings everyone else in town—bloodshed and more hunger.

The town grows even quieter as autumn ends, and winter creeps in from both the east and the west, settling hard and still in the river valley. Occasionally, a cohort of soldiers marches by the shop, their clothing so tattered and shabby they look more like refugees from Germania than Roman infantrymen. Claude and Ruggie still make regular weekly trips up the hill to deliver tallow and take more candles than ever for the fort, which keeps Melia busy and helps fill her little tin box with coins. Cooks and slaves like Melia still walk to the market and to the town well to pull water. The mortuary cart that collects the town's dead still clatters up the streets early each morning.

Otherwise all activity in town seems suspended in anticipation of an invasion. Even the young folk stop gathering in Dodi's bar on Sunday afternoons, now that the soldiers aren't allowed to leave the fort.

Still, Mogantiacum doesn't feel calm. It hums with nerves and fear. Market shoppers avoid each other's eyes. The sharp commands of officers training the town recruits inside the fort echo off the town's walls and up its cobbled streets. The curs that once ignored her as they fought over carrion in her path now slouch away when Melia approaches, their heads bowed to the ground and their ribs protruding.

There is so little food for sale at the market that Melia cuts back her trips to a couple of days a week, and instead of the usual diet of meat and poultry, she and Matildis rely on bread, and a stew of onions, turnips, and carrots to fill their stomachs. Nearly all the meat that makes it into town is requisitioned by the barracks.

Merchants travelling with meat, grain, and amber from Germania avoid Mogantiacum and the hordes that huddle across the river, choosing now to enter the Empire by crossing the Danube at Castra Regina, where Stilicho has amassed the better part of the Roman legions, or far north of Treverorum where the Franks have built a stronghold and a kind of peace on both sides of the river. Dodi's father's guesthouse and tavern are closed to guests.

Only Dodi, Melia, Theo, and Ruggie still meet at the tavern on Sundays. Ruggie is kind and respectful, but Melia senses he is growing impatient when she ducks and pulls away from his attempted embraces. One afternoon, when Theo and Dodi disappear into one of the guesthouse rooms, as they did for an hour or so every Sunday, Ruggie tries to kiss Melia again. Anticipating the sensation of his lips on hers, she closes her eyes, her heart racing. But when Ruggie's warm breath blows against her cheek, in her mind's eye she sees Hermann's face closing in on her.

"No!" She blocks Ruggie's advance with a shoulder.

"What is the matter?" he asks quietly, backing away. "I must misunderstand you. I thought we were drawing close, that perhaps you cared for me."

"I do," she says. She searches for words to explain. "But…
There is something you don't understand." She looks down at
her hands and picks at the dry callouses on her fingers.

"What is it?" Under Ruggie's calm reaction, Melia senses his
frustration. "What don't I understand?"

Melia doesn't want to tell him. How can she explain her rapes,
the nightly visits? The rough kisses that turned her stomach?
And if she does, Ruggie will know what she has become, who
she really is—Hermann's whore. Just like Matildis says.

She sits mute and avoids his eyes. Ruggie watches her face,
and she feels her cheeks blaze under his scrutiny. She wants his
embrace, maybe she wants even more from him, but she doesn't
know whether she ever will be able to distinguish his touch from
Hermann's, if she can accept his caresses without cringing in
horror.

Ruggie stands up and walks behind the bar to refill her mug.
He returns and sets it in front of Melia.

"Drink up, my dear," he says. "It will give you the courage to
tell me why you refuse me."

Melia takes a big swallow of the warm beer, but she still can't
fathom how to explain what is in her heart. She does care for
Ruggie. Perhaps she could even come to love him. But being
touched by a man means only two things to her: pain and
humiliation.

They sit in silence for several minutes as Melia struggles to
form sentences that express her pain.

"I know you." Ruggie finally breaks the silence for her, his
voice barely above a whisper. "I know you are a slave. I know.
You have been hurt and used, and you have had no choice."

Melia looks at him, puzzled. Could he know what she has
suffered? Is it obvious in the way she looks or carries herself, or
is it obvious to Ruggie because he knows the ways of the world?
Because he is a slave himself?

"I didn't want—I don't—," she stutters. Her eyes fill with tears.

"You didn't want what?"

Melia takes another long swallow of her beer and a deep, staccato breath. At once, she wants to explain and she doesn't. She is no different from any other woman—married or slave. Men do to them what they want.

She looks away and swats at the tears falling down her cheeks. "I hate him, and he forces himself on me, and I fight, and I fight, and I can't—." A huge sob fills her throat, blocking another word.

"I know," Ruggie says, reaching out with both arms and pulling her to his chest.

Howls burst from Melia's lungs, and she lets herself lean against him. He holds her gently while she cries.

Finally, Melia's tears stop, her sobs subside, but they stay locked together, his arms around her, her arms limp at her sides.

Melia feels relieved. She hasn't shed as many tears since she was pulled away from her mother in the Danube forest. Now she feels drained, not only of speech and energy, but hate as well. In Ruggie's arms, she is calm.

"Well, for now, you are safe from him," Ruggie says finally. "If the bridge is breached, he will most likely never come back home from the garrison."

"And if it's not breached? If there is never a crossing?"

"Then, you will …" Ruggie's voice trails off. He starts again: "I don't know what you'll do, but I will help."

For a moment, Melia is filled with hope and gratitude. But quickly it dissipates. He has no more ideas than she does about how to extricate her from her enslavement. It will be up to her to figure it out.

That is nothing new. No man has ever saved her—not her father, who turned her over to the Burgundians. Not the priest who blames her and Fritigil for their own abuse. Certainly not Hermann. Since the Huns first come to her village on the Danube, men have only put her in danger. At least Ruggie isn't doing that. At least he is someone she could move toward rather than run away from.

That is something new, something positive.

Ruggie rests his chin on the top of her head. His breath tickles as it moves her hair. "I believe you are the strongest woman I have ever known," he whispers.

Melia looks up at him and nods. Maybe she is.

"Someday you will overcome your fears, the hate, the pain," he continues. "And someday you will let me show you how much I care for you. Not today, perhaps, but when you are ready, Melia."

THE THIEF

December, AD406 - Mogantiacum

The temperatures have stayed well below freezing for days. Melia's thick animal-skin cloak provides little protection against the cold blasts that billow down the street from the west, but as she picks up her pace, climbing the hill from the market, she warms up enough to stop her teeth from chattering.

Her sales of candles dwindle as Mogantiacum's residents flee before the expected invasion and only women and children inhabit the homes. The fort is Melia's only large customer left. She has more free time, and without Hermann's visits at night, she is rested, calmer. She spends more time with Ruggie. Some days, he meets her at the water well and carries her water yoke up the hill. She introduces him to Canuto. A few late afternoons, they meet outside the garrison walls and walk to Dodi's tavern together for a beer before Melia returns home to prepare

Matildis's meals. Ruggie's kind attention erodes her reticence, and eventually, she craves those moments when he turns to her and, with his finger under her chin, brings her mouth to his. With Hermann's nightly visits further and further in the past, she begins to imagine Ruggie's arms around her at night. Instead of dread, she imagines the thrill of him undressing her, and spreading her legs with her name on his lips.

Most days, now, she stops to visit with Fritigil and Briggeta on the way down to the market. The two Franks have developed a quick friendship, thanks to their shared tongue, and Melia is relieved to know someone watches over Fritigil as she nears the end of her pregnancy.

Still, Fritigil looks pale and, except for the huge belly of babies, skinny. Too skinny. Julius hasn't returned from Treverorum to see her for weeks, and Fritigil sinks into a sullen mood that neither Briggeta nor Melia can brighten.

"Is she eating anything?" Melia whispers to Briggeta while watching Fritigil rest on Julius's abandoned bed.

Briggeta shakes her head, but Melia doesn't know if she was answering the question or indicating she has no idea what she'd been asked.

Melia realizes she was wasting her voice. She turns to Fritigil. "Do you think we should call for the midwife?"

"No," Fritigil answers and says something to Briggeta. Briggeta shook the little coin purse that hangs by her side. It sounded nearly empty.

"There's no money for that," Fritigil says. "Julius sends just enough to pay the housekeeper and to buy bread, barley, and a little meat. But you know how much everything costs these days. I have sent the messenger to tell him we need more now that prices have risen so high, but he hasn't answered."

"I'll see what I can do," Melia offers. "I don't have to feed Hermann anymore, so maybe I can make our money stretch a little. The only problem is candle sales have dropped. Other than the fort, I have had no customers for weeks. I'm not sure how long the money I've made will last us."

The rising price of food, the empty streets, the echo of training exercises at the fort, and the frigid air are wearing on everyone's nerves. Even the priest seemed more melancholy than ever when she last delivered a few votives.

"I don't think we'll be needing many more for some time," he said, waving his arm at the empty street as he opened the church door for her.

"But it's advent," Melia said. "Aren't people preparing for Christ's mass? They always burn a candle after confession."

"Not this year," the priest said, leading the way to the side altar. "Anyone who is still in town is either down at the fort learning to be a legionnaire"—a smirk betrayed his opinion of that—"or is huddled at home awaiting the invasion."

"But they will come out for the mass, won't they? And how about the feast of Saint Stephen?"

"I doubt there will be any feasts either," he said. "Who can buy meat? The villas are abandoned, the livestock have been herded far into Gaul. What's left is going to the men at the fort. They are eating the rest of us into starvation."

Melia realized that arguing with the priest wasn't going to change their bleak reality. She took the coins the priest offered, and instead of burning a votive for Fritigil, as she had planned to do, she unloaded her delivery and headed back to the shop.

Back at the house from her visit to Fritigil, Melia strips off her cloak to keep the relative warmth from making her sweat. They are lucky; since candle sales declined, the wood supply was now more than she needs to keep the tallow vat boiling. They burn more logs in the house.

When the temperature in the shop had dropped too low for sleep, Melia moves her mattress into the kitchen, close to the fire, and although Matildis's snoring in the loft wakes her from time to time, at least the wife doesn't complain about her company. Ingoberga hasn't visited for many days, either due to fear or the penetrating cold, and with Hermann gone, Melia is the only companion Matildis has. She quits treating Melia with as much derision and scolding. She doesn't upbraid Melia for imagined violations as she has in the past. On the other hand, she is still doing little: she stops malting and grinding barley for beer since Hermann left. Melia takes on the extra task—she has the time since she is making fewer candles.

Instead of heading into the shop to dip candles after delivering the church candles that day, Melia sits down near the fire to braid strings of cotton into wicks. It takes her a few minutes to realize she hasn't heard Matildis moving around. She glances into the back corner where Matildis usually sits, either napping and snoring, or stitching a repair in a piece of her own clothing. Her chair is empty.

Melia doesn't worry at first. Perhaps Matildis has gone next door to visit Ingoberga. Hermann's gone; he can't keep her cooped up in the house. Alone for a rare moment, Melia closes her eyes to soak in the peace, the warmth, and the silence. She gets up to make herself a cup of cider to go along with the pleasant afternoon. The deep freeze outside has kept the cellar colder than usual and the ampere of juice she purchased a few weeks before is staying sweet longer.

Melia places her clay mug on the firepit wall to warm up and returns to braiding wicks. Once the aroma starts to steam off the top of the mug, she sets aside the braids and takes it in both hands. She sits back against the bricks of the firepit, more contented than she has felt in the house ever. What if her mother never arrives, but Hermann never comes back either? Could she get over the disappointment and stay with Matildis? Could she continue to make candles and earn her keep? With

Hermann gone, would she still feel like a slave? Or even be one?

More importantly: Would Ruggie stay in Mogantiacum with her even if he could go to Castra Regina? If he does leave, could she go with him? She remembers the last kiss they shared, when his hands had found their way under her cloak to her breasts. He had brushed her nipples with his fingers, and she had jumped at the sweet sensation.

She drinks the warm cider slowly. Finished, she puts the mug down on the floor beside her chair and leans back to enjoy her daydream.

THE FRONT DOOR CRASHES NOISILY against the wall of the shop, yanking Melia from her accidental nap. She hasn't slept during the day since she left the village on the Danube with her family. For a moment, confusion clouds her thoughts. What is she doing sitting by the fire? Where is Matildis? Melia stands quickly and tries to shake off her drowsiness. She smooths down the front of her wool dress and turns to face…

Ruggie?

"Melia!" he shouts, at the door to the kitchen.

"Yes!"

She holds up her palms. He doesn't have to yell. She stands only a few feet away from him.

"You have to come and get Matildis."

"What? Where?" Dizzy from standing up so quickly, she struggles to understand him.

Ruggie puts his hands on her shoulders and shakes her gently. The cold clinging to his cloak sucks the warmth out the air.

"She's at the jail. Hurry and get your cloak."

Melia stumbles toward the hooks by the door and pulls her cloak over her shoulders.

"I don't understand. She never goes near the market or the center of town."

"She was caught stealing a leg of lamb. The merchant called the count's men, and they are holding her in the jail. Do you have any money? You may have to pay to get her released."

Still groggy, Melia turns to pull the household coin box out from its hiding place under the tinder for the fire. She counts the coins.

"I don't have much here," she says. She holds her palm to show him.

"That isn't going to be enough," he says. "The merchant will ask twice the usual price as punishment."

Melia starts to protest. "There isn't any m—" and then realizes what she must do. She steps into the shop. The freezing air blowing in the open front door finishes waking her.

"Close the door, Ruggie," she says. "I'll get some more money."

She reaches into the chest where she keeps her clothes and cedar oil and pulls out the small tin that holds her secret stash— the coins she has skimmed here and there over the past two years from candle sales. Before Hermann left, she'd never kept enough to draw attention to her thievery, but over time, she had hoped it would be enough to help buy her freedom.

Ruggie looks over her shoulder as she pours the money into her hand. He clucks his tongue.

"Are you sure you want to do this?" he asks. She looks up into his eyes. He is wise; he knows what her stash represents.

"We don't have a choice," she says, her voice cracking with pain.

Ruggie and Melia slide and slip down the icy street toward the urban police headquarters and jail, which sit just outside the main gate of the fort. Melia has never been inside the building, but she knows of the place. Men and women accused of crimes but not yet sentenced are held in two separate cages behind metal bars until a judge for the diocese makes his weekly visit to

Mogantiacum to hear their pleas. If they are sentenced to more imprisonment, they are shipped to the catacombs below the municipal building to serve their time. If they are condemned, the sentence is carried out quickly and without ceremony on the gallows behind the building.

Clinging to Ruggie's arm to keep from sliding onto her butt, Melia wonders why she is rescuing Matildis. If the woman is sent to jail, Melia might have time to get far away, and Hermann—if he survived his recruitment—would never find her. Freeing Matildis might cost Melia her one chance at freedom. She has dreamed of escape from the time she was thrown onto the shoulder of the rough Burgundian, but options have been few. Escape is unlikely even for strong, healthy male slaves with access to horses or friends who can hide them. And where would she go? Punishment for run-away slaves can be anything from whipping to losing an arm to death. An escaping man has to have a great deal of luck and a good plan, or a tremendous amount of stupidity to try. A run-away woman must be insane.

The building that holds the jail is less impressive than Melia expected. Ruggie raps with the heavy knocker on the door, and they hear a clang as it is unbarred.

Melia steps into a long, narrow room that holds only a desk and chair. Along the wall, rows of hooks are hung with metal cuffs used to shackle those accused of real or imagined crimes. Most of the space is taken up by the jail cells. Women crowd in the one closest to the door, the one down the other end of the narrow room encloses men. The air reeks of urine, feces, and unwashed bodies.

In the dark room lighted only by the weak sunshine coming through the door and a small window high on the wall, the butcher stands with his back to Melia. Waving his arms up and down in the air, he argues his case in Burgundi-accented Latin so rapidly that Melia can barely follow. One of the count's cohorts sits slumped at the desk, looking at his feet and yawning.

"We work hard (blah, blah) this meat (blah, blah) customers!" Melia catches the gist of what he argues. "This thief (blah, blah) punished and (blah) pay! Get the candlemaker! He's rich. His woman (blah, blah) money."

Melia peers around the man into the women's cell. Hunching on a stone bench at the back of a jail cell crowded with ragged women, Matildis sits, her eyes wide with fright. She looks more miserable than usual.

It serves her right. She accused Melia of lying about how much money she needs at the market and how little there is to buy. Now, acting on her hubris, she has found out Melia is right—food is expensive, so expensive that Matildis opted for stealing it. Melia feels a smirk crawl up one side of her face.

"Hello, Ferdinius," Melia says to the butcher's back.

He spins around. "Oh, Melia! Where is Hermann?" He looks around behind her at Ruggie.

"He's at the fort being trained for battle," Melia says. "Why aren't you there? Matildis and I are on our own now."

"Is that your excuse? Did you send her down to steal from me? You think I feel sorry for her?"

Melia considers the absurdity of those questions. Answering is impossible.

"What do you want her to do?" Melia says, nodding at Matildis who stands up and smiles weakly at her.

"She pays for that meat, and she stays in jail!" Ferdinius bellows.

"I understand," Melia nods. She tries to hide the involuntary smile that spreads across her face. She imagines a night in the house without Matildis or Hermann. How peaceful that would be. Maybe Ruggie would stay with her. Blushing, Melia banishes the thought.

"How much does she owe you?"

"Ten *denarii*," the butcher claims quickly.

"That's four times what that meat should cost!" Melia steps back. She had expected him to inflate the price to punish Matildis, but ten *denarii* is nearly all the money she has saved to help buy her freedom.

"Seven *denarii* and a night in jail."

It is still too much, but what bargaining power does Melia have? She is a slave, and everyone in the room knows it. She is the real prisoner of the Empire, but she is buying Matildis's freedom.

Melia considers the butcher's offer. If she gives him the ten *denarii* he asks for in the first place, Matildis could probably be spared spending a night there. Does Melia feel generous enough to pay that? Doesn't Matildis deserve to stay a night? And more?

But if she doesn't rescue Matildis now, Melia imagines how difficult life with her will be once she returns home. It has been bad enough up to now; Matildis will make it worse.

She looks back at the mostly toothless women crowded at the front of the cell, watching and listening to the negotiation, their filthy, claw-like nails hanging over the bars. Some chuckle with a creepy snort; others laugh heartily. But most of them stare with empty eyes. Melia wonders how long they've been in there.

She imagines the maggots, lice, and fleas that swarm just below the surface of the dirt floor and crawl in the worn wool blankets thrown around their shoulders. Whatever their crimes— vagrancy? prostitution? theft?—they could all be exonerated and released if someone like Melia showed up with money in hand. But for the town's lull in commerce and population, the healthier and cleaner ones might have sold themselves into slavery in return for the coin needed to pay off their debts and fines.

Melia shivers. Compared with the hopeless women watching her with hard, cold eyes, she is lucky, although it is the first time in two years she has thought that.

Melia turns to the scowling butcher, who stands with his hands on his flabby hips. "Seven *denarii*, and she goes home with me," she says. "So does the lamb. That's all I can pay."

CLIMBING UP THE HILL TO the house behind Melia and Ruggie, Matildis says nothing. Melia hopes she will be grateful for her rescue, and they will live more peacefully, at least if and until Hermann returns and Matildis regresses to her usual nasty behavior.

Ruggie and Melia walk ahead, and although they aren't physically attached, Melia feels like they are dragging Matildis up the street. The wife shuffles her feet and pants, which isn't surprising, as it is a longer walk than any Matildis has done since Melia came to take over her water collection and shopping duties.

"How did you know that she was in trouble?" Melia asks Ruggie in Suevi.

"Theo, by chance, was in the jail when the merchant and one of the urban cohorts brought Matildis in. The count's cohorts told Theo who she was."

"I'm not sure I should thank you," Melia says, winking at him. "I might have had a few days of peace if she'd ended up having to wait for the magistrate."

"Yes, but eventually, she'd be free," Ruggie says, missing her humor. "She would only be nastier in the long run."

"Yes." Melia lets out a loud sigh. "And now I have very little coin left."

"I'm sorry."

"You know I was hoping to help my mother buy my manumission."

"I thought as much."

They walk in silence for a few minutes. "But now?" Ruggie finally asks.

"But now I will have to hope that my mother doesn't need my help."

Ruggie leaves Melia at the front step of the shop with a brief brush of his lips to hers and runs back down the hill to the garrison. Melia opens the door and waits for Matildis to catch up and shuffle past, aiming for her chair in the back of the house.

By that time, Melia should have been done preparing the evening meal. Now there isn't enough time left in the day to cook a bit of the leg of lamb on the spit over the hearth. Melia hangs it on a hook in the cellar and returns to the kitchen with an armful of root vegetables and the hindquarter of a chicken left from the day before. She stokes the coals and builds a fire, fills a small pot with water, and sets it over the heat. She cuts up the vegetables and chops the chicken meat and bones and tosses them in the pot.

Matildis sits, pouting on a stool at the table, waiting to be fed.

Melia had hoped for but doesn't expect an apology or thanks. Still, Melia hasn't expected the first words that come out of Matildis' mouth when she sets the bowl of stew in front of the woman an hour later.

"Are you going to apologize?" Matildis growls.

Melia sits down on her stool hard, her surprise knocking her legs out from under her. "What? You think I should apologize to you?"

"You told me there was no meat at the market. There was meat."

"Not meat that we could afford. I have to conserve *denarii* now that candle sales have dropped," Melia says.

"But you had the money. You had money to pay that butcher."

Melia knows there was no way she can explain the money she used to buy Matildis' freedom. Admitting that she's been skimming coins from candle sales all along? Although it hasn't been much—it has taken her two years to collect just ten *denarii*—

any amount constitutes thievery. The amount won't matter as much to Matildis as the subterfuge itself.

"And now we have no money at all," Melia says. She feels her anger build at the disagreeable woman. "We will have to make do with what we have in the cellar until I get another order from the priest. Now my only customer is the garrison, and it's not paying. It says Rome is sending no money."

"That is not my problem," Matildis says, raising her voice. "You need to work harder. You sleep too much, and you eat too much." She takes a swipe at Melia's bowl of stew as if to knock it over, but her big chest hits the edge of the table, preventing her from reaching across. Melia steadies her bowl and pretends not to notice. "And who was that slave who came with you? Are you his whore, too?"

Too? Matildis can't still believe that Melia invited Hermann's nighttime visits!

Melia says nothing. She spoons the rest of her stew into her mouth and stands to wipe off her dish and store the remainder of the stew in the cellar.

"You didn't answer me!" Matildis howls.

"I am no one's whore," Melia says, her voice low with anger. "But now I regret what I did."

"Tempting Hermann into your bed?"

"No," Melia says, as she gathered up her mattress and opens the door to the shop. "I mean I regret paying the butcher the money to free you."

Matildis screeches and lumbers up from the table toward her, but Melia is too quick. She closes the door between the house and the shop. Quickly she pulls her work stool over and slides it under the handle, locking the latch in place.

Why hadn't she thought of that before? Could she possibly have kept Hermann from coming to her mattress at night?

Probably not. Much stronger than Matildis, he would have

crashed through the door, smashing her stool to pieces.

But for one night, at least, Melia will sleep without interference from either him or his disgusting wife. It will be cold, and she'll sleep in her clothes and cloak, but at least it will be quiet.

PART 2

INVASION

CAMP

December, AD406 - East bank Rhine River

Greta hates this camp even more than all the others.

As she walks back from the small clearing the migrant camp has designated for the open-air latrine, she stumbles over a snow-covered log and falls to her knees. It is enough to bring on another bout of sobs and tears. She sits back on the heels of her wet, freezing feet and cries.

When they first reached the east bank of the Rhine months before, it was muddy from spring rains. Now summer and fall have passed, and winter on the river has arrived. The mud has frozen to hard, immovable hurdles, thunderstorms have turned to blizzards, and daytime has turned into perpetual dusk in the coldest winter anyone can remember.

Blocked from entering Gaul by the Romans, surrounded by Alans and Vandals with their strange hair styles and difficult dialects, the Suevi are cold, hungry and anxious. The men fight and argue, and the women quibble and fume.

But Greta just grieves. She's lost a son, her husband, her sister, and her home. The only thing keeping her from tying a rope around a tree branch and hanging herself is her need to rescue her daughter from slavery as she promised. But how can that happen if they are never able to cross the river?

After many minutes, Greta runs out of tears, and her knees have stiffened on the cold ground. She bends her neck back and peers through the dark branches overhead to the low, grey clouds above. "God of Constantine," she whispers, "why do you punish me so?"

"What are you doing there?"

Greta recognizes the voice behind her. "I tripped," she answers. She turns to Milo, her brother-in-law, the widower of her slain sister.

Milo reaches down and helps her stand. "You should get back to the fire," he says. "This cold can kill even the strongest of men."

Greta grabs his arm and steadies herself on her feet. He is right. Just a few minutes kneeling in the snow has stiffened her joints. Members of their tribe have died after wandering out of the camp and getting lost in blowing snow. They were found within hours, but not before the cold winds had sucked their breath from their lungs.

"Thank you, dear brother," she says. "I'm sorry you always find me this way."

"What way?"

"Wallowing in my sorrow. You have lost your wife, too, and yet you walk tall. I never see you weep."

She smiles weakly through sniffles. Milo has been kind to her since Vertila and Ballomar were killed in the raid by the Franks. He discourages other men from approaching her around the fire at night. He sleeps near her wagon at night and checks every day to be sure she is eating enough and has enough dry animal furs to keep warm. She isn't surprised by his attention. Everyone had expected him to defend her. All they have now, other than a couple of aging uncles and a few cousins, is each other. Yet, lately, he's acted increasingly reserved around her, as if he has grown afraid of their bond.

"I am grieving, too," he says, securing her arm under his. "But I have run out of tears."

Greta nods and digs into the pocket of her cloak to pull out a rag to wipe her nose and eyes. She takes a step toward the center of the camp, but Milo stops her.

"I'm glad to get this chance to talk with you alone," he says.

Greta frowns. "What do you want to talk about?" She fears more bad news from the joint council the tribal kings have formed to plot their move across the river. As they wait in this dismal forest, her tribesmen have morphed from farmers and migrants into bloodthirsty warriors. War and revenge, not farming, are all they talk about.

Milo pauses and scratches his head under his fur cap. He rocks from one foot to the other, avoiding her eyes, until she laughs.

"Out with it before we freeze!" She blows her nose.

Milo looks back toward the camp and takes a deep breath. He looks down at her and holds her eyes in a solemn gaze.

Finally, Greta understands. What he has no words for, his eyes communicate.

She nods shyly, and Milo steps forward, puts his hands on her shoulders, and kisses her softly.

AT FIRST, GRETA IS ASHAMED of the renewed passion that has blossomed amid their sorrow. But Milo counters that they deserve some happiness; they have suffered plenty. They marry in a simple of ceremony of shared oaths, blessed by the village's high priest.

Milo's arms transport her away from her personal tragedies and from the brutal reality of their stymied migration. Squeezing her thighs around his slender waist and pulling him inside rewards her with brief respites from her grief. The fierce longing to reach his soul through her body surprises and thrills her.

Even though winter's brutality deepens, their love grows, and she allows herself to hope for a bright ending to this journey. As she joins the women of the camp to gather what nuts, berries, and tubers they can find in the forest, and whatever small animals they can catch in their traps, she plots her search for Melia. The Burgundians had brought Greta the news that her daughter was bought by a Germani candlemaker. That information is now two years old, but it is the snippet that keeps Greta hopeful. She isn't sure how she would find a candlemaker in Mogantiacum; she's never been in a city. Neither does she know if anyone there speaks Suevi. And she has no money to buy her daughter out of slavery.

But none of that is going to stop her from trying. Once she gets across the river, she will start looking, even if it means being left behind as their horde spreads out into Gaul.

Getting across the Rhine, though, has proven more difficult— it may even be impossible—than the Suevi had imagined when they first fled the Huns. Back then, they didn't plan to enter Gaul empty handed or as an invading army. They had expected the Romans to heed their request for land to settle and grant them entry. Gaul is rumored to be full of abandoned farms and villas. But even though the Suevi and other tribes have filled the Roman slave ranks and served in their legions for decades, the Romans have turned their backs on them.

When they aren't out hunting for the increasingly scarce

forest animals to feed themselves, the men sit around campfires night and day and debate various strategies to get around the Romans' blockade. At first, they thought the Empire would decide it would be better to allow the tribes to settle in Gaul peacefully rather than encourage an angry invasion. They had done so with the Franks on the lower Rhine, the Alamanni in the upper Rhine, and the Goths on the Danube.

"Kings" were chosen to bargain with the Romans, the negotiations had ended in stalemate, and the migration stalled. The single bridge at Mogantiacum is easily defended, and the Roman garrison, even in its reportedly depleted state, has the upper hand.

Now starvation is more likely than crossing the river, and freezing temperatures of the early winter have reinforced the determination of the tribes. Greta doesn't like the new belligerent tone of the discussions around the night fires. Instead of settling and farming, the men talk of looting Gaul for food and treasure and pillaging for revenge. Arguments over strategy and timing wage deep into the night. Tired of the repetitive debates and war talk, she retires to the wagon she shares with Milo long before the wood burns down and the men fall asleep in heaps next to the hot pile of coals.

On the night of the winter solstice, however, she stays at the campfire. The tribes have nominally converted to Arian Christianity decades before, but they still conduct the rituals of their ancestors. So, even as the temperature falls and icy crystals form in the air just beyond the heat of the flames, they gather to celebrate the deepest winter night with a sacrifice of a lamb, a reading of its entrails, and the banging of drums.

And therefore, when the scouts return that night from the river's edge with news that might finally break the stalemate with the Empire, her heart leaps with joy. She won't have to wait much longer.

CHRISTMAS EVE

December, AD406 - Mogantiacum

Christmas mass is cancelled. The unusual cold spell that has hovered over the town for more than three weeks makes it dangerous for worshippers, already weakened by hunger, to venture out of their homes. A majority of the town's Roman families have left the region to return to Rome, Milan, or other, more prosperous cities. And under the cloud of an anticipated invasion by the Germanii, the urban cohort imposes a curfew on everyone except their night watchmen.

"I'm sorry, but we don't need these," the priest tells her when she shows up with her wagon full of candles he ordered early Christmas week.

Melia looks down at the neatly packed tapers and votives and holds back tears. So much work went into making them perfect—the pretty tapers thin at the top, the votives filled cleanly. With no other paying customers to serve—the fort still takes candles but has no money to pay for them—she took her time making this week's batch the best ever.

"I understand," she says. She turns to pull her load back up the hill. The sad knot in her chest turns to angry, and she spins around to face the priest.

"If this Empire of yours would let those people on the other side of the river come in, I'd have customers, you'd have worshippers, and the market would be crowded again. I don't understand why Stilicho is refusing them."

The priest takes a step back, almost tripping on the threshold. He stands with his mouth open and his hands held out in front of him as if to protect himself from a physical blow. Once he realizes that Melia isn't going to hit him with anything but words, he relaxes and steps forward again.

"Young woman," he says tersely. "You should not speak to things you don't understand." He shakes his head as if with pity. She expects him to shake his finger at her next, but instead, he clasps his hands behind his back and sticks out his chest.

"The pagans will destroy Mogantiacum and all of Gaul," he continues. "It is the Lord, not Stilicho, who keeps them bound to their backwardness. As uncivilized as they are, they have no place in a Christian empire of laws and culture."

"But they're not pagans." Melia snarls. "They have converted to Christianity, even though Constantine doesn't rule over Germania."

"They are Arians, and their conversion is political expedience," he says, his face exuding disgust for her ignorance. "That's all it was. Tonight, look across the river at their bonfires celebrating the winter solstice. You will see. They're still pagans, and God knows it."

The priest raises his hand to the sky, and Melia fears he will bless her—the last thing she wants from him. But if he does, he will do it to her back. She stomps up the hill, pulling her heavy wagon, its rattle overpowering whatever benediction he utters.

She returns to the candle shop in time to catch Claude and Ruggie as they arrive with a load of fat slabs.

"I'm afraid I don't need any tallow," she says, holding back tears of self-pity. "The priest just refused this week's entire production."

Ruggie leaps down from the wagon, asks Claude to wait, and walks into the shop with her. She lets him fold her in his arms, burying her face in his thick fur cloak. Worried that Matildis will see them like this, she takes a deep breath and composes herself. She pushes herself away and smiles at Ruggie.

"Thanks for being my friend," she says, wiping the last tears off her cheeks and pointing to her full wagon. "You should take these back to the fort so they are enjoyed by someone." She shrugs. "I guess it's not all bad. I don't have to work so hard now. What do you think I should do with all my time?"

Ruggie laughs. He lowers his voice to a whisper and looks sideways, conspiracy in his eyes. "Maybe you can leave."

"That's foolishness," she says. "I have no idea where I'd go or how I'd get there."

"You could come with me."

"Are you leaving?"

Ruggie looks over his shoulder to Claude, who sits on the wagon, squirming with impatience and the cold.

"Perhaps soon," he says. "But I'll know more in a couple of months—earlier if the Germanii cross over. I may have a chance to go to Castra Regina, finally."

She has wondered if he will ask her to go with him, and now he has. She should be thrilled, but instead, she is overwhelmed with sadness. She can't run, and she has no money left to buy her freedom. There is no reason to talk about something that is nothing but a fantasy.

"Claude is waiting for you." She hangs her head.

"We will talk about it later," Ruggie says. His voice is encouraging. "I'll come by for you Christmas Eve," he said. "Theo has a cart and horse, and we're going to have our own little party."

CURFEWS DON'T RESTRICT THEO, WHO has been elevated to second in command at the garrison, or his friends. As promised, Ruggie, Melia, and Dodi ride in his cart up the hill to the western town wall. Theo steers the draft horse up a rough dirt path to an outcropping of granite that lies in a copse of scrub oak. They hop down, gather up the blankets and tankards and an amphora of beer.

Above them, the stars twinkle joyously in the freezing, crisp air, and far below them, along the far banks of the Rhine, tall flames of the camp bonfires dance, their bright light reflecting off the ice-clogged river. Perhaps no candles burn in the priest's church that night, but the world gleams as if to celebrate the birth of the Christian God's son.

After a few boisterous toasts, the little party settles down to survey the frigid but glorious scene before them. Ruggie and Theo plant themselves on the cold stone, and Melia and Dodi snuggle between their legs to watch the clear, tiny sliver of the moon rise over quiet Mogantiacum.

"My mother is over there," Melia says, pointing across the icy river at the dancing flames. She stifles a shiver, and pulls her mittened hands close to her body, twisting them into her old fur cloak under the musty blanket.

"God speed her journey!" Ruggie whispers sympathetically.

Theo laughs and makes a show of shaking his head.

"I pity you, Melia," he says, the tone of his voice both sympathetic and pessimistic. "Yes, she may be a stone's throw away, but you likely will never see her on this side of the Rhine."

Theo points up the river to the north. "The bridge guard will hold. They've trained for this. We don't need more barbarians in the Empire."

Melia is accustomed to Theo's denigration of the Germanii. He seems to forget that both she and Ruggie are "barbarians," and some of his ancestors likely were as well. She waits to let his words sink in the frigid air and considers how to respond. She knows that Theo was Ruggie's champion; he refuses to let Ruggie train for battle, arguing that the troops need him brewing their beer far more than they need him dying at the point of a sword of the barbarians. But Theo seems to forget that nearly everyone around him, including his betrothed, is part Germani.

"Did you ever think that perhaps the Romans came to Gaul to build some character?" she asks him. "That warm climate in Italia could turn men into weak fawns, don't you think?"

Ruggie pulls her close, his chin burrowing into her hair. "Don't tease Theo tonight," he whispers. "He could leave us up here to freeze to death."

"Yes." Theo chuckles at Ruggie's comment. "You are lucky to have a sturdy stone house to sleep in. Didn't you live under the same grass roof as the farm animals back on the Danube? That must have been much colder."

"I remember when it was this cold one year, back in the village," Melia offers. "The barbarian village. But even then, it was warm inside. And the air was moist, not bitter and hard like it is here."

"But it stunk!" Theo doesn't hide his condescension.

"Well, not in the summer. Then the cattle and goats would stay outside," she retorts. "And you do know that the candlemaker's house reeks of suet and Matildis's nauseating odors? I breathe tallow fumes every day. Do you think that smells any better?"

Theo laughs. "I hadn't thought of that."

"Did it look like this?" Ruggie asks, waving his arm over the valley below, covered with snow. "The land around your village?" Even though he has no allegiances to the Germania of his birth, Ruggie has frequently asked Melia about her Suevi village. His warm attention is melting her resolve to avoid his bed—or keep him out of hers. He comes to the shop to see her nearly every day the last month. And each day it is clearer that his touch is not like Hermann's.

"Melia?" Ruggie draws her attention back to his question. "Was your village like this?"

"Very much like this," Melia answers. "The Danube is as wide, and the valleys as broad. This time of year, it would have been snowing for weeks. I think you would feel very much at home there."

"Maybe, I will someday," he whispers. "And maybe you'll go with me."

Ruggie's arms tighten around her waist and Melia feels her body melt into his. Hermann has been gone for weeks, and now as Ruggie holds her against him, warmth creeps up her spine. The sensation of Ruggie's soft lips on the back of her neck stir something vastly different from the repulsion she felt with Hermann. Is it desire or is it love? Are they the same?

Feeling a tumble in her chest and the sudden need for more of him, she twists around, and pulls Ruggie's face toward hers. Melia absorbs his kiss. He slips his tongue between her lips, and she reaches under his coat to press her hand on his erection.

After several long minutes, they pull their lips apart and, sighing in unison, settle back into their original position

Next to them, Dodi and Theo are locked in a tight embrace. Melia doesn't look toward them, but her friend's moans and the rustling of their clothing under the blanket send her heart racing and the soft tissue between her legs throbbing. She takes a deep breath to calm them both.

Eventually, Theo and Dodi also quiet and rearrange

themselves to return their attention to the scene below them.

"More beer, my friend?" Ruggie asks.

"Yes. No need to ask." Theo picks up his tankard, and Ruggie refills it from the amphora.

"And you my dear?" Ruggie whispers in Melia's ear, his lips so close his breath moves the hair.

Melia sits up and lifts her mug to him. As she settles back down against his chest, she points down at the Rhine. Something catches her attention.

"Where are the ships?" she asks. "Is no one patrolling the waters?"

"Too much ice," Theo says. "The ice floes can tear a hole the size of a horse in the most magnificent ships in the fleet. We have sent them down the Rhine, north to Aggrippenisium, where the channel is wider, where the ice breaks up."

"But will the river freeze solid?" Melia asks.

"It never has," Theo answers. "Well, some say it froze over thirty years ago, before we were born. But I doubt it ever did."

Melia wonders, though. If the river freezes, the Germanii won't need that well-defended bridge.

How their lives would change if that happens! Suddenly she realizes if she is ever going to let Ruggie love her as he wants, now is the time.

She turns around on Ruggie's lap again and kisses him in a way that clearly tells him that.

MELIA WAKES TO LOUD POUNDING at the shop door.

Sleepily, she rolls away, untangling herself from Ruggie's arms and slips off the mattress. The cold of the room shocks her awake, and she feels around the bed in the dark for something to cover herself. She grasps the cloak she had shed the night before in their rush to undress and throws it over her nakedness.

Has the river frozen over? Is it her mother at the door?

Stepping quickly across the stone floor, her feet nearly sticking to it, she wraps the scratchy wool around her body. Standing on her toes, she peers out the peephole in the door to see Briggeta huddled outside, hugging herself and rubbing her hands up and down her arms against the cold.

Instantly, Melia knows why she is there.

Melia throws the heavy bar up off its holder and opens the door.

"Hurry, come in!"

The cold draft that blows in from the street stings her face, and Melia slams the door closed.

"Fritigil!" Briggeta cries.

"Of course. I'll get dressed."

Melia kneels by the tallow vat, uncovers a coal in the ash with a tong, and lights a candle. The flame flickers in the swirling air. In the weak light, Melia pulls on her boots and her wool shift, and wraps the cloak back over the top. She pulls a heavy knitted scarf off a hook by the door.

"Let's go." Melia glances back as Ruggie struggles to sit up.

"What's going on?" he asks in a croaking voice.

"It's Fritigil," Melia answers. "Come find us at Julius's house. We might need some help."

"The babies?"

"Yes." Melia fights the urge to stoop for a quick kiss.

"Now?"

"I don't know yet. But I've got to go."

Briggeta has already opened the door, and the women rush out.

The night air crackles with cold and Melia sticks her hands under her armpits. She's forgotten her mittens, but she won't waste time going back for them. In a matter of a couple of minutes, they push though Julius's mansion door and run up the stairs.

Fritigil writhes on the bed, her bare legs and arms glistening with perspiration in the candlelight. The room is much warmer than the candle shop, but not warm enough to account for her sweat.

"Tell me what's happening," Melia says, leaning over and feeling her friend's cold forehead.

Briggeta cries and shakes her head, not understanding. Melia notes the large bloody stain spreading under Fritigil's hips.

"Did you go to get Helga?" she asks Briggeta, who stares wide-eyed at the blood, as if she hasn't heard the question.

"The midwife! Did you go to Helga?" Melia shouts.

Briggeta shakes herself out of the trance. Melia knows that she doesn't understand much that Melia says, but she knows Helga's name.

"No Helga," she answers.

Melia has worried that this might happen. The midwife has no reason to stay in Mogantiacum since most of her business fled to Arles, Treverorum, or the Aquitaine.

So, they are on their own. And if Briggeta is going to be any use to Fritigil, Melia is going to have to keep her moving and busy.

"Go down to the kitchen and put a large pot of water on to boil," she orders the young cook. "And while it's heating, bring me all the cloths you can find. I'll try to figure out what to do here." Melia doesn't know if Briggeta understands any of those words, but the girl heads down the stairs. Perhaps she's been around enough childbirth to know what's needed.

Melia's hands shake as she sits on the edge of the bed and feels for a pulse at Fritigil's neck. Even as the girl squirms, her heart is beating slowly—too slowly.

"I'm going to spread your legs and take a look," Melia says, smoothing Fritigil's blonde hair off her forehead. "Can you help?"

Fritigil tosses her head back and forth on her mattress. "No! I can't—"

Melia stands and pulls Fritigil's knees up to form a tent of her dress and gently pushes them apart. She can't see anything in the widened birth canal except for a slow stream of blood. Is this normal?

Holding back panic, Melia tries to remember anything she had overheard back in the village. Screams. Push! Almost. Keep pushing! It is all she could remember. It isn't any help.

Briggeta runs back into the room with an armful of fabric and tosses it on the floor. It appears that Melia's word for "rags" and Briggeta's are similar enough for the girl to understand.

She had apparently not understood "water." What should I do now? she asks, not in words but in wide eyes.

"I really don't know," Melia says. "I have no idea what we're doing."

TWINS

Melia sits helplessly at Fritigil's side. She has to let nature take care of this. Fritigil is too weak to talk, and she doesn't seem to hear anything Melia says. For many long minutes, Melia watches her writhe, sweat and bleed, stroking her friend's forehead and arms and repeating, "Relax, Fritigil. Breathe. Relax. Breathe."

Too exhausted to fight, Fritigil slips into semi-consciousness, and her bleeding slows down. Is that a good sign?

Downstairs, a door crashes open, and Briggeta shrieks.

"Where is she?" It's Ruggie.

Melia jumps up and yells down the stairwell. "Up here."

Hearing his heavy steps on the stairs, Melia cries with relief, tears streaking down her cheeks by the time he storms through the door.

"Can you help? Do you know anyone who can help?"

"Matildis is coming. Ingoberga and Matildis."

More heavy footsteps at the door and up the stairs. Ingoberga rushes into the room first, breathless from the run down the hill and up the stairs. Then Matildis appears. Her eyes slip past Melia and directly to the tented skirt above the blood-soaked mattress.

"Out of here!" she orders Melia. "Get out and have Ruggie bring hot water. Ingoberga, check to see where the babies are."

A stream of sweat runs down the back of Melia's neck and she backs away, yielding the room to the older women. Matildis has changed her dress for the first time in weeks. The woman still smells bad, but Melia realizes she probably does, too. Sweat and sex. A pungent combination.

She hears Ruggie pumping water down in the kitchen. After a few minutes he comes up the stairs.

"The water is heating," he tells Matildis.

Melia nods toward the two women hunched over Fritigil's side. "How did you know to bring them?"

Ruggie shrugs, his eyes focused on the bed scene. "I didn't know if you would need help, but I didn't think it would hurt." He nods at Matildis. "She had to get dressed and bring Ingoberga. That's why it took us so long."

Melia falls weakly against him, and Ruggie wraps his arms around her and kisses the top of her head.

"This isn't good." Matildis whispers her verdict to Ingoberga, but Melia hears it, and a sob escapes her throat.

"Ruggie!" Matildis yells. "Where is that water?"

Ruggie lets go of Melia and runs down the stairs. A few long minutes later, he lugs a heavy pot of steaming water up to the bedroom and sets it on the floor.

"You can leave now," Matildis says. "Men don't belong in here." Ruggie obliges without an argument.

"I have to get back to the fort before dawn," he says to Melia and Briggeta in Suevi. "I'll come back if I can. But the cook may have other things for me to do. We're trying to build up some extra supplies in case."

"What?" Briggeta asks, struggling to understand.

Ruggie doesn't answer, and Melia doesn't need him to. As he slips away, she steps back inside the room to watch Fritigil. Her cries and moans weaken to whimpering and an occasional guttural growl.

"Push!" Matildis orders her. "You have to push. Babies don't come out by themselves." As far as Melia can tell, Fritigil doesn't obey.

"I see the crown," Ingoberga announces, excited.

"Good." Matildis places her palms on the upper side of the bulge of babies and pushes. She lets up and pushes again. Can Matildis accomplish what Fritigil is too weak to do? Melia remembers times when mothers were cut open and babies lifted out of wombs; in those cases, the mothers never lived to see the cause of their misery. She closes her eyes and prays silently to Wodin: Don't let this end that way.

Matildis leans against Fritigil's bulge, sweat building up on her brow and neck, and her hair falling out of its knot into wet strands around her face. She applies pressure, lifts up, and pushes again, but Fritigil's moans only grow weaker. Melia feels Briggeta's breath on the back of her neck and turns to see tears flowing from her wide-open eyes. Melia reaches for her hand and holds it in both of hers.

"Can you pray?" she asks the girl, using hand gestures she thinks Briggeta might understand. Briggeta nods and sinks to her knees.

"Aa-aa-aa!" A pained, staccato shriek flies from Fritigil.

"It's here!" Ingoberga catches the first tiny infant in a towel, pops a slap on her butt, and rewarded with a tiny wail, lays it down on the bed. She takes a knife from her apron and deftly releases the babe, tying the cord tight against its belly.

"Melia, come here," she orders. "Grab a rag and clean her off. Then wrap and hold her."

It is a girl, then. Melia hasn't thought once about whether the babies will be boys or girls. She has been so concerned about Fritigil's health that their sex hasn't entered her imagination. She grabs a rag and holds out her hands to receive the squirming infant.

"Don't we give her to Fritigil?" Melia realizes how silly the question is as soon as she asks it. Fritigil is not finished yet. The baby's afterbirth slips onto the bed between her legs, and she seems to slump farther into the mattress.

"Come on, girl," Matildis orders. "You have one more. Then you can relax. Push!"

Fritigil isn't pushing. She is barely moving.

"Is she going to be all right?" Melia asks over Matildis's shoulder.

The woman ignores her. "Push!"

"Give her a rest a minute," Ingoberga says, reaching out to pull Matildis back. "It might take an hour. Maybe more. I've seen twins born hours apart."

"That is true." Matildis sits on the edge of the bed, with her hand resting on Fritigil's stomach, and takes a few deep, slow breaths. Melia wonders who is working harder to deliver these babies, Fritigil or Matildis.

Melia lays the bawling baby on the floor. She dips a fresh cloth in water and wipes the crinkly red skin gently. She wraps the tiny creature in one of the larger rags and hands her to Briggeta, showing her how to hold it against her chest. Soon, the baby will need milk, and Melia wonders if Fritigil is going to be able to feed her. Sitting down on the floor, Briggeta leans her back against the wall, both arms wrapped around the bundle of baby.

"Get us some beer," Ingoberga says, looking around Melia at Briggeta.

Briggeta shakes her head. She knows that word. Apparently there isn't any left in the house.

"Go back to the house and get the amphora," Matildis tells Melia. "Briggeta, stay here and hold that babe."

Exhaustion spreads from her core down to her legs, but Melia runs down the stairs and out the door. It already was late when she and Ruggie had returned to the house earlier that night. And then, as natural as it was, their lovemaking took time. Ruggie was patient and gentle, turning what Hermann had made frightening into a slow, seductive dance. He waited until she begged him to enter before he rose above her and teased her with his erection. Eager for him, she pulled him in and wrapped her legs around his waist. It was nothing like she had expected. When the sensations finally collapsed, pulsing around him, she wrapped her arms tightly around his torso and wept.

How could he feel so different from Hermann? As she runs back up the hill for the beer, she shudders, remembering. Now she understands better what Fritigil was talking about with her babies' father. Now she understands how the act of making babies can be addictive.

As she brings the beer amphora up the stairs back at Julius's house, she hears Matildis shout. "She's contracting again!"

"Good," says Ingoberga. "Let it build. It's too soon to start pushing."

"Where's that beer?" Matildis says just as Melia runs in the room, huffing from her trip.

The second baby, also a girl, comes with as much difficulty as the first, and Melia accepts, cleans, and swaddles her. Melia sits next to Briggeta against the wall and watches the girl's face as the younger girl's anxiety has turned to wonder with the first baby in her arms.

Once the last after-birth is expelled, Fritigil lies motionless, her breath slow and shallow.

"It's over. You have two beautiful girls." Matildis leans close to Fritigil's face and brushes back the hair clinging to her forehead. "Rest now. We'll take care of them."

Fritigil doesn't respond, and Melia knows she never will. She will never hold her babies.

MELIA AND BRIGGETA CARRY THE infants away as Matildis instructed, their tears making it hard to descend the stairs and walk out the door. It took hours for Fritigil to deliver them, and only a few minutes after the second one was born for her to pass from this world.

As they walk through the freezing streets toward the convent, Melia wrestles with the juxtaposition: the wonderous way babies are made when it is a mutual act of love, which she had come to know only hours before, and the gruesome way they come into the world, as she had just witnessed, with women suffering all the pain and the danger alone. What god would design a world like this?

Wodin is entertained by humans, but he has no interest in their fate. He craves their loyalty and praise, but he ignores much of what goes on down on earth and cares nothing for their misery. She can accept a god that ignores them, but the God of the Christians supposedly reigns over everything that happens. He makes the rules, tempts men to break them, and then punishes them for grabbing the bait. A viper he created tempted Eve to eat an apple he also created, and when she obliged, he made all women who came after her suffer the pain of childbirth and let death award them for their suffering.

As long as she lives, Melia swears, she will not swear allegiance to any deity. If it means damnation, that couldn't be any worse than what she had just watched Fritigil endure.

At the convent door, Melia lifts the big knocker and lets it fall back with a bang that echoes down the quiet street. The sun has just risen on this Christian holiday, and soon the death cart will roll up the street to Julius's house and take the indigent, abandoned Fritigil away.

The small window above the knocker opens inward, and words in Latin float out: "Bless this day in Christ." The dark interior masks the face that delivers the benediction.

"Matildis, the candlemaker's wife, sent us to deliver these infants," Melia responds in the same language.

Silence. Melia waits, wondering if the nun on the other side of the door has understood her.

"Sister?"

"I will call for the abbess," the nun responds. She closes the window.

"It is cold out here!" Melia shouts after the retreating nun. She has no idea whether she is heard through the door. She supposes it isn't any way to talk to a nun, but with little experience handing over orphans to a convent, she was bound to make a mistake or two.

Melia and Briggeta bounce on their feet, quieting the babies against their chests and trying to keep warm. Finally, the window opens again, and this time, the woman on the other side sticks her nose out to appraise the visitors.

"Bless this day in Christ's name," she says.

"We already heard that," Melia mutters. "Yes, bless this day," she says more audibly. "We have been ordered to deliver these little lambs to your care."

"And to whom do the babies have to blame for entrance into the world?" the nun asks.

Melia smiles. Yes, blame is the right word. That is just what she thinks Julius deserves. Blame.

"Julius, the diocese's inspector," Melia says. "He is away in Treverorum. We don't expect him back for some time. Meanwhile, the mother, the slave girl who bore him these children, has died."

The abbess says nothing. She closes the little window, and for a moment, Melia thinks they are being refused. She glances at Briggeta and realizes the girl doesn't know enough Latin to follow the conversation.

"Father. She asked who the father was," Melia says, knowing that in all their dialects, "father" sounded about the same. "I don't know what—" She stops midsentence as someone on the other side of the door releases the lock and pulls it open. It complains with a groan of breaking ice. It has probably been days, maybe weeks, since anyone has passed through.

Two nuns—Melia assumes the one who addresses them is the abbess—stand inside the door and reach out to accept the babies. Melia and Briggeta hand them over; Melia is at once grateful, and then worried. What will happen to them? Will they receive the care, the feeding they need?

"We will expect remuneration," the nun with the abbess's voice says. "Julius should come as soon as he is in town. I will talk to the priest to make sure this is so."

The two nuns step backward, and the door closes, seemingly on its own.

DETENTE

Melia hadn't expected the delivery of tiny, innocent humans to the convent to end on such a pecuniary note. But then, she's not had much interaction with nuns. Her only relationship with the Catholic Church has been as the candlemaker to the priest at the basilica. She knows nothing about the life and concerns of the sisters other than that they always seem to have food and shelter when others in town are going hungry.

When she and Briggeta return to Fritigil's house, it is empty. The death cart has come and gone, and Matildis and Ingoberga have cleaned up the bed and left. They left a pile of bloody towels and rags on the floor near the door. Briggeta and the housekeeper will decide whether to wash them or burn them. If it were up to Melia, they would go into the fire.

Melia walks into the candle shop not knowing what to expect from Matildis. The woman's calm care of Fritigil surprised her. How had she learned how to deliver babies? After months of refusing to help Melia cook, shop, get water, and clean the house, Matildis had left her with the impression that not only did she want to do nothing, but that was all she could do. Melia had been proven wrong.

Muting her new appreciation is the pain of losing Fritigil. It isn't until she was safely back in the house, away from the night's horror and the eeriness of the streets, that she allows herself to feel her own sorrow. She sits on her work stool, her cloak still covering her shoulders, and weeps. Any residual joy she may have from her night with Ruggie is sucked from her heart. She doesn't deserve to be happy when Fritigil will no longer enjoy another moment on this earth or see her babies grow into pretty, giggling girls.

Finally, shivering from the cold, Melia rises, dries her eyes, and takes a deep breath to fortify herself. She pushes open the door to the living space and steps inside, not knowing what kind of reception to expect from Matildis.

Matildis stands with her back to Melia, grinding dried malted barley in the large mortar she uses to make beer. She is humming to herself, a tune that Melia has never heard. She seems not to hear Melia come in.

"Matildis," Melia says quietly, not wanting to surprise her.

Matildis turns around, puts down the pestle, and walks to Melia. She raises her arms and Melia steps back to avoid a blow.

"No," Matildis laughs. "Come here. I only want to comfort you. Your friend has passed, and you must be sad."

Cautiously, Melia lets the wife surround her with her excess flesh. It might be comforting, if the woman didn't smell so ripe. It isn't her fault that she's been up to her elbows in blood and sweat all night, Melia knows, but she is pungent. Melia holds her breath and stands still, letting Matildis shelter her.

"You are a good woman," Melia says as Matildis releases her and she can breathe. "I don't know what we would have done without your help. And Ingoberga, too. You were brave and skilled. I was neither."

"You have learned a great deal today," Matildis says without turning around. "Someday maybe you will have babies of your own, and you will know to take better care of yourself."

Melia frowns. Does Matildis think that Fritigil's death was her own fault—perhaps that she had starved herself in her pregnancy? Yes, she was very skinny, but wasn't that a consequence of having twins and Julius's neglect? She wants to argue with Matildis, but she doesn't want to ruin any possible détente. Perhaps someday, she will ask Matildis to explain what she thinks Fritigil had done to bring on her own misery and death.

"I'm going to go down and get water for your beer," Melia announces, pulling a single water bucket off the hook by the heart. "It feels like it's going to get colder yet today and tonight. I want to go now while I can still breathe without freezing my lungs and the well isn't frozen."

The frigid air stings back of her throat as she runs down the hill to warm up. While the cold is painful, at least it keeps much snow from falling. It will have to warm up a great deal before the sky can shed the flakes that she imagines are swirling in the hard, dark clouds above the city.

Melia drops her bucket into the well in solitude. If anyone else needs water that day, they are either done or doing without it. The bucket hits a sheet of ice, and Melia pulls it up and lets it drop again. It takes four times before the bucket breaks the surface of the water.

That reminds Melia of the river.

Has it frozen over yet?

THE INVASION

Winter all over Gaul and Germania has been particularly brutal this year. But for the tribes camped on the east bank of the river, it was deadly. Toddlers died of exposure, women died in childbirth, and everyone was on the verge of dying of starvation.

Families huddle, twelve bodies to a wagon, at night to stay warm, any notion of intimacy thwarted as much by the rancid cloud of body odor as by the lack of privacy. The men keep the fires fed day and night, and the women stray from its heat in the day only when they have to gather the frozen bodies of the small animals they trap for food and fur and when they join their families in the wagons at night. They lodge the cooking pots up as close to the fire as possible, scooping the floating ash off the top before tossing in some barley and the skinned and eviscerated carcasses for squirrel and rabbit stew. Greta lusts for the taste of a vegetable, or even a spoonful of stew that isn't infused with smoke.

The men keep warm during the day cutting wood to feed the fires, and as the frigid weeks stretch on and the surrounding trees are felled, the forests shrink away. Now, blizzards regularly blow unblocked through camp, and when the snow flies, it forces men, women, and children back under the putrid blankets and tarps of their wagons, even in the daytime.

But as the winter solstice passes, hunger displaces the cold as the tribes' greatest preoccupation. Just as their bodies need more insulation and more fat to burn, their main food source—wildlife—dwindles. The traps have culled most of the small animals that once scurried about in the woods and the larger ones—deer and wild pigs—were either eaten or had fled away from the camp.

Stories about the wealth of Gaul had fueled this journey as much as the marauding Huns had from the start. But as their meager possessions and food supply disappear, the imagined riches on the other side of the river have gone from tempting to essential.

Greta fears the growing desperation and belligerence will turn the tribes against each other, and instead of being united against the Roman blockade, they'll fight amongst themselves. But just as futility threatens to turn Suevi against Alan, and Alan against Vandal, the scouts delivered the news that the river was freezing solid. The Roman fleet had been sent downstream where the wider channel is still open.

News of the freezing river whips the men—farmers-cum-warriors—into a frenzy. Their behavior hasn't changed overnight. It degraded as the days grew shorter, food scarcer, and the temperature dropped. Now instead of talk, the night air resounds with war cries.

The garrison in Mogantiacum, reported by the scouts to be down to a few dozen soldiers and some local recruits, can keep the tribes from crossing the narrow bridge with just a few guards and well-aimed arrows. But the ice on the river has created a natural bridge a few meters across and miles long, and there aren't enough men in all the forts of the Roman *limites* to defend a frontier that expansive.

In a few days, the tribes forge a plan. The warriors will cross over the ice at midnight with pitched torches, the leaders in the front, their loyal tribesmen close behind. They will attack the guards at the bridge first, clearing the way for the wagons. The old men too weak to march on the front lines will drive the wagons across at daybreak, followed by the women and the few surviving toddlers born during the migration.

The day before the midnight crossing, the women pack the wagons, bundling their babies and securing them deep in rags and blankets, and prepare their last meal in Germania—the gods willing and the ice strong enough to hold the men. By mid-day in camp, the pots have been emptied and stored in the wagons along with their small cache of dried meat and any belongings they had not burned for heat. The warriors tie points to newly hewn arrow shafts, reinforce their shields with thick bark, and sharpen their swords and hand axes. Their weaponry ready, they prance around, warming their joints for the charge.

The newly nominated kings of the three tribes circle the camps, shouting orders peppered with bellicose shouts of hatred for the very Empire they crave to settle in.

"Aren't there spies amongst us who will report to the Roman legions?" Greta asks her new husband. "Why do the men shout their plans?"

Milo looks sideways at the Suevi leader and nods. "Some think the Romans are stupid and will think the shouts are the start of ritual feast of Kalends." He pauses, sad in face. "There is much pride and glory before the charge. Spies or not, many on both sides will fall before we breach the walls of the city. But without this excitement, our mission would be doomed before it starts."

"Of course." Greta moves close to him and puts her hand on his back. She has nearly forgotten about Kalends, the celebration that greeted the start of a new year and the eventual return of the sun's heat. Over the months of their journey, they observed solstices, equinoxes, births, deaths—all the occasions that call for ritual—despite their struggle for survival. But on this night, the eve of their crossing, the ritual chants are replaced with war cries.

Side by side, Greta and Milo stand at a distance, watch, and listen as the leader of the Suevi waves his arms and shouts down from a large rock, the young men looking up at him, their eyes glassy with the madness of battle. Cloaked in a heavy bear skin, with leather hosiery secured from his ankles to his crotch and a horned helmet atop his head, the Suevi king looks frightening enough to send effete Roman legionnaires retreating without a fight. Or so Greta hopes.

Milo puts his arm around her shoulders, and they survey the preparations. Greta squeezes her husband's waist with one arm. Ballomar, as one of the leaders of the tribe, would have been in the middle of the boisterous men, but Greta is grateful that Milo's role is different. As an older warrior not yet considered an elder, he is assigned to take the bridge once the warriors have cleared a safe path through Mogantiacum. He and a few others will hurry the wagons across the bridge and point the way toward the farmlands of Gaul. Milo won't be in the vanguard, crossing the ice with a torch and sword, but his will still be a dangerous assignment.

"God speed your journey," Greta prays aloud.

"Wodin or the God of Abraham?"

"I don't much care," Greta whispers, tears forming and burning the lids of her eyes.

"When you get across," Milo says, "I know you will want to find Melia. I will wait at the bridge for you to get word to me. I'll come to get you as soon as all our wagons are across and heading west."

He turns to kiss her quickly and walks away. Greta watches until he disappears into the midst of the gathering war party and focuses again on how she might retrieve her daughter on the other side.

THE MEN THROTTLE THEIR WAR cries and start across river in silence just after midnight. Greta and the women in the wagons watch as the light of their torches follows the bank's slope down, and disappears for a few minutes, finally reappearing as they reach the flat ice and slip quietly toward the opposite bank. They can see the torches bobble in the dark as the men scramble up the Roman side.

Just as the leaders reach the flat plain on the far bank, the war cries rise again, and Greta knows the battle has been engaged. Axes clang on shields, arrows sting the air and cries of anguish and victory float across the frozen river, and the torch lights blow cold. For hours, the war rages, but by the time the sun's first rays hit the other side, word is sent back that the invaders have entered the city, thrown open the gates, and whatever battle continues is taking place inside the city's walls. Now they wait for the signal that the wagons should cross, and the tribes will finally claim their place inside the glittering Empire.

Greta imagines how she will wave to her husband as she passes into Gaul and heads for her reunion with Melia. She closes her eyes and does something she hasn't done in a long time: she thinks about their future.

BAR THE DOOR

December 31, AD406 - Mogantiacum

Matildis and Melia finish their evening meal in pleasant silence, Melia grateful for the peace that has settled between them since Hermann had left and Fritigil's babies came. She feels guilty for the joy she finds in the man's probable and imminent demise, but it seems that Matildis, too, has brightened, perhaps even blossomed, in the wake of his departure.

As Melia washes out their bowls and mugs, Matildis retires to her usual chair, and lights a lamp to illuminate her mending. Melia has hauled her mattress back into the warm house and looks forward to lying down early.

As she settles into sleep, Melia wonders what Matildis thought when Ruggie woke her at that early morning hour before Fritigil gave birth and died. Matildis hasn't mentioned seeing Ruggie, even though it is a crime for anyone to sleep with a slave without the owner's permission. Only Hermann has a right to force himself on her.

The door to the shop shoots open, and the blast of cold air blows the door to the house open as well, startling Melia and eliciting a scream from Matildis.

"Who is—," Melia stifles her shout when Ruggie steps inside. She sits up on her mattress, blushes at seeing him. Has he come to stay with her again?

"Melia," he says, his voice deep with urgency. He takes her hands in his and pulls her to her feet. "Matildis," he adds, looking back at her. "You must prepare yourselves. The Germanii are rousing for a crossing, and the legions are preparing to let them pass."

"What do you mean? They're not putting up a fight?"

"No, they will protect the fort and the garrison, but the town recruits will have to protect the streets. Theo and the Camp Prefect expect the Vandals and Suevi will head south through Gaul toward Hispania not stay in town. So, we'll let them pass through. The field army is coming up from Pannonia, but they won't be here in time. We don't have the manpower to resist an invasion."

Matildis cries out. "Hermann is being fed to the barbarians? You're making him face the barbarians alone?"

Ruggie nods. He isn't the one sending Hermann to his death, but he doesn't argue. Clearly, he wastes no sympathy on the man who repeatedly raped Melia.

"How do you know they're coming?" Melia's heart is pounding from both fear of the invasion and anticipation of seeing her mother.

"The Romans have had spies amongst them for some time. They're coming soon. Maybe as soon as tonight."

He puts his hands on Melia's shoulders and looks her in the eye. She's never seen him so serious.

"Listen to me," he says. His tone is demanding. "Your survival depends on it, and I very much want you to live."

"All right." Melia's heart pounds harder. "What?"

"You must put out the fire. Smoke would tell the invaders someone is living here, that there'd be food. Throw the shop door bolt and this one"—he gestures at the house door—"and stay inside. I'll knock down the candle shop shingle outside so they won't know this is a shop. You should stay up in the loft. Take some beer or cider or whatever you can eat from the cellar, and pull up the ladder, and stay silent and hidden, whatever happens. Don't move from there until I come back."

"How do we know you'll come back?" Matildis asks.

"I will be safe," Ruggie says, looking down in Melia's eyes, and grabbing her hands in his again. "I speak Latin, Suevi, and Burgundian. I can be anyone I need to be if I run into someone out there."

"How will we know it's you?" Matildis asks.

"I'll go into the alley and shout up at the loft. You'll hear me. No one else would call your names."

"Except Hermann," Matildis ventures.

Ruggie shakes his head. "I don't think Hermann will be coming back," he says. "I don't think many who are sent out of the barracks will be going home."

"Noooooo!" Matildis sinks to her knees and leans forward, her face in her hands. Melia feels sorry for her, but she can't feel bad for Hermann. She can't imagine that he deserves anything else, even if his death will be horrible.

"What will happen to the town?" Melia asks. "Will the Germanii pillage? Will they raid our houses? What will happen to the church? The convent?"

"We don't know, Melia." Ruggie lets go of her hands. "I think they will be pretty belligerent after being held back and starved for so long. Now, get ready as I said. I have to get back to the barracks. I'll come back as soon as I can."

Melia follows him to the front door of the shop. He turns, takes her shoulders in his hands, and kisses her forehead. She lifts her head to accept his lips; she hopes it won't be the last time. He slips out into the dark, leaps up to knock the shingle off its hanger, throws it into the shop, and closes the door.

"Bar the door, Melia!"

"I love you!" she shouts in response.

"And I love you!"

And he is gone.

MELIA DOES AS RUGGIE SAID, barring the shop door and then the door to the living quarters. By the time she gets inside, Matildis has tamped down the fire and scattered the coals. It won't take long before there will be no smoke rising from the roof to betray them. And it won't be long before the house will be too cold for comfort.

"I wonder if Ingoberga will be okay," Matildis mumbles. "Flavius is in the barracks too."

"Do you want to run out and talk to her?"

"Yes." Matildis looks unsure, and Melia realizes how frightened the woman was.

"Do you want me to go?" Melia asks. Matildis doesn't say anything, but her eyes plead for Melia's help.

"I'll go." Melia throws on her cloak, unbars both doors, and steps outside. She was right about the weather. It had been getting colder and colder all day; a thousand needles sting her cheeks as she runs to Ingoberga's house and pounds on the door.

As she waits for Ingoberga to answer, she can hear shouts floating across the river and over the silence of the town's streets. Are her tribesmen celebrating Kalends, or are those battle cries? It sounds more like the whooping, warring Huns than her own village farmers.

Melia pounds on the door again and shouts for Ingoberga. Still no answer. She backs off the step and looks to see if there is any smoke coming out of the roof. Convinced that Ingoberga has already gone—perhaps to her daughter's home—Melia runs back to the relative warmth of the shop, bars the door, and closes herself and Matildis in the house.

"No one there," Melia says. Matildis only nods. With fear in her eyes, she is busy tying ropes to the handles of the beer fermenting vat.

"What are you doing?"

"We'll have to hoist this upstairs together," Matildis says. "You climb up to the loft. I'll lift it and you pull."

Ingenious! Melia is impressed. It continues to surprise her how different Matildis is now with Hermann gone.

Melia helps Matildis slide the vat across the kitchen to a spot beside the ladder to the loft. She climbs up with the ropes in one hand, and sits down at the edge of the loft, her legs under the banister and her arms over the first rail. She pulls up on the ropes, but the vat doesn't move.

"Can you lift it a little more?" she asks. Matildis nods. With a groan, she manages to lift it off the floor. With Matildis lifting and Melia's pulling, they raise the vat level with the loft, but Melia can't get it over onto the surface herself. Melia ties the ropes to the post that supports the ceiling. "Come up and help."

"I'm coming." Matildis climbs the ladder, stands next to Melia, and together they pull the vat to safety.

"We did it!" Melia laughs. She stands and hugs Matildis, forgetting for the moment how bad the woman smells.

"I think I'm going to pull my bed up here, too," Melia says. She must avoid spending an entire night sleeping on a mattress next to Matildis!

It is getting late by the time the women establish themselves upstairs. Melia brings up the small amphora of cider and a basket of bread, carrots, cabbage, and dried meat that comprises their remaining food supply. They stash some candles and a flint in one corner, and their sewing projects in another. Finally, Melia thinks to bring up an empty bucket for their waste. If they have to stay up there until Ruggie returns, they won't be visiting the privy.

Matildis sends her back down one more time to retrieve a large ceramic plate before they pull the ladder up and store it away from the edge of the loft.

"What for?" Melia asks.

"We will cover the waste bucket between times."

Apparently, even stinky Matildis has a limit to the odor she can tolerate.

Shouts, mortal screams, and the clatter of horse hooves in the distance wakes Melia in the middle of the night.

The invasion has started. Matildis sits up in her bed.

"They're coming," the wife says. "We must pray. It's the only thing that can stop them now."

Melia shakes her head. "My mother might be—." She stops midsentence. She never told Matildis that her mother was one of the Suevi in the camp, or that she promised to come and buy Melia's freedom.

Melia doesn't know if her mother has survived the trip to the river and the raid by the Franks. So much could have happened in two years. She could have become a slave herself; she might have died from disease or starvation; she may not have the money she needs for Melia's rescue and might pass through without looking for her.

Although they had shared birth, death, the threat of incarceration, and the rising tide of fear over the past weeks, Melia doesn't know if Matildis will grant her freedom, even if it is paid for. Can Matildis find or buy another slave now that trade with the Burgundians will be interrupted and she has no *dinari*? Even if she can find another slave, what are the chances they can find a scribe in the town to record Melia's manumission?

Melia cringes as a loud crash down the street interrupts her thoughts. Has the noise come from the church? Will the Christians among her tribesmen attack a sacred altar as well as everything else?

Matildis waits until the noise settles down little before asking: "What did you say about your mother?"

Melia decides to reveal only what she knew to be true. "My mother was among the Suevi who headed from our home to the river," she whispers. "I don't know if she made it; I don't know if she will look for me."

Matildis says nothing for several minutes, and in the dark, Melia can't read her face.

"If she finds you, that will mean nothing."

"I will be glad to see her," Melia says to deflect Matildis's implication.

But Matildis responds flatly. "I can't let you go. I have no one to help me. If your mother comes, I will send her away."

"But perhaps she will give you money to buy a new slave, one who is better at cooking and making candles."

Matildis huffs. "You may not be a good cook or a hard worker, but I won't be able to replace you for a while. There will be no slave auction for a long time. There will be no markets of any kind for a while. I foresee a terrible winter ahead for Mogantiacum."

Melia had those same thoughts. But beyond that, she hasn't considered what the town might be like after the migrants pass through and she leaves. She had been singularly focused on her mother coming into town, not on the likely pillaging that arrives with her. Melia was naïve, thinking she had no stake in the fate of Mogantiacum or in the Empire. She was spoiled by the ease of the marketplace, the security of their stone house, easy passage on cobblestone streets, and the ready availability of tallow and grain and meat. She has become Roman.

She doesn't know how long it will take for the markets to reopen. No one will know how many farming villas will survive, unnoticed and unmolested by plundering tribes, and how many will have meat and vegetables to sell again. Or how many homes in Mogantiacum will be spared. Melia doesn't think of her tribesmen as barbarians, but they will be hungry and angry after more than a year in a stalemate with Rome. They have deaths to avenge. The Empire has done nothing—offered nothing—to help them, and the migrants will have no sympathy for anyone on this side of the river.

Although the chaos sounds like it is still far down the hill near the fort and the market, Melia can't sleep. She fears the barred doors and lack of fire won't be enough to protect them. Now she worries that Matildis will quash the dream that has carried her through two and a half years of hard work, rape, and shame. She's been stupid about so much. Just as she thought she and Matildis had developed new respect for each other, she is slapped with the reality that she is never going to be anything other than a slave to the wife. Even if Hermann never returns, she will still be Matildis's chattel, with which Matildis can do anything she wanted—including turning her into a prostitute. There are few limits to an owner's power over a slave.

Melia has known that for some time, but she's ignored it. How did she think she was any different from any other slave?

Matildis, on the other hand, falls back to sleep, her snoring a third thing to keep Melia awake. At dawn, when it is light enough to see, she gets up and uses the waste bucket. She wonders how much danger there is in going back down the ladder. It seems that the stone walls of the house should protect them. It would be hard to burn down. And if the bars on the doors don't hold, any Alans or Vandals who want to reach them can do it with a simple bit of teamwork: standing on each other's shoulders, or throwing a rope over the banister and pulling themselves up. Why did Ruggie think staying up in the loft would help?

She is about to let down the ladder and descend when Matildis wakes with a snort and a cough.

"Did I sleep?" she asks hoarsely.

"Yes, in spite of everything." After their conversation in the middle of the night, Melia's opinion of Hermann's wife has turned sour again.

"What is happening?"

"I have no idea. I'm up here, too."

The sound of battering rams and axes is moving closer, up the hill. Smoke seeps in through the cracks around the ceiling and around the frames of the doors. Melia hears wood splintering nearby and realizes that even if the heavy metal bar across their door holds, the wood door itself can be broken through with an axe.

Her heart pounds as it sounds like the raiders reach the house next door. Moments later, she hears what she imagines is an axe bashing into Ingoberga's door. Melia hears a shout in the Burgundian accent of her owners. "No farther, scum! Back off!" Is she imagining things, or could it have been Hermann?

"That's Hermann!" Matildis whispers.

The command is answered by the whistle of a dozen arrows and the laughter of a horde of Germanii. Was Hermann the target? Melia holds her breath, trying to pick out his voice again. Instead, someone shouts above the laughter: "We are finding nothing of value here. Let's go back to the church."

Melia recognizes those words too; they are Suevi.

The raiders don't climb back up the hill toward them again that day, but Melia and Matildis stay in the loft. Matildis sobs and snorts, but Melia feels nothing. She is relieved that Matildis stayed quiet when the Suevi moved close. But the possibility of being attacked by her own people, now seeming a real threat, leaves her numb.

Toward nightfall, the pillaging sounds as if it moves to other parts of town, and Melia decides to climb down and get away from Matildis's weeping. If the raiders return, she'd scurry up the ladder, pull it up to the loft and return to the back corner. But she surmises their neighborhood holds no allure for the invaders. They would be looking for treasure, not mattresses, tables, or stools. If they move on to southern Gaul, as Ruggie predicted, they'll be looking for food or livestock, and the market and the villas outside of town are better targets.

Matildis is curled up on her bed, with only brief respites in her sobbing, when Melia slides the ladder back over the edge of the loft and slips the bolt into the hole that holds it in place.

"Where are you going!" Matildis shouts.

"Shhhhh!" Melia orders. "You don't want anyone to hear you."

"Are you thinking of running away?"

"No." Melia hasn't even considered it. With the Vandals and Alans running through the streets, she'll be no safer than Hermann had apparently been—if it had been Hermann they heard outside.

"I will send the cohort to find you." Matildis threatens.

Melia laughs quietly. The cohort had locked Matildis in jail; how likely are they to hop to her command with a horde of barbarians on their hands? They aren't even likely to survive. She has little to fear from Matildis; only slightly more from Hermann if he is still alive.

The long night and day of their voluntary imprisonment confused Melia's emotions. She swung from fear to optimism to pessimism and now to a sense of calm. She no longer needs her mother to save her. Once she knows Hermann isn't coming back, she will walk out the door. With Mogantiacum's security forces likely decimated, Matildis will be powerless to stop her.

But where will she go? Castra Regina with Ruggie? Into Gaul with her mother? Until this invasion is over—how long will it take?—she has no way to know.

HUNGER

January, AD406 - Mogantiacum

The second night of the invasion passes a little more quietly than the first. Melia hears occasional shouts in the distance, and the smoke in the air grows thicker, but little happens around them.

The next morning, she and Matildis lower the beer vat back down to the main floor, and Melia carries the basket of food and the amphora of cider down the ladder. She lowers the waste pail by rope, and taking a calculated risk, she opens the door onto the rear garden and tosses its contents out onto the ground.

As Melia tears a small piece of dry bread off their remaining loaf, Matildis reaches across the table and slaps it from her hand.

"No more for you until you go find us food," she says.

"How?" Melia asks. "Any food that can be found has already been stolen by the raiders or by our starving neighbors. We just have to hope Ruggie comes from the fort before we starve to death. He will bring us something."

"Or Hermann will."

Melia looks at Matildis with pity. Does she really think Hermann is alive?

"I think you will have to figure out how to live without Hermann," Melia says quietly. "He's not coming back. And you have nothing and no one to provide for you."

"You will."

Melia looks across the table and narrows her eyes at Matildis.

"While you knock bread out of my hand? Tell me why. Why would I help you?"

"Because you belong to me."

"Yes, I do. But if I walked out of here, there's nothing you can do to get me back."

Matildis sits back and scowls. In a matter of hours, their detente has fallen apart.

Inside the house and outside, everything has changed. Matildis had control over Melia back when the Empire controlled Mogantiacum. Now, Melia calculates, there is no law; there is nothing Matildis can do to hold her. Perhaps someday, the Empire will regain control over all of Gaul. Stilicho could call the legions back and order would be restored. But until then, Melia is as good as free.

Matildis must have come to the same conclusion. "I'm going to go find Hermann," she announces.

Melia shakes her head. She would be happy to be rid of the difficult woman, but she doesn't want Matildis to attract attention to the shop. "You are a foolish old woman. You will die out there. No one will stop a Vandal who decides he wants to take you the way Hermann took me."

"That's all you think about. Hermann in your bed."

"If you believe that, then both of us are whores, Matildis,"

Melia answers. "Neither of us had a say in his way with us. Once you chose to marry Hermann, he owned you just as much as he owned me."

Matildis scowls, but Melia sees a hint of sadness in her expression. Matildis doesn't have to be a slave to feel like one.

Matildis stands up and pulls her cloak down from its hook. Melia doesn't try to stop her. When the woman struggles to pry the heavy bars from the doors, Melia doesn't help. After she leaves, Melia re-bars the doors and returns to the kitchen.

She picks up the piece of bread that Matildis had knocked to the floor and sits down to gnaw at it. Melia's listens to the voice in her head argue back and forth: care about Matildis, don't care about her. When she came to understand Matildis's fate is not much better than her own, she had started to feel sorry for her. But now, she cares little. What has changed?

"Freedom," Melia says out loud. Once she glimpsed the possibility of freedom, it is all that matters. Her empathy has evaporated.

How will she figure out what to do when her future and her desires swing wildly?

Sleep. Melia nods to herself. Her problem is a lack of sleep. She climbs back up to the loft, flops on her mattress and falls asleep before fully prone.

MELIA WAKES ONCE AGAIN TO banging on the door. She sits up with her heart pounding. How long has she slept? She looks out the high window in the loft. It is still daylight. She hasn't been out long.

Who is it? Ruggie? Hermann? Matildis? A Vandal? Her mother?

She climbs down the ladder, her legs shaking. She sets the bolt back from the first door quietly, and tiptoes across the floor of the shop to the peep hole.

Matildis.

For a moment, Melia considers not letting the wife back in the house. What could Matildis do? Would anyone come to her aid?

But, as much as she despises the woman, Melia can't let her die on the front step. She takes the chance that Matildis isn't being followed by the horde and opens the door.

"Did you find Hermann?" Melia asks. Her tone is cold, but she can't muster any warmth for either of her owners. She throws the bar down across the door and follows Matildis back into the kitchen.

"No, I didn't see Hermann," Matildis forces out over heaving breaths. Has she run back to the house? "The dead are all over the streets." Matildis's eyes fill with tears. "Dead men, dead horses. The smell is horrible. Dogs are eating..." She chokes on the words.

"How about the raiders? Are they gone?"

"I don't know. Their wagons of women and children are coming across the bridge now. I could see them across the valley. No one is stopping them."

Melia's heart leaps. Maybe one of them carries her mother.

"How about the fort?"

"I didn't get down that far. It was too dangerous, and I couldn't stand the smell. The church is burning; that's where most of the smoke is coming from. Ingoberga's door was broken. I looked inside. Everything broken or gone. We are lucky. They were coming here next. Maybe Hermann stopped them."

Melia doubts it. Probably it was just chance that saved them. "And the priest?"

Matildis shrugs. "I saw no one. There isn't a Roman soldier in sight, either. They have abandoned the streets and left us to the barbarians."

Ruggie had been right. Stilicho's field armies have to travel up from Illyricum and Pannonia and won't get to Mogantiacum for weeks. If they are coming at all. Until then, the soldiers here on the frontier will hunker down and wait. Melia wonders what has happened to the soldier's wives and children who live in their own part of town. Have they been killed? Kidnapped? Their houses burned?

Melia and Matildis sit at the table, their heads in their hands. They survived the onslaught of the invasion, but to what end? Unless Ruggie comes to help them, they will starve in this house. Anyone else who survives will starve as well.

For the next two days, Melia and Matildis don't argue. They don't speak to each other except when necessary. Hungry and anxious, they walk around in circles like ghosts. They finish the turnips, cabbage, and carrots they have left. They drank most of the beer Matildis made before the invasion and sleep fitfully for hours to pass the time. Frugally, they sip the remaining well water.

Finally, Melia announces she will light a fire. Although the worst of the cold snap has passed, and the weather is warming slightly, days without heat has turned the stone walls to icy blocks that suck the remaining heat out of their bones.

"No, don't," Matildis argues. "It'll alert the barbarians."

"Who? The women and children?" Melia asks. "My guess is the warriors have passed through. We have nothing to fear from the families."

Matildis nods, a rare concession to Melia's logic. All they have to worry about now is freezing and starving to death. Even thirst will be a problem soon. The cider is spent, and the water is running low.

Once Melia gets the fire going in the pit, Matildis pulls her chair in from the back room and sits close to it. Melia pulls her mattress closer, too, lies down, and closes her eyes.

She wakes as the bar on the kitchen door hits the flange at the top. Matildis is heading for the front door.

"Where are you going?" Melia yells.

"I can't stand this. I'm going to find Hermann," Matildis says. "I can't stay here and starve." She struggles to lift the heavier bar that lies across the outside door. Melia reaches her before she succeeds and pulls the big woman away. The bolt clangs back into place.

"There is no Hermann," Melia says. "Not anymore. We have to wait for Ruggie."

"It's been four days since we saw him. Ruggie isn't coming," Matildis says. She scratches wildly at Melia's arms, trying to get past her to the door. "You were only his whore, not his wife."

Melia's eyes burn with hatred, and for a moment she considers opening the door and pushing Matildis out. But once again, her hate wavers.

As difficult as Matildis is, she is better than no company at all. If Matildis leaves, if Ruggie never comes back, and if her mother never makes it across the river, she'll be alone. That now seems more frightening than the horde.

"No! We stay inside. We stay together," Melia says. She sounds crazy, even to herself.

Matildis stares at her. Melia grabs her arm to pull her back into the house, but Matildis surprises her with a hard slap across the face. Melia reaches up to stop the sting, and Matildis slugs her in the stomach. With Melia bent over, Matildis slips out of her grasp and lifts the door bar again. She throws it up with a strength Melia has never seen in her.

Melia flies at her back, knocking her into the door, and the bar falls back in place. Matildis spins around, her back to the door and growls. Startled by the sound, Melia backs up, and Matildis turns to unbar the door again. But this time, she gets the heavy metal only part way up to the flange before she loses her hold on it. The bar falls back down, smashing onto her head.

Matildis crumples to the ground.

Melia holds her stomach, catching her breath, waiting for her head to clear and for the woman to get up. But Matildis doesn't move. It takes a few seconds before Melia realizes she isn't going to. Melia kneels and twists the woman over onto her back. Matildis's eyes are closed, and Melia feels her neck for a pulse. Good. She isn't dead; just knocked out. Serves her right; she should have stayed put. They should both stay where they are until Ruggie comes. If he comes.

Melia sits back on her heels. What should she do? She can't leave the woman lying on the cold floor by the door. She has to get her back into the house by the warm fire.

Matildis has lost weight over the past couple of months, with so little food in the house, but it is still hard work to pull her across the shop floor. Melia lifts her under the arms and leans back, digging her heels into the breaks between the stones on the floor. Matildis' head flops back, and Melia worries she might break her neck. It is a little easier to pull her along the smoother stone floor in the kitchen. She gets Matildis to the fire and rolls her onto Melia's mattress. She flips Matildis over onto her back and straightens out her arms and legs. She looks as if she's just laid down to take a nap.

Taking a deep breath, Melia stands up straight and stretches her back. She looks down at the wife and mutters, "I hope you don't die on me, Matildis, because I don't want to have to drag your body out of here."

Melia sits at the table and stares at Matildis' chest as it rises and falls shallowly. Perhaps she will stay unconscious until Ruggie gets there. Melia will leave with him. Castra Regina or anywhere else would be better than this. And then, Melia won't have to argue with Matildis about food or Hermann or anything else.

But now she worries about something else: Is she going

insane? Matildis is hurt, perhaps mortally. And it is all because Melia panicked about being left alone. She should have let the woman leave without a fuss. Melia remembers the vacant stares of the crazy women behind the jailhouse bars. Is that what she looks like now?

She leans forward, her elbows on the table and her forehead in her hands.

"God," she implores, praying to the one Matildis worships. "Don't let this woman die by my hand. Take her if you wish, but don't make me a murderer."

Then, she switches gods and says a prayer to Wodin, but this time only for her mother, Ruggie, and herself.

THE ACCIDENT

Someone is pounding on the front door to the shop. Melia shakes herself awake. She has fallen asleep with her head and forearms resting on the table. When she sits up, her stiff shoulders ache. She pushes her arms down to her sides, painfully.

"Melia!" It could be Ruggie.

Her stiffness vanishes. Melia throws the house door open and runs through the shop.

"Ruggie?"

"Yes, it's me. You can open the door."

Melia tosses back the heavy bar as if it were a feather and throws the door open. Ruggie steps through, and Melia grabs him, burying her head in his chest. She surprises herself by bursting into tears.

"Hey, hey!" he says. "Are you hurt? Did someone get in?"

"Matildis!" Melia sputters and backs up, pointing into the house. "I don't know if she's okay."

Ruggie rushes around Melia and into the kitchen. He kneels by the mattress.

"What happened?" he asks as he feels Matildis's neck for a pulse and runs his fingers over the back of her head.

"She tried to go out, and I tried to stop her, and the bar fell on her head, and she's been like this for, I don't know, hours."

"And she'll be like this forever," Ruggie says. He rolls back on his heels and stands up. He takes Melia by the shoulders. "She's dead."

"But she doesn't even look hurt."

"She has a very large bump on the back of her skull. My guess is she bled in the brain. We see this in the legion. Sometimes even after fights between the men. It's actually better if a head wound is open and the blood runs out."

"Oh!" Melia looks down at Matildis, panic rising in her chest again. "What do we do?"

"Sit," Ruggie orders. "Sit and take some deep breaths. I don't want you to faint. We need to think."

Melia nods and plops down on a stool. She feels like she is in a trance; she can't stop staring at Matildis' body. Ruggie paces a little, sits down, and gets up to pace some more.

"In the scheme of things, Melia," Ruggie says, his voice low and sympathetic, "this isn't as bad as it might seem."

Melia breaks out of her trance and frowns. "How can this not be bad?"

"There are virtually no authorities in Mogantiacum right now, no one to arrest you or judge you or punish you. It's chaos and anarchy out there. You're as good as free, Melia. Your master and his wife are dead. No one will care about your disappearance for months. If ever."

Melia listens and considers what he says. Her owners are dead, or at least Hermann is most likely dead. Who owns her now? Did Hermann have any heirs who can claim her as inheritance? She has no idea what happens to slaves when their masters die.

But she shakes her head. "No. Someone will eventually discover her body. I'll be the only suspect, and Stilicho's men will search for me. Wherever I go in the Empire, I'll be looking over my shoulder, waiting to be returned and hanged for murder."

"No," Ruggie says. He sits down across from her. "It will be a very long time before things settle down in Gaul. Already a man named Constantine from Britannia has crossed the North Sea and is marching toward Milan to claim the title of emperor. Stilicho has much bigger problems than Mogantiacum or you to worry about."

Melia says nothing. How can he be so sanguine about Matildis' death? Is he crazy, too? This invasion, these horrific events have made them all insane.

"And, I have some news," Ruggie continues. "Some really good news."

She stands up, turning away from the table. Nothing good can come from all of this.

"No, here, look!" Ruggie reaches into the lining of his cloak and removes a folded piece of paper. He opens it and hands it to her.

She takes it reluctantly and glances down at it. It looks official, like a military document or maybe a court document. "I can't read, Ruggie. What is it?"

"My freedom. Theo has given me my freedom."

"He can do that?"

"Since the Castra Prefect has been called to Milan to answer for the invasion, Theo is the highest-ranking officer of the garrison. He won't be for long, but for now, he is. He can do anything he wants."

"That's good, Ruggie. You're a freeman again. You can go to Regina." Suddenly she realizes he will leave her now. Why would a freeman want the burden of an escaped slave on his hands?

But Ruggie argues otherwise. He explains how he didn't have to buy his way out of slavery. Theo had given it to him. And then Ruggie used his money to buy a horse and wagon from one of the recruits in the garrison—a man likely dead. This is his plan: He will bring whatever dried meat, beer, cider, and root vegetables he can smuggle from the fort's larder. Together, they will head east across the Rhine against the hordes of women, children and old men still streaming over the bridge, and then follow the Main River east. Once the snow melts in the spring and they cross over the mountains to the Danube, they will find a barge to take them down to Castra Regina. Theo has sent a message ahead to let the brewery there know he is coming and is eager to offer his brewing services as an apprentice.

"And you can go with me," he concludes.

Melia feels nauseous, her head spinning. Too much is happening too fast.

"What about Hermann? Is he dead?"

Ruggie shrugs. "There were no townsmen who came back after the warriors passed through. We know some of them may have joined the migrants, some went to protect their homes. If he didn't come back here, he's dead."

"Isn't anyone identifying the bodies?"

"Melia, there are too many. Migrants and infantrymen and the town recruits. Horses, too. The stench is bad enough to force a man to stop breathing."

Melia tries to process all he is telling her. She had been sequestered in the house since Fritigil died. She has no mental picture of the carnage he describes.

"Wait!" she cries. "What about the wagons of women and children? Have they all passed through?"

"Many more are still coming," Ruggie says. "Before he left for Milan, the prefect ordered us to let them pass through. There's no reason to stop them from moving farther into Gaul. There's no food here, nothing for them to stay for. They can only cause more problems."

"So, my mother may still come."

Ruggie reaches for her and pulls her to his chest. "Yes," he says into her hair. "It is possible. But we can't wait. We must run now before Stilicho gets close with the field army. It will be much harder to travel then."

Melia's eyes fill with tears. "But what if she comes?"

"I love you, Melia, so I don't want to say this," he squeezes her tightly. "But I don't think your mother is coming."

Melia pulls away and sits down. She tries to think. If she is crazy, one way to prove it would be to stay in this house with a dead woman and wait for her mother, who probably wasn't coming, while letting Ruggie go. That would be foolish, maybe even suicidal. There is no food in the house. Soon, she will either have to pull Matildis outside and let the dogs and crows feast on her putrefying body—she shivers at the thought—or she'll have to leave. Where will she go? Where could she find food?

"Yes," she says. She lets the word hang in the air and waits to see how it feels. "Yes, Ruggie, we should go together. There's nothing here for me. Right now, you are all I have."

She looks up at his wide grin with dry eyes. "My mother traded my life for hers," she says. "I owe her nothing."

Before he leaves, Melia and Ruggie light the coals under the tallow vat long enough to soften the fat, and together they lift Matildis' body and tip it in. One way to preserve meat is to store it in lard; the heavy grease keeps water out, and rot requires water.

Melia watches Matildis sink under the surface. It seems an ignominious burial, but waiting for the death cart would be futile. So many bodies, and no one left to mourn them or pray over their graves. At least Matildis lost consciousness quickly. If she felt any pain at all, it could only have been for a moment.

Designating the tallow vat as Matildis' final resting place was Melia's idea. She didn't want to spend the night with the body putrefying in the house. The smell would have overwhelmed her. But when the tallow hardened again it would seal Matildis's odor in there with her. Finally, Melia will be free of the wife's stench.

"Can you be ready to leave in the morning?" Ruggie asks once they'd dowsed the fire.

Melia looks around at her few belongings: the broach her mother gave her the only precious thing she owned. She has two dresses: a linen one for warm months and a wool one for winters; a few undergarments; a cloak; and a comb and her sewing needles.

"It won't take long to get ready to go," she says. "I'll bring some candles, beeswax and votives. Perhaps we'll need them later. And we can take whatever you want from the house. The cooking pots and the stools, perhaps? Whatever will fit in the wagon."

Ruggie leaves her lips burning with a passionate kiss and skips out of the house as if he inhabited a much brighter world—one not filled with rotting bodies and burning buildings.

Melia starts right away, throwing her belongings in the little wagon she used for candle deliveries and folds up all the blankets in the house except for the one they wrapped around Matildis before dropping her in the vat.

She lifts the smaller pots off their hooks over the kitchen fire and uses a stiff brush to knock the ash and char off the bottoms. Then she throws her mattress over the hearth onto the coals and watches it catch fire. She has spent only one pleasant night there—with Ruggie—and many miserable ones. How many times she wished to die while lying on it, anticipating and bearing Hermann's visit? But it was Matildis who died there, not Melia.

Melia would sleep in the loft that night, and they could take that mattress with them as well. Perhaps it would air out in the wagon.

Melia lugs all the pots, blankets and her meager basket of possessions to the front door, ready to load in Ruggie's wagon. She fills a large burlap sack with a bag of sulfur crystals, the beeswax she has left, rosemary, almond oil, and a stack of votives.

She finishes about the time the weak winter sun dips below the hills to the west, and she sits down to chew on the stringy dried beef Ruggie brought for her. It is tough, and it isn't much, but it is the first meat she's had in more than a week.

Her last days with Matildis have been mercurial and tricky: but in the end, Melia thinks they had reached an understanding about their common misery. Theirs was far from an intimate bond, and it was kept shallow and fragile by their mutual distrust. Thinking about the woman, Melia's sudden tears surprise her, and she lets them fall as she finishes eating.

In the pot that remains over the fire Melia heats the last of her water supply. When it is warm, but not yet hot, she lifts the pot down from the hook, pulls the pins that hold her hair up in the knot on her head, and undresses. She dips her long hair into the warm water, sprinkles it with the last of Matildis' witch hazel that had come all the way from the Far East on the Silk Road, and gives herself a long scalp massage. She rinses out the herbal fragrance and uses the sweet-smelling water to wash her body from her face to the bottom of her feet.

Since her mother pushed her away into the arms of the Burgundians back on the Danube, she has not enjoyed a single bath in warm water. This is what freedom feels like, she thinks as she dries herself off. Freedom to take care of herself. Freedom to let herself think. Freedom to sleep with a man she loved. And freedom to let go of her past.

Melia combs out her hair and leaves it down to dry. She snuffs out the candle, climbs the ladder, and falls into Matildis' bed.

GRETA

Pounding on the shop door surprises Melia again. Ruggie isn't due until morning, and as far as she knew, no one else knows she is there. Hermann? Ingoberga? Invaders?

At first Melia considers staying in the loft, pulling up the ladder, and ignoring the knock. But just as she is resolved to do that, she sits up straight.

Mother!

Melia slides down the ladder, unbolts the door to the shop, and runs to peek out the hole in the front door. It is still dark, but even then she recognizes the shape of the face and the angle at which the visitor holds her head.

Melia throws up the bolt, opens the door, and flies into her mother's embrace.

Her throat swells with emotion, and Melia can't utter a word. The two women stand on the step of the shop, and cry, wrapped in each other's arms.

Finally, their sobs subside and, taking her mother's arm to lead her inside, Melia feels how thin Greta is. She bars the doors, and they stand in the kitchen at arm's length, staring at each other. Greta looks lean, tough, weary. Dark circles around her eyes and deep lines down the sides of the mouth age her far more than Melia would have expected in only two years.

"I'm so happy to see you," Melia cries.

"It took so long," Greta agrees. "It has been hard and brutal. You can't imagine how many of us perished. How hungry we've been. But you have been comfortable here, haven't you?" Greta looks around the house as if she were viewing a palace. Melia imagines that it looks to her mother the way Julius's mansion looked to Melia.

"It has been—," Melia stops. She doesn't want to talk about her abuse by the candlemaker, yet. There is too much pain. She wants to enjoy her mother's arrival without complaint. "It has been … I have survived." She changes the subject. "I knew you would come." That is a lie, but her mother doesn't need to know that.

Melia leans forward to be surrounded by her mother's arms again, and Greta stumbles backwards. Melia catches her, realizing she has grown taller than her mother, something else she hadn't expected.

"Oh, Mother, I'm sorry. You are so weak. You must sit down."

Greta sits and smiles through her tears. "You have grown into a beautiful woman, my daughter."

Melia smiles back, a little shyly. Her mother has no idea what a woman she has become; first and unwillingly, a concubine; and now by choice, the brewer's lover.

She pulls the last piece of jerky and the last heel of bread out of the tin box and puts them in front of her mother.

"I wish I had something more to give you to eat," Melia says. "But food is scarce and with the invasion, there has been no chance to go to the market."

"Invasion?" her mother asks, eyeing the meager dinner.

"The barb—," Melia catches herself. Her mother doesn't know all of Mogantiacum calls the migrating Germanii barbarians. "Your crossing of the river."

Greta nods with pursed lips. She understands. "It was supposed to be a peaceful entry," she says, her voice both weary and angry. "Do you know that?"

Melia shrugs. "I have heard there are so many dead."

"Yes," Greta says. "There are. Suevi, Alans, Vandals. We've all lost many. Perhaps some Romans, too?"

She hesitates before continuing, and then her story starts to pick up momentum and her voice turns sour. "We waited for the Empire to let us move across the bridge and settle in the plains beyond here. But we were held back and starved. There finally was no choice but to slide across the ice. I'm afraid by then our warriors were angry. I see they burned your church. And bodies litter the streets."

Melia has yet to see the carnage herself. Even if her mother excuses what happened, Melia can't accept that her own people are in fact barbarians. She heard their voices outside the shop in the first hours of the pillaging, and she understood their anger. But this violence is of a kind she had never seen among her villagers.

She doesn't want to argue. Instead, she asks, "How did you find me, Mother?"

"The nuns. I went to the convent, which has been spared. I was fortunate that someone there spoke our language. I asked how to find the candlemaker's shop, and she pointed me here, even though she seemed reluctant to tell me."

Melia nods, remembering her reception at the convent with a baby in her arms. She smiles as she realizes that if the convent survived, Fritigil's babies were spared as well.

"Will the candlemaker want money for you?" Greta asks. "We

were going to sell the last of the livestock in the market, but it is abandoned. I have nothing to offer the man."

"It won't be a problem," Melia answers.

"Where is he? Is he willing to let you go?"

"He's dead," Melia states flatly. She doesn't try to look sad. She isn't.

Greta sits back, her head tilted in confusion.

"And he had a wife?"

"Dead too." Melia decides not to tell her mother about the body in the tallow vat. She will be well gone before decomposition finally betrays its location.

"How?"

"The invasion."

Greta pauses for a moment, apparently getting used to the word. Then, she leans across the table and takes her daughter's hands. "So, you will come with me?"

"Where are you going?"

"We are going south through Gallic territory abandoned by the Romans. We will find places to farm far from the Huns. We will settle again."

"You and father?"

Greta looks at their entwined fingers.

"Your father was killed by the Franks. They charged us at the behest of the Romans. Many of our people died, and more would have but for the Vandals and Alans."

Melia tries to remember more about her father than his looks. She recalls only that he was a big man who stood before others at the community fire at night and orated. He had never held her. He hadn't been particularly kind to her mother, either. But perhaps she doesn't remember their lives together correctly. Of course, she had just been a child.

"My sister was killed as well," Greta adds without looking up. "I am now married to Milo."

"Vertila? And my uncle Milo?"

"Yes. I hope you will love him as a father."

"Oh." Melia tries to sense how that might happen. Her father's death is a surprise, but she isn't particularly sad about it. She barely knew him. But her uncle? She knows her Uncle Milo had been kind to her aunt, but otherwise she has little impression of him either.

"You aren't angry about that, are you? I had no one else to go to."

"No, Mother," Melia says. "Women have few choices. It is men who decide these things."

Greta looks up and studies her daughter's face.

"I suppose you have learned that by now."

"Mother." Melia stops. Suddenly she is angry. Yes, she has learned many things. Things she never should have had to learn. She stands up and turns away from her mother.

She tries to sort through her feelings. Is she right to be angry at her mother?

"So, Mother," she says finally, still facing away, her voice shaking as she tries to hold back sobs. "You sold me into slavery." She pauses, deciding whether to continue. "You now want me to love another man like a father. Mother, I am too old now for a father. I—."

She stops and takes a deep breath. She turns back to face Greta.

"You have no idea how I have been treated. Listen to me for a minute." Melia narrows her eyes and composes herself. She sits down. "I was raped by the candlemaker nearly every night for the past two years."

Her mother's eyes widen, and her mouth forms a straight, indecipherable line.

"You don't have to say anything, Mother." Melia's voice rises. "Let me tell you how it was. He was a brute of a man. He slapped me, he beat me, he cut me. He made me take him in my mouth. He entered me in ways men enter beasts. I am sorry to tell you this, but I am not a girl anymore. I'm not your daughter anymore, and I'm not—never will be!—Milo's daughter."

She stops and sobs erupt in her chest. She lays her head down on her arm and cries.

Greta sits still and says nothing. Melia realizes her mother remembered her as a young girl, and innocent child, one who played with the younger kids and the dogs in the village courtyard. But she isn't that child anymore. She is now a woman, a misused and abused woman, but wiser, and from now on, she will make her own decisions. She can't trust a woman who sold her into slavery to make decisions for her.

"One more thing, Mother," she says, lifting her head to look her mother in the eye. "I am leaving tomorrow with a man I love. We, too, have been in my bed together. But it is different. I am cherished and loved. And I am ready to make a life with him."

"But you are just a child," her mother insists. "You can't know this now."

"Children should be virgins, Mother. I am not. I am not a child. Look at me!" Melia stands up and pulls back the sleeve of her dress. "See this?" She slaps the slave stamp tattooed on her forearm. "This is proof that you have no right to tell me who I am."

Greta stares at the dark stain. She leans forward, and her tears fall onto the table in big splashes. Melia looks away.

"I am sorry, Melia. Surely you don't think I had a choice." Her mother's voice is halting and pleading. "It was not my decision to send our children away. I don't know if any of the others survived. You may have been abused, but you are alive. Think of that!"

"I am supposed to be grateful to be alive?" Melia says, her

back turned toward her mother. "You have no idea how many nights I lay on a filthy mattress in there"—she points at the door to the shop—"and wished I were dead."

The room falls silent except for Greta's low sobs. Melia walks to the firepit and stirs the coals. The room has turned cold without her notice. She places a couple of logs on top of the coals and fans them with the billows.

When she turns back and sees her mother's face just an inch from the table, she feels her anger lift. It is spent. Just as she had with Matildis, she feels something in common with the crying woman who used to be her mother—something that has to do with womanhood, with not having choices, with sadness and loss.

Melia pulls a mug down off a shelf and fills it with the last of the beer. She was going to save it for the morning, but her mother needs it now.

"Here," she says. She sits the mug in front of her mother and places a hand on her shoulder. "Drink up. It's not good, but you look like you need it."

Greta sits up and pulls the mug toward her. She sniffs the yeasty liquid and grimaces, but she takes a swig. She looks up into Melia's face.

"Thank you. I have not had beer in a long time."

Melia's heart softens, and she sits down again. She waits in silence as her mother sips the distasteful brew. Finally, Melia speaks.

"Perhaps you can tell me now about your journey. Tell me how you have spent the past two years."

"Almost three," Greta answers.

"Yes, almost three."

GRETA AND MELIA SIT UP well into the night. Melia feeds the fire with logs that she will be leaving behind if they don't burn them, and Greta tells the story of the slow caravan up the Danube, through the Alpines, and down to the Rhine, and the constant pursuit by the Huns and Franks. Hunger, fear, bitter cold. Horses and oxen plunging to their deaths over cliffs and down muddy slopes. The camp on the river, the rape and slaughter of her sister by the Franks, and her escape.

"Our people have been changed by this," she says. "The camps, the hunger, the death. Most of the men have lost their minds. They talk only of killing Romans, looting, getting revenge."

"And Milo?"

"Somewhat less." Greta pauses. "I think he has seen enough death. Some men see nothing but the glory of battle, but Milo is not a warrior at heart. Maybe none of the men are as they lie with their wives at night."

By the time Greta's story winds down, Melia's eyelids are drooping. She's slept little and poorly for more than a week. She leads her mother out to the privy behind the shop, and then, back inside, they climb the ladder to get some sleep before Ruggie comes to get Melia in the morning, and Milo comes to get Greta.

Melia pulls the ladder up and rests it against the banister. She lies next to her mother and puts her arms around her. It is likely to be the last night they will ever spend together, and it is only a minute before both women are fast asleep.

Arooster announces sunrise, and Melia smiles before opening her eyes. She is glad to know at least one creature had survived the onslaught.

Melia descends the ladder and pins her clean hair up into a tight knot on her head. With nothing left in the house to eat, she clutches at her empty stomach. Ruggie will arrive soon with supplies for their trip. Melia will introduce him to her mother, and they will all leave Mogantiacum and its tragedy behind.

Greta comes down the ladder a few minutes later and puts her hand on Melia's face.

"I hope you will be safe, my daughter," she says. "I will think of you every morning for the rest of my life."

Melia shudders at her mother's touch and turns to walk to the front door of the shop. Her mother's comforting words irritate her, and she needs to get away for a few minutes before her anger wells up again. She steps out onto the street for the first time since the invasion. The extreme cold has broken, and Melia turns her face up and to the east to feel the gentle warmth of the morning sun on her face.

As her eyes settle on the scene in front of her, she gasps. Scattered on both sides of the cobblestone street, lumps of human bodies lie distorted, with arms above their heads, legs twisted at grotesque angles. Matildis told her of the stench, but she is still shocked by its potency, even though the air is still freezing. She covers her nose with the sleeve of her cloak, but her eyes still burn.

At once both repelled and curious, she creeps across the street toward the remains of a man splayed in the street. What felled him—an axe? arrows? a sword? There is no way to know. The murderer—or murderers—had not only retrieved their weapons, but also took whatever boots and the coat the man had worn into this battle. His tunic, torn and splattered with blood stains, is tangled around his body as if he's been turned over and over as his killers looked for other valuables to strip from him.

He lies face down but as she grows closer, Melia finds the size and shape of his shoulders and back familiar. Was it Hermann, then, they had heard shouting that first night of the invasion? Had he, in a worthless but noble effort, tried to save them from the looters? Trembling with the cold and fear, she tentatively pushes at a shoulder with her foot to turn the grizzly lump over. Frozen solid, the man's body flops heavily onto his back, and Melia's heart jumps into her throat.

It is Hermann—Hermann more frightening than ever, his eyes wide open, his mouth gaping with a frozen scream. The skin and cartilage of his nose are scraped away, and the mangled bone looks more like the knuckles she bought at the market than a human proboscis.

She feels dizzy. She backs away, turns, and bends at her waist to keep from fainting. Breathe, she tells herself. Breathe and get back in the house.

Melia staggers, bent over, into the shop and slams the bar down across the door. She leans her back against it and squeezes her eyes closed against what she has seen. Matildis had to have walked right past Hermann when she went out that day, looking for him. Why hadn't she recognized his bulk? Perhaps she had been too afraid to turn over the bodies on the street; perhaps she had avoided looking, not wanting to believe he could be among the dead.

Melia knows the corpses won't stand up and start wandering the streets, but now the house doesn't feel safe with them out there. She shakes her head against the nonsense and tries to think. Does she believe in spirits or ghosts? No. Does she believe the dead can hurt her? Perhaps only with the smell and the disease that rises from them. She tries to remember if anything had been said around the fire at night back in her village on the Danube about death. No, she realizes. Nothing. Nothing about death, dying, what happened to people when they died.

"Melia?" Her mother peers out the kitchen door into the shop. "Are you all right?"

Melia blinks a few times and pulls herself back into the present.

"Yes," she says with a shaky voice. "I just saw Hermann's body out there. I feel sick."

Her mother walks across the shop and pulls Melia close. "It is horrible," she says. "I know. I have seen too much death. You have seen too much death."

Melia stands still in her mother's arms, leaving hers stiff at her side. It is odd to be comforted by Greta. Odd and far too late. Greta had been far away when Hermann was abusing her. She'd sent no word; Melia hadn't even known if she were alive or dead. For a long time, all Melia thought about was being back with her mother, in her arms like this, protected again. Now, those arms make her nearly as nauseous as the corpses outside. They seem insincere at best, manipulative at least. She doesn't need to be protected or comforted by her mother now. She hasn't needed it for a long time.

"Mother," Melia says through clenched teeth. "Leave me alone. I am too old to be held like a child."

"Everyone needs to be held," her mother says. But she lets go of Melia and backs away, fear and confusion in her eyes. "You'll feel better when you leave this place and its sorrows behind you."

Melia shakes her head and latches onto her mother's eyes. She wants to slap her, pound her fists into her stomach. The pain and fear of the past two years and the gruesome scene outside is too much to hold in. She needs to lash out, flail, strike something. Afraid of what she might do, she pushes past Greta to the kitchen.

Melia sits with her head in her hands, her eyes dry, and her heart pounding. She takes deep, open-mouthed breaths that catch in her throat coming in and catch going out. Hadn't she managed to quash this anger the evening before? Why is it resurfacing now? Is it going to be with her the rest of her life?

"I'm going to get ready to leave," her mother says quietly behind her. Melia hears her climb the ladder and pull her shift over her undergarment. She looks up and watches her mother fasten a small purse to the belt around her waist and come down again. Greta shuffles around the kitchen, gathering spoons, bowls and mugs into Melia's market basket. She glances over at Melia, catching her eye. "You might want these when you get to Regina," she says. "I'll set them by the door."

Melia sits still and lets her mother scrounge through the rest of the house, looking for anything valuable enough to carry away. Slowly, Melia's anger evaporates again, and still she sits, numb and spent. Finally, she stands and steps into the shop. She wrapped the tapers she hasn't sold in two canvas cloths—one for herself, one for her mother—and lays them with the other things to go in the wagons. Her mother hauls the kitchen stools to the front door, and Melia adds her work stool.

"I don't know if we'll have room for them," Melia says. "But I'll let Ruggie decide."

"If you don't, we'll take them with us." Her mother speaks cautiously, as if she were afraid to upset Melia again. "We have burned nearly everything we brought from the village for heat. Once we settle, it will be good to have something to start a new home."

Once they finish moving everything to the front of the shop, Melia stirs the coals in the fire and throws the last log on to burn. Silently, they lean against the table and wait for Ruggie and Milo to arrive.

At the sound of horse hooves and the clatter of a wagon coming up the street, Melia feels her heart leap. She rushes out the door without considering the wagon might not be Ruggie's. It could be Milo's or one of the barbarian families taking a wrong turn through town.

It is Ruggie. Melia waves and runs down the street to meet him, her eyes refusing to acknowledge the bodies splayed in the gutters this time.

"My mother is here!" she yells up to him. Ruggie pulls the reins and stops the horse and cart. He sits silently, looking down at Melia. She reads the concern in his face. She reaches up for his hand, climbs up beside him.

"No, I'm not leaving with her," she says, realizing how sad she sounds. "I'm happy to see her," she adds quickly, "but I'm going to Castra Regina with you, my dear."

Ruggie's quick smile flashes brightly, and he leans over to kiss her lightly.

"I'm so happy for you," he says. "Now you know she made

it. She told you where she is going?" Ruggie slaps the reins, and the horse continues up toward the shop.

"Yes, she's headed with the Suevi and Vandals into Gaul. They are looking for land to farm."

Ruggie nods. "There are lots of empty villas. Anyone who wants a farm in Gaul today can find land." He pulled the reins again and stopped the wagon by the shop stoop.

Melia jumps down.

"Mother! Come! Ruggie is here."

Greta steps out of the shop, squinting, a hand shielding her eyes against the morning rays.

Ruggie gets down and rounds the back of the wagon to greet her, but Greta falls back. Her hand slaps her mouth.

"No!" she screams through her fingers.

"What? Mother, what?" Melia yells, grabbing her by the arms. "What's wrong?"

"No," her mother says again, quietly this time. She backs away from Melia's hands, tripping on the front step and landing hard on her butt. She stares at Ruggie, her hand still hovering over her open mouth.

Ruggie and Melia lean down together, each putting a hand on her shoulder, but Greta only looks at Ruggie.

"Mother, what is the matter? You look like you have seen a ghost." Melia forces a laugh.

Greta's eyes flash at her and then back at Ruggie.

"He is my son," she says, now barely whispering. "You are my son."

Ruggie steps back, shocked, and Melia looks from her mother's face to Ruggie's.

"What do you mean, your son, Mother? I am your only child. Yes, he looks like Father. I noticed that too. But you have no son."

Greta shakes her head slowly, her eyes not leaving Ruggie's

face. She takes Melia's hand to stand. "Let's go inside, Melia, Ruggie. I must tell you a story." Her voice shakes. "It is a long one."

Bewildered, Melia holds Greta's trembling arm and helps her into the shop. Ruggie follows and closes the door. Greta sits on one of the stools they had put near the door, shock on her face. She clears her throat and launches into her tale, staring into a space between Melia and Ruggie, her eyes focusing on nothing. The story comes out so effortlessly, Melia wonders if she's been practicing it for years. For just this occasion.

"Back when you were just born, Melia, the Huns came to the village for the first time," her mother starts. "They came in the middle of the night, the pounding of their horse hooves shaking us out of our sleep. They shouted like warriors as they dismounted, and they burst into the huts, one by one, and dragged us out into the moonlight. We stood there, barefoot, huddled against each other, ready to die.

"One of the ugly beasts spoke our language, and he announced that each household would have to give them a child or they would slaughter us all. If there was no child to surrender, they would take the woman in the family as a bride." Greta looks at Melia. "I was holding you. You were just a baby, still suckling at my breast, unable to survive on your own. I knew I couldn't let them take you. But I didn't want to lose you, either, Ruggie. I shuffled my body in front of you, hoping to hide you from their gaze. Then I realized that if I didn't let you go, they would take me, and Melia would surely die, and eventually I would, too. The Huns were cruel to women. And they were not interested in raising babies."

"You don't know that Ruggie was that little boy," Melia interrupts. "There were hundreds of Suevi boys kidnapped for the slave trade. He probably didn't even come from our village."

"Let me finish," Greta says, not impatiently. "First, a couple of Huns grabbed your father's arms and held him back. One of the Huns came straight up to me and pushed me aside. He grabbed you, Ruggie, and tucked you under his arm. Then he pinched my nipple, making milk squirt out, and he laughed. It hurt like a stab in my breast and I shrieked. He said something I couldn't understand, but his clansmen laughed with him. If I hadn't been holding you, Melia, I would have fought back, but they would have killed both of us. Maybe your father, too."

"Still—" Ruggie tries to interrupt her, but Greta waves him silent. Clearly, he doesn't like the implication of Greta's story any more than Melia does.

"I could hear your screams and cries as they rode away," Greta says. "And every night in my sleep, I would see and hear the scene again. Your father and I never mentioned it to Melia, as we didn't want her to grieve a brother that she never knew." She nods at Melia. "So, we never told you."

She turns back to Ruggie. "But you have your father's face. Your hair has never lost its bright color. I know your eyes as if they were my own. I know who you are. You are my son."

Melia and Ruggie stand shocked and silent for a moment. Then Melia speaks.

"There is no way your son is Ruggie," she says. "He would recognize your face. Babies' faces change a lot over the years, but mothers' don't. Children never forget their mother's face." She doesn't know if that is true, but she is desperate for an argument that will make things right again.

"I don't remember anyone who looked like you, Greta," Ruggie agrees. "I have never seen your face in my life. And I remember my mother's face. I still see it in my dreams."

Melia looks over and takes his hand on hers. "See Mother. This is only something that you wished for. You hoped you'd find Ruggie someday. But it's not something you know."

Greta looks at her with sympathetic eyes. "I know you don't

want to believe this," she says. "But there's more. Years later, a woman who had been taken by the Huns that night returned to the village. She had escaped during one of their raiding forays and ended up in Burgundian hands. The Burgundians were happy to bring her back to her husband for a fee. She knew a lot about what had happened to the children the Huns took." She looks at Ruggie. "She told me you were sold to a trader on his way to Treverorum's slave auction. I assumed I would never find you—that you would have ended up in the land of the Franks or sold to Goths in Italia. I had no idea I would find you here."

She pauses. "And your real name is the same as your father's. Ballomar."

Melia watches Ruggie's eyes widen and his face turns white. What has he heard? He fingers the leather bracelet on his wrist. Melia has noticed it; it is carved with runes, but she can't read. Does it carry some significance? She holds her breath and waits for him to protest, but her mother continues.

"It is not your fault, children, but your sin insults your tribe. You cannot marry. Your love is incestuous, and that would offend everyone, even the Huns. But you must come with us, my dear son. You must return to us."

Ruggie's face turns to stone. He pulls his hand from Melia's and steps away from her. He turns to her with watering eyes. She never expected to see tears on his strong face.

"Melia," he says, so quietly she can barely hear. "This bracelet is carved with the name Ballomar. I never knew what it meant. I only knew I had heard it before I heard anything else. It is my first memory. 'Ballomar.' I'm sorry, Melia, but..."

Ruggie blinks a sudden heavy load of tears down his face, turns stiffly, and marches outside. Melia stands stunned for a moment, and then runs to follow him.

"Ruggie, stop!"

He jumps up onto the driver's seat and gathers the reins

before he looks down at her. She holds onto the post of his seat. "I don't know what to do! What can we do?" she pleads.

"You may think she is wrong," Ruggie says. "But we don't know. I do know how long you've waited for her. Go with her, Melia." Melia turns to see her mother, tears streaming down her face, leaning against the door jamb.

She turns back to Ruggie. "No, wait. Let's talk. Let's talk about this. If she is your mother, you can't leave us now."

"You must decide." Ruggie glares at her with swollen eyes and waits. "If you believe her, how can you want to go with me? If you don't believe her, come with me."

Melia's heart pounds and the rush of blood to her head clouds her thoughts. She hides her face in her hands. What choice does she have? Leave with a man who might be her brother? What kind of a life would that be? Or go back to the mother who abandoned her years before? Finally, this is her chance to choose her own future, and she doesn't want it.

She looks up, and Ruggie shakes his head. Is that love in his eyes or sadness? Melia hesitates. Ruggie snaps the reins and the wagon jerks forward. Melia loses her hold and falls back, barely avoiding the rear wheels of the wagon.

"No, Ruggie! Wait!" Melia throws up her arms. When he doesn't stop, she hoists her dress up to her knees and runs after the rumbling wagon, but it moves much faster, and quickly she runs out of breath. She stops, huffing, holding her stomach, and watches him disappear into the distance. Surrounded by the stench of death, she stands in the street and waits. Perhaps he will come back.

But she knows he won't. She walks back to the shop, surrounded by the bodies and stench of the street. She rounds the side of the house and vomits in the garden.

PART 3

GAUL

MIGRATION

West of Mogantiacum

Before dawn the morning after Ruggie left, Melia is hit with another wave of nausea. She leaps up from her mattress by the hearth and steps out the garden door just in time to retch in the dirty snow piled up against the back wall. Having eaten so little for days, she spews little more than watery bile, but she suspects its cause: Her conscience is exacting revenge for her incest.

But is Ruggie her brother? The name Ballomar was common among the Suevi; she knew seven Ballomars from her own village. Yes, Ruggie does look like her father—with his blonde hair and blue eyes—but so do most of the men she's ever known before she crossed the Rhine in the slave traders' wagon.

Moments after she comes back into the house, Milo and one

of her mother's ancient uncles arrive with an ox-wagon, eager to catch up with the migrating horde. Greta opens the door to greet them, and Milo bends down to give her a quick hug. He acknowledges Melia only with a nod before starting to load her things, lifting her small furniture and candle-making supplies over the wagon's sideboards with ease as she and the uncle stand and watch.

"Stop!" Greta cries, leaning against Milo's strong frame. "We must find Ballomar. We cannot leave without my son."

Milo stops, a stool in his hands above his head, and looks at her quizzically. "What are you talking about, Greta?"

Quickly, Greta spills out the story, even confessing Melia's illicit relationship with Ruggie. Milo sets the stool on the street and sits on it to listen, his arms crossed over his chest.

"You don't know that he is your son," he says calmly at the conclusion of the tale. "And we must go now. The garrison still harbors soldiers. They could decide to come after us any time."

He stands and tosses the stool into the wagon. Greta turns and stumbles back into the shop, sobbing into her cloak. Melia doesn't budge.

"Milo, if Ruggie is your nephew, now your son, we can't leave him. Don't you want him to join us?" Melia says, now regretting how she let him leave without her the day before.

Milo shakes his head and drops his voice. "No, it is best if we forget him. Amongst themselves, the gods may tolerate incest, but the Suevi do not."

Milo tosses the last bags into the wagon and walks into the shop, returning with the sobbing Greta. He helps her climb into the wagon. How can he be so tender and, at the same time, so ruthless in leaving Ruggie behind? He motions for Melia to follow her mother, and climbs up to the bench, offering her no hand.

Melia hesitates. She crosses her arms over her chest, holding her cloak against the cold, and stares off in the direction Ruggie had left. She and Greta haven't said a word to each other as they waited for Milo's late arrival. Greta slept in the loft, and Melia slept slumped against a wall near the firepit, hoping for any residual warmth it might hold. With nothing to eat and nothing to say to each other, the hours crept by, accompanied only by muffled sobs of mother and daughter.

Now, she has to decide. If she stays, can she find Ruggie? Will he take her with him after her doubts of the day before? Unlikely, she thinks. Unlikely on both counts. No. She'll be alone. She'll be hungry, cold, and alone. Forever. Or for as long as she survives. Which wouldn't be long.

"Hurry up, girl!" Milo's patience is spent. "Get in or say goodbye to your mother. Now!"

Melia has barely found a decent perch among the household belongings before the wagon lurches forward.

Through tears, she watches as they climb up the dismal street toward the west gate of the city, leaving behind the houses and shops more familiar to her now than the shady circle of her native village. She came to feel at home in Mogantiacum, to enjoy its market and its orderliness, and to love many of its people. Not just Ruggie, but Dodi, the women and children at the town well, Briggeta, who now cared for Julius, and Fritigil, who had been her best friend for more than two years.

Now dozens of townsfolk lie rotting in the streets. Ashes smolder around the few marble blocks that remain standing. Fine homes scattered, smashed by hand-axes and battering rams, the stone of their walls strewn into the street, and their broken treasures littering the cobblestones.

This is how her people have left this fine city on the river. If this is who the Suevi have become—raiders, pillagers, rapists, everything Matildis claimed they were—does Melia want to be with them?

But what choice does she have? Ruggie turned and drove from her, taking away what she had thought only days before was her bright future.

Years before she longed to be part of this migrating, barbarian horde again. But now, it is nothing to rejoice. Instead of feeling grateful for her rescue, Melia blames Greta for everything: for putting her in Hermann's hands, for chasing Ruggie away—even for running from the Huns in the first place. She winds her scarf around her head tightly to keep her ears warm and block the sound of her mother's voice as the wagon lumbers through the open, unguarded city gate.

Melia's nausea doesn't pass until shortly before midday, hours after they have left the gruesome carnage of Mogantiacum behind. Leaving the valley of the Rhine, the Suevi wagons wend their way south along the west bank of the river through territory the Romans have ceded over the past century to Alemanni and other Germani tribes.

Thick tangles of shrubbery block the view to the sides of the road. Melia wonders if Gaul was as prosperous as promised. The wide, level roads are ostensibly paved with stones, but they're now snow-packed and as treacherous as the mud paths they'd driven along the Danube. Occasionally, they come to a sturdy bridge fortified with huge blocks of granite, which speaks to some affluence. But otherwise, there is no evidence of the grand stadia, baths, temples and aqueducts to prove the glory of Roma's empire.

For days, and all day long, the crack of whips and angry shouts drift back from the front of their band. The oxen pulling the wagons tire quickly in the deep snow, stumbling and bellowing their agony. The women, toddlers, and old men trudge in the wake of the sluggish wagons, managing the few cattle, sheep and goats that have survived the journey, and keeping an eye out for wild animals that might thin the herd further. At night, the wagons pull around a large fire, and families huddle together under blankets atop the loads.

The pace doesn't improve that week or the next, even when a warm spell moves in under heavy skies. Then, the sun emerges to turn the road to slush—slush that refreezes into deep icy ruts overnight. Twice progress halts when teams of oxen slide off the slippery road, bellowing as they crumble into a tangle of haunches and horns, breaking their necks or legs, pulling loaded wagons down on top of them. The animals are quickly put out of their misery and butchered on the spot. Their loads are redistributed and the wagons disassembled for spare wood and wheels before the tribe gets moving again.

Melia clomps along with the old men and women, seeing nothing but wagon tracks in the snow and the hind end of oxen. She is filthy and damp from the hair on her head to her boots, sores burst open on the soles of her feet, and her legs ache with fatigue. At night, memories of her miserable mattress on the floor of the candle shop haunts her dreams—Hermann hovering over her, his swollen penis in his hand. In other nighttime chimera, Matildis strikes her with the back of her hand, and Fritigil lies sweating and hallucinating on a perpetual birthing bed, bleeding and pleading for Melia's help. Melia wakes before the camp comes back to life, her heart pounding, afraid to return to the nightmares.

But during the day, Melia remembers her life in Mogantiacum as comfortable and productive compared with the drudgery and misery of migration. She thinks less about her experiences as slave and victim, and more about her work as a candlemaker. Despite what Matildis had said, the townspeople had known her not as Hermann's whore, but as a skilled maker of graceful tapers; smelly and effective fumigating candles; and beautifully scented votives. Even as her status tied her to hours of hot, dangerous labor, it allowed her to make friends and move freely about Mogantiacum. And who is she now? Not a valuable member of the community, a craftswoman, but a useless, soiled woman whose place in this diaspora is nothing but a burden, staring at cattle's asses and slipping through their droppings with blistered feet.

Escaping from the candlemaker and Mogantiacum was supposed to set her free. But instead she is trapped. Out in the frozen forests, bears, lions and wolves crouch, savage and hungry, and in camp at night, lecherous men ogle and grab at her. When one catches her eye, she looks away quickly, but not before catching a glimpse of the greedy desire that reminds her of Hermann's nightly snarl.

Her first night in Mogantiacum, Greta lamented the change in the men of her village, and Melia now sees it for herself. Once they had been farmers and cattlemen; now they think themselves warriors and conquerors of foreign lands. Melia once played with the boys in the village open, but now they strut with conceit and violence, their pride fed by their conscription into the warring ranks. A few years older than Melia, they were too big and strong for the Burgundians to grab, and the tribal leaders had thought them too precious to trade for passage to the Rhine. After months on the trail along the Danube and over the Rhine with the belligerent Vandals and Alans, the boys have morphed into pillagers and raiders, never talking of settling down, driven only by thoughts of looting along the way. Their chests swell with hubris, and at night in the camps, they brag to their own mothers about the women they rape in the city.

The fast-moving horsemen of the Alani have moved ahead, leaving the Suevi and their wagons behind. But the Suevi men—especially the younger ones—have been infected with the Persians' bellicosity.

It is also the Empire's doing—this transformation of a peaceful people into barbarians. By refusing them entry into

Gaul for months, Stilicho starved them and turned young men mad.

"They think they are as brave and powerful as the Alani," Greta muses at the camp one night. It is so cold, even Melia huddles close. "I remember how hard they fought the Franks on the other side of the river, but we have encountered no enemies since, and the troops in Mogantiacum didn't even come out of the fort to fight. But I think they fool themselves. The Romans in Hispania won't be so easily pushed aside."

IT IS NEARLY A MONTH after leaving Mogantiacum before Melia sees Canuto. His parents had died before the crossing of the Rhine, but an aunt found him at the stables. At first, too weak from hunger to walk, he shivers in a wagon, covered with blankets. But once he recovers his strength, he and Melia find each other, and he clings to her side. They fall to the back of the trail of women and old men, and keeping Canuto next to her created a shield against the crude advances of the men.

It seems to work, until it doesn't.

It is early spring, and the air holds a small bit of warmth past dusk. The advance party of raiders have returned to the campfire, pumped up by that day's windfall of a few head of cattle, a bag of Roman coins, and a cache of axes and arrows. A young man who was called Granulo in the village, but now calls himself the war-like name Gaidus, has been gawping at Melia since Mogantiacum. But this night, his hubris inflamed by beer and pillaging, he slides up behind her as she walks away from the camp to fetch water from the nearby creek.

"You! Slave girl," he growls into her ear. "How long has it been since you spread your legs for that master of yours back in Mogantiacum? Aren't you hungry for it?"

He grabs her between the legs from behind and squeezes. Melia spins around and throws the water in his face. He steps back, sputtering, his arms flailing at his sides as he tries to keep balance. Melia drops the pail and runs toward the fire at the center of camp. He stumbles clumsily, drunkenly after her, but she slips, and he's right behind her again. She turns to face him, holding him off with a stiff arm.

"What? You think a Suevi can't satisfy you after you've had so many Romans?" He spits out a laugh and grabs his crotch. "I think you'll be—" His speech is interrupted by a fist to the head. Melia realizes it was Milo who struck him from behind, and Granulo sprawls, face down, on the ground.

Shaking, Melia waits for her uncle to hit him again, but Milo only stands with his hands on his hips and glares down at Granulo. Even though elders aren't paid as much respect as they once had in the village, it seems Milo's status in the tribe has not diminished.

The young man crouches under his glare and grins. "I was only pointing out what she is now." He shrugs and spits in Melia's direction. "A whore. A slave."

Milo kicks Granulo in the ribs, and the young man rolls away and struggles to his feet. He lunges at Milo, who steps quickly aside, letting the drunk fall to his knees. Circling around behind him, Milo gives him another quick boot in the rear, which leaves him prone, his face deep in a muddy rut.

Not waiting to see more, Melia sprints back to the wagons where the women are preparing the evening meal.

"Where's the water?" her mother asks.

"I was attacked on my way back from the creek," Melia says breathlessly, her hands on her knees and her heart pounding from fear and her run. "I dropped the pail."

"What attacked you? A bear?"

"No. Granulo."

Greta puts down the knife and the turnip she was peeling and turns to face her daughter. "You must be careful, Melia," she says. "I've warned you before. You need to behave like a woman now, not like a silly girl playing with the boys around the village."

Melia's fear flips to anger. "That's what you think happened? Do you think they are still boys? Do you think I was playing with him?"

Greta stares at her, her eyes cold and her mouth a rigid line. Finally, she turns back to the turnip. "I don't know what happened, but clean yourself," she says over her shoulder. "Put your hair back on your head and go get the water."

For the first six weeks of the slow slog down the western flank of the Rhine, Melia's frequent nausea morphs into regular morning sickness, and then it stops. By then, Melia knows she is pregnant. Whenever the thought of it surfaces, as it does several times a day, her heart pounds violently. She stops and puts her hand to her chest to contain it. Giving birth in this wilderness would be even more perilous than it was back in the city. Would she die outside in a wagon, in a pool of blood like Fritigil?

As worrisome: she doesn't know who the father is.

It is possibly Hermann, despite her faithful use of the silphium and cedar oil. Could it be Ruggie? She had only lain with him once, though. She has grown so thin that her monthlies had become irregular over the past year, so that provides no clue to the time of conception. Either way, Melia despairs. A baby with Hermann's blood would be a constant reminder of his abuse; a son or daughter with Ruggie might be a child of incest.

She told no one but her mother of her abuse by Hermann, and only Greta and Milo know about Ruggie. Still, her fellow travelers won't be surprised once her pregnancy is evident. Slavery is rare east of the Rhine, but in Gaul, the rape of slaves by their Roman owners is so common that even Granulo knows of it. Everyone, she supposes, will assume her baby to be her slaveowner's.

Of course, Greta suspects differently. "Is that your brother's bastard child?" she asks Melia one morning as they—both pregnant now—return from vomiting in the woods together. Melia wipes her face with a damp cloth she carries for that purpose. She is surprised that her mother has so clearly abandoned her grief over losing her son for a second time—or the man she thinks is her son—that she would insult Melia that way.

"You don't know he's my brother," Melia snaps. "And if you spread that nasty idea around the camp, I'll be treated worse than I am right now."

"Well, we'll know when you give birth to a monster, won't we."

Greta's disdain hurts, and Melia suspects it was about more than possible incest. Over their weeks on the road in Gaul, Greta has turned cold and cruel. Melia tried to understand: the mud and cold and constant movement are even harder on Greta, given her age, than on Melia. But it pains her that Greta, like Granulo, believes that she is now unclean because of her enslavement.

In some ways, Melia needs her mother now more than she had in Mogantiacum. There she had a purpose and some respect—at least from her customers and friends. But on the trail, Granulo has shown how vulnerable she is. Milo acted quickly to defend her that night when Granulo attacked, and her uncle watches her more closely now. She would never see him as a father, but she appreciates his protection. Perhaps now Granulo will leave her alone.

It isn't long before she learns otherwise.

It has been a long day on the trail, and Canuto has jumped in one of the wagons to take a nap, leaving Melia alone at the back of the horde. With dusk approaching, she steps into the woods to relieve herself before darkness makes it treacherous.

She kneels behind a dense bush, and as she finishes, pulling her dress and cloak back down, two men approach on horseback through the shadows, their faces obscured by darkness.

"What are you doing here?" She tries to sound strong and sure of herself, but her voice wavers.

"We were sent back to gather stragglers," one of the men says blandly.

"And look what we found! A straggler!" the other exclaims.

Melia knows that voice!

With a flash of terror, she watches Granulo swing a leg over his horse's back and jump to the ground. She is trapped. "I believe we deserve a bit of fun after this long day, don't you, man?" He looks back at his companion and laughs.

"You go ahead." The other man encourages him from his perch atop his horse. "I'll watch."

Granulo walks toward her. Melia turns to run back into the woods, but he grabs her cloak. She twists out of it and pulls away, tripping over a fallen branch and falling to her knees.

"Aha! Right where I wanted you!" he shouts, pushing her face down into the muck. She twists her neck to see him grinning down at her. He lifts his jacket and pulls down the top of his trousers. Already he is erect; the excitement of the short chase has hardened his greed.

He drops to his knees behind her. She struggles to push herself back up, but he slugs her in the middle of the back, and she falls into the slush.

Melia screams. He reaches around and covers her mouth with a filthy palm. She fights to breathe, and shakes her head, trying to throw his hand off. The man on horseback laughs boisterously. His horse steps closer.

The violence is over quickly, but it stings no less for its brevity. Granulo gives her a final push into the slush, stands, and rearranges his clothing. He laughs as she rolls over and pulls her skirt back over her legs. She tries to stifle her sobs as the men ride back through the trees and disappear down the road, chatting idly as if nothing unusual has happened. By the time she pulls herself to her feet, she knows she will be far behind the last stragglers in the horde. She peers ahead in the growing darkness and sees no one on the road.

Melia brushes slush, mud, and forest detritus off her dress and searches the ground for her cloak. Pulling it around her, she steps carefully toward the road. She knows not to run, which might attract a four-legged predator, so she walks briskly, and in a few minutes, she spies the wagons ahead. Finally, she catches up to her mother and the other women.

"You look a mess!" Her mother reaches over and pulls a wet, muddy leaf off the back of her head. "What happened to you? Where did you go?"

"I went to relieve myself, and I fell," Melia says, lowering her voice to a whisper. "I'm sorry if I worried you."

"You deserve this, Melia." Greta wags her finger. "You've already learned this, haven't you? There are men in this tribe who will take advantage of a woman alone. You know that already, yet you behave as if you want them to."

Melia wants to cry, to scream that she's been raped. But something in her mother's scold warns her that Granulo won't be blamed for what happened. Just as when he attacked her before. Just as Hermann was never to blame for his assaults.

At camp that night, Melia hangs close to Milo, barely lifting her head for fear of meeting Granulo's eyes. What has happened to her in the woods that afternoon crushes her already low spirits. The young warriors are gathered around the chief, gaily plotting the next day's raid on a villa the scouts have reported ahead. None of those men would see Granulo's act as anything out of the ordinary. On their long journey from their village on the Danube to this soggy camp, they've lost sense of the village's rules. They can take anything they want; they can attack, maim, rape, and kill. The old mores that had held their tribe together are forgotten—out here, they have no meaning.

Melia has nowhere to go. She can't walk away and set out on her own. All she can do to protect herself, she realizes, is not to be caught alone again. Not until she is old and crippled as the ancient ones at the back of their horde will men leave her alone.

SETTLING

AD407 - Near Lugdunum

Melia's stomach balloons, her back aches from her growing load, and her feet and legs swell. She hardly notices the arrival of spring—budding trees, longer days, and warmer nights, and a bit of heat in the sun's rays.

As she expected, her baby bulge hasn't improved her status with the tribe's other women. Her slavery purchased the tribe's passage into Gaul, but instead of buying her respect or gratitude, it has ostracized her.

But food is now plentiful, as the tribe's loot from raided villages and abandoned villas grows more robust as they head deeper into Gaul. Once she stopped vomiting in the morning, Melia has been able to eat better than she had for nearly three years—since they left the village back on the Danube. And now that she can better estimate her month of conception, she is optimistic she is carrying Ruggie's child, not Hermann's. Her breasts plump out and her mood lifts.

The slog of travel, however, is still taking a toll on the tribe. Her old uncle, her father's older brother, succumbs to the hardships of the trail, and the man who had been appointed king for the purpose of negotiating with the Romans dies in a raid. Hastily, the tribe builds funeral pyres along the road. As they leave the ashes behind, Melia wonders why they keep pushing farther into Gaul. They've passed many abandoned villas where they could have settled and become farmers again. Other women mumble with the same thoughts as they slog into spring. As the now-fallow fields around them sprout with volunteer grains, and temperatures rise, the women gaze at the greening valleys with longing.

"The men have their eyes on the plains of Hispania," Greta shares what Milo has told her. "But even when they get there, I doubt they will be satisfied. Where will they want to go then? Will they ever want to be farmers again?"

As they wend farther into abandoned provinces, turning southeast along the Roman Vienne-Aoste Road that the Romans built centuries before to speed legions and supplies, the Suevi wagons move swiftly. Many residents of the territory have fled to Hispania, Italia, or farther south in Narbonensis in advance of the swarming Germanii; or they run to the hills and hide until the horde passes.

Expecting at least a remnant Roman presence in Lugdunum, the tribe pulls away from the Roman road onto muddy livestock tracks that bypass the city. The men again shout angrily at the oxen dragging their burden of loot through the thickets and muck. The progress is so slow that on many days, the women stay in camp from dawn to dusk, waiting while the men fell trees to lay a path across the mud so the wagons can pass through. Once they circle the city, they turn north and join the stone-paved Lugdunum-Sainte Road, heading west over the mountains and dropping onto the plains of Aquitania, once again traveling quickly.

Five months on the trail in Gaul should have been enough to ignite the women's rebellion, but it is a grisly scene they come upon in the road that finally triggers their demand for a halt.

Usually evidence of the men's raids lay off the main road in nearby villages, and it is easy for the women to push the origin of their provisions from their minds. But that day, villagers have pursued the Suevi raiders back to the road in a futile effort to recover their stolen livestock, and bloody and tangled bodies litter the migrants' way. The tribe's raiders continue ahead to rout the remaining fleeing villagers without stopping to clear the road for the wagons, and the women are left to pull the carnage out of the way.

It is gruesome work. Melia ties a scarf over her nose and mouth to try to block the stench of flesh rotting in the late spring heat. It doesn't work, and she stops several times to vomit in the bushes. That night, the women sit mute around the campfire, stricken and sullen. Melia can read the story of what their tribe has become in their wide, sunken eyes.

Two days later they come upon a beautiful villa—one of the hundreds that have been abandoned and then looted by earlier waves of migrants. From the highway, Melia points out a graceful archway in a high stone wall that surrounds the homestead. The women peel away from the wagons to inspect it, leaving the livestock to rest and graze under the watch of the old men.

Melia leads them through the weed-choked arch. Inside, what remains of geometric gardens flank a long stone pathway leading to another gate. Next to the perimeter walls, tree branches sag with heavy clumps of fragrant apple blossoms. The women follow the path through the second gateway. An exquisite tile mosaic of flowers, vines and geometric designs decorate the front of a large stone house, now partially obscured with tall thistles.

"Let's go inside and look," Melia says. They step over brambles and through the open door. Sticking together, they explore the rooms, and investigate the grounds. At one side of the villa lies a small chapel. It has been stripped of whatever precious sacramental objects might once have benefited its purpose, but its bright frescos of religious and pastoral scenes glow on its walls. On the other side of the grounds is a large bathhouse, its pools still flowing with water from a hot spring. Behind the house stands granaries and pens, now devoid of grain and livestock, infested with scurrying rodents, but sturdy and useful.

That night, just a short distance down the road from the villa, the women prepare the evening meal and argue among themselves. Later, as they sit around the late afternoon campfire and wait for the scouts and raiders to return to camp, the women say little, but a buzz like that in the wake of a lightning strike charges the air. Finally, Greta stands to speak.

"We will let the raiders continue without us," she says. "We are tired, and this pillaging is like that of the Huns we ran away from. Our men are now no better."

No one disagrees, and Greta continues. "We are rich enough. We did not cross the Rhine to wander forever. We came to create a new village. I want to stay here, plant our vegetables and grain in these abandoned fields, and raise our new babies."

Melia turns to watch the elder men, expecting them to tell Greta to keep quiet. But she sees only shy nods of agreement. They, too, are sick of travel and looting. They, too, want to settle.

When the raiders return hours later, Greta starts the discussion. She describes the women's position more as a decision than a proposal. It is met with vociferous debate.

"You will not be safe here," one of the men argues. "The villa's owners will return. They won't let Germanii live here."

But another of the warriors disagrees with him. "The weak Romans are long gone. They won't come back, even if Stilicho sends them."

"Women don't make these decisions," another man boasts. "You will go where we take you."

"But the women slow us down," Granulo argues. "We can move much faster if we don't have them and the old men dragging behind." It strikes Melia as strange to hear him agree with the women, even if it shows how little respect he has for them.

Greta smiles as some of the men take her side. She stands again once they've all had their chance to talk. "If we stop now, we will have just enough time to sow fields for harvest this fall," she says. "If we keep going to the territory held by the Hispano-Romans, we will starve."

Melia considers adding her own argument: that she and the other women will be much safer with the likes of Granulo far away. But she says nothing. She has yet to earn any respect among her fellow travelers.

"What about the livestock?" one of Milo's nephews asks. "Will we leave the cattle and goats behind?" He sounds like he hopes they will. Even though the men might want the meat— perhaps they'll have bad luck hunting in territory the Alans and Vandals have already traversed—the cattle and goats slow the raiders down, and animal husbandry no longer interests them.

"You should leave them," Greta says. "We have adequate pasture here, and they will sustain us while our fields mature."

After an hour of letting everyone voice their various opinions, Milo, now chief, following the death of the ersatz king, hasn't yet spoken. Finally he stands. "The women will need protection from the Germanii following in our wake, the Franks in the north, and from the Romans to the south," he says to the men. It is a tacit acceptance of the women's decision. "A few of us should stay with them. I relinquish my leadership as you move on. We'll wait for word from the rest of you. If you find a better place to settle, we will decamp and join you."

Melia wonders if anyone else heard the false promise in his voice. By now she knows her uncle well enough to see he, too, is anxious to settle down, weary of the constant march. He is aging, tired of raiding, and weary of the belligerence of the young men who have forgotten anything but warfare and looting.

It is unlikely that those who settle here will pick up and move south once they establish a new farming village. Melia smiles at the thought.

At first, the entire travelling horde—now numbering about a hundred men, women and their toddlers—move into the abandoned villa and corral the livestock on adjacent, overgrown pastures. They all sleep inside the villa on the beautiful mosaic floors, which, although hard and cold, are an improvement over the crowded, smelly wagons. Melia feels safer with a roof over her head and the whole tribe around her at night. Constantly surrounded, Granulo doesn't have a chance to attack her again.

Only a few dozen young warrior-aged men, including Granulo, plan to continue south, raiding and warring, following in the wake of the Alani who are plowing through any remaining Gallic resistance. They stay only long enough to help hew a few stools and tables from the hickory and chestnut woods and enclose the livestock in pens. The morning they leave, neither the newly settled tribesmen nor those leaving shed tears.

Milo and Greta take the lead in organizing the new settlers, and Melia's respect for them both grows. Milo directs the management of the fields and herds, and Greta plans the community's joint cooking and housekeeping, and then puts two of her cousins in charge of them. Melia and Canuto repair the chicken houses. As the tribe's midwife, Greta prepares a room in the villa where expecting mothers will deliver their babies away from the sleeping rooms. As their pregnancies progress, Melia sees an improvement in her mother's attitude toward her, but doesn't acknowledge it for fear of seeing it reverse.

Once the fields are planted and the men have time, they build new longhouses outside the villa's gates like those they left behind in Germania. Only Melia's family, including her few remaining cousins, take up permanent residence in the villa. Eventually many of the villagers who fled the nearby town return, and the newcomers make an uneasy peace with them. The Suevi, one-time invaders, promise to help defend the village against later waves of Vandals and Alans that continue to pass through toward Hispania, and the Gauls warily accept their assistance.

That summer, Melia and her mother suffer through the heat and humidity of the low, verdant plain, at times even waxing nostalgic for the snow and ice of the harsh winter. On a hot, sultry August night, as they sit outside in the courtyard, wiping sweat from their faces and swatting at swarms of mosquitos, Melia tells her mother about Fritigil's death in childbirth.

"I don't want to die like that," she concludes her story.

"We are well-fed and safe, Melia," her mother assures her. "We will both survive. I don't want you to be afraid, but you mustn't be foolish. When the time comes, you will have to do as I say, no matter how painful or frightened you are."

"Tell me now so I can be ready."

Greta shifts her swollen body around and faces Melia.

"Together, you and I will bring the other babies of our cousins into the world while we wait for ours," she says. "Experience will help."

Melia nods, wanting to believe her. "But I'm still afraid of what my child will look like."

Now that Melia believes her baby was conceived in late December with Ruggie, she worries her child of incest will emerge as a monster. Legends tell of some born with six toes, split lips, or swollen heads, and some who never learn to walk or talk. In many cases, they are strangled or drowned as soon as they enter the world.

Melia leans closer to her mother and whispers. "What if my baby is a monster? What will we do?"

"We will do what we have to do," Greta whispers back. "But you bring evil by talking about that now. Don't tempt the fates."

In the middle of September, just before dawn, a warm liquid spreading across her mattress under her hips wakes Melia. She rises, throws a blanket over her shoulders, and tiptoes to where her mother sleeps on her side, curled against Milo's chest.

She rocks her mother's shoulder.

"Mother, it's time," she says. "It must be early, but it's time."

Greta bolts upright, fully awake in an instant, and groans as she pulls her own swollen body to her feet.

"Go to the birth room," she says. "I'll light a lantern and be right there." Melia hears Milo mumble as Greta awakens him and orders him to heat a kettle of water.

Just as her first contraction sends her swooning onto the mattress, Melia sees the monster. A massive red beast hovers over her in the darkness, its huge tongue writhing in and out of its mouth, sliding back and forth between huge canine teeth, dripping blood that hovers in the air and doesn't fall.

Melia screams and rolls onto her side, pushing her knees up under her massive belly against the pain. She squeezes her eyes tight to avoid the ugly visage, but it hovers there, and she recognizes the dark, protruding, greedy eyes.

The monster isn't her baby. It's Hermann!

Melia pants and shakes her head violently to dispel the image. Why is it appearing now? Is it an omen? Is she giving birth to Hermann's monster?

Greta enters the room with a lantern. "Melia, you have to calm down." Her mother's voice is stern, bordering on angry. "We've been through this many times. You know what happens. Now breathe deep."

Still, the monster hovers, sometimes dipping close enough to touch Melia's huge stomach, snatching at her with its massive teeth, and sometimes rising high above her and cackling. Every time he dips, Melia screams.

"Melia!" Her mother slaps her face.

"It's Hermann!" Melia yells, huffing to catch her breath.

"Look at me, Melia," her mother orders. "Open your eyes and look at me. It's not real. Whatever it is you are seeing, it's not real!"

"But my baby is a monster! It's a monster! I don't want to do this! I can't do this!"

Greta slaps her cheek again, and Melia's eyes blink open in surprise. The monster disappears, and Melia stares at her mother's face. Another contraction grips her, and as Melia closes her eyes and strains against the pain, the monster hangs over her again. She shrieks, and the red creature looks startled. It rises and dissolves into the ceiling.

"Breathe, Melia!" her mother demands. "You have to breathe. Come on, you know how this works. Breathe!"

Now, the contractions come closer together, forcing Melia's eyes closed each time, but the monster doesn't reappear. Relieved, she crouches on the edge of the bed and feels the wet baby slide out of her and into her mother's open hands.

"It's a boy!" Greta exclaims and holds him up for Melia to see.

He looks vaguely like the monster—glossy and covered in red, his mouth wide, and the long, bloody rope undulating in the space between them. Melia stares, blinks, and stares again. Slowly, the mass starts to resemble a baby with arms and legs, its eyes squeezed shut against his harsh new reality. Melia falls back onto the mattress, as her mother expertly flicks her knife through the swaying cord and lays the tortured infant on Melia's chest.

Another contraction expels the afterbirth, but Melia hardly notices. She pulls the baby's fingers open in her hand. She counts. Five. She lifts one of his churning legs and feels for the toes. Five again. She lifts an eyelid and marvels at the bright blue irises that stare back at her.

"Good, Melia," Greta says. Melia watches her mother wipe the baby clean and lay him back on her chest. "You did fine. I've never seen a baby come so fast."

Melia nods, and her eyes fill with tears. It will be some time before she will know much about the little creature squirming on her chest, but at least he doesn't appear to be the monster of her visions. At least he has the right number of fingers and toes.

Within days, Melia comes to trust that—with an unusually full head of blond hair, bright blue eyes, and long limbs—the baby's father was Ruggie. She names him Ballomar.

"He's perfect," she coos.

Her mother laughs, bouncing her own little Milo in her arms, born a day after Melia's baby. "They always are at first. It won't be long before you're chasing after him and cursing the day you conceived."

Melia closes her eyes and remembers that day. That night. She longs for Ruggie's arms.

THE SUEVI

The heat of summer breaks early that autumn and in blows winter, one even more harsh than the season of the Suevi's wait on the east bank of the Rhine. As the waves of passing migrants slow with the deepening of winter, and the travelling merchants dwindle with the pullback of the Empire's forces, the Gallic villagers adjust by reviving the old skills they had let go dormant when Roman trade was robust—smelting, weaving, leatherworking and herb-gathering.

The villagers and Suevi come to depend on each other, the Suevi supplying meat and protection, and the villagers showing the newcomers how to use nature's regional gifts, like bitumen to seal the gaps in the stones of the walls of their houses. The tar smells horrible at first, but as the walls grow cold, it becomes less noticeable, or, perhaps, everyone gets used to its stench.

Melia finds an old iron vat in one of the outbuildings at the villa, and Milo helps her set it up to resurrect her candlemaking.

There is plenty of fat from slaughtered calves, sheep and deer, and the rosemary she once had to buy at the market in Mogantiacum grows right through the winter in protected spots around the villa, next to the villa's stone walls and along the stone fences that encircle the summer pastures.

Before her return to candlemaking, after little Ballomar arrived, Melia was listless and, at times miserable. It isn't unusual, Greta said, to fall into despair after giving birth, but Melia was lonely. Even if she wanted to replace Ruggie with a husband to fill her lonely nights, her choices were few. The young warriors who left months before did not return from Hispania—quite possibly they didn't survive their foray into former Roman territory now dominated by Vandals.

But once Melia makes candles again, her mood improves. Once in a while, she asks little Canuto to help her, which cheers them both. By the first snowfall, she has produced enough tapers and votives to last the tribe two months. They will be needed in the long, dark nights on either side of the solstice.

Greta watches both babies—her own whom she names Milo, and Melia's—most of the day, and when she isn't in the candle shop, Melia joins the other women in the villa's main room, spinning, weaving, and braiding candle wicks, rotating seats every so often to share the meager heat of the firepit. But most of the women have never warmed to her, and Melia feels more at home in the candle shop.

A blizzard early in January keeps everyone inside day and night, the men arguing and playing dice in front of the fire, leaving only to break the ice in the livestock's water troughs and throw out forksful of hay. The women hang strips of meat to dry by the hearth, bake bread, stir batches of stew, and brew beer. Melia escapes the cacophony of the abode for the peace and warmth of her shop, stopping work only for a few minutes to nibble on a dry biscuit and slices of turnip, and a few times each day when Greta brings little Ballomar to her for nursing.

One evening, as the light fades, she lets the fire under the tallow vat burn down to embers before closing the door to the shop. Shivering against the shocking cold, she wraps herself in her heavy wool shawl and stomps through new snow down the narrow path to the house. Passing the open arch in the perimeter wall, she spies a figure slogging through the deep drifts toward her. At first, she thinks it is one of the deer that occasionally brave the proximity of humans to find a sliver of hay or a clump of grass laid bare by the heat of the villa and the longhouses. She stops and stands still, not wanting to frighten the hungry animal, but as it approached, she sees it had two legs, not four. The man isn't coming from the village or the Suevi longhouses but from the road they had taken many months ago on their migration from the north.

Melia scurries through the archway into the villa.

"Milo!" she calls. "Milo! A stranger is coming down the road."

Milo's long strides take him to the door in seconds, and Melia shrinks back in relief. Strangers travelling at night might be scouts for the Franks, who are known to be pushing south from the Liger in cahoots with the Romans—no friends of the Suevi. Scouts, however, are stealthy—usually more rumored than seen. Given the way this man plunges forward with no effort to conceal his approach, Melia guesses he was one of the many displaced Gauls who come seeking help from the settlers.

"Hello, good fellow!" Milo bursts through the arch and calls out.

The man waves his arms over his head, signaling friendliness. "Hello! I come in friendship," he shouts.

In Suevi! The man speaks Suevi. Or at least a few words of it.

He continues toward the villa, and Milo steps outside the wall. Melia waits just inside and hears the two men greet each other. From the tone of their voices, it appears the stranger poses no danger. She steps back as Milo returns through the arch, and behind him walks in—

Her father?

Confused, startled, Melia can't decide whether to run toward the man or away from him. Her father is dead. She knows that, but his face is right in front of her, his blue eyes staring down into hers. Icicles of blond hair stick out below his cap, and he wears a bearskin coat, closed with a broach, the likes of which she's never seen before.

In her bewilderment, her feet catch in the trail of her shawl, and she stumbles and falls to her knees. Together, the men step forward and lift her by her elbows until she steadies herself. She stands up straight and stares at the stranger while he and Milo continue to talk in low tones. The stranger's tongue is heavy with a foreign accent, but he speaks Suevi.

"Who are you?" she interrupts.

"Ballomar," he answers, slightly bowing his head toward her. Surely, he is not a soldier or a mercenary. His attitude is more servile than belligerent.

"Ballomar was my father," she retorts. "But he is dead, and you are too young to be my father."

"Melia, we must let him come in and get warm," Milo interjects. "He has come from the north, from an encampment of Franks with news for us."

Still confused, Melia gathers her shawl and scrambles ahead of them into the warmth of the villa.

"Greta!" Milo calls across the room. At the large firepit, Greta and another woman turn, and Melia sees her mother react exactly as she had—with confusion and surprise. She drops the ladle onto the floor and stares.

"Ballomar?" Her eyes open wide. "How can this be? A ghost? My husband has come back as a ghost!" She steps back and stumbles against the bricks, just inches from the fire.

The stranger reaches out to steady her. "How did you know my name?"

Greta leans away, but lets the man hold her by the arm. "How can this be?" she repeats, looking to Milo.

Milo takes Greta's other arm and leads her to a stool at the long table in the center of the room. "Sit, and we'll let him explain," he says, gesturing to the man to take a stool as well.

"Thank you." Ballomar sits, but as he stares at Greta, he, too, looks as if he sees a ghost.

"Now tell everyone why you are here," Milo orders. He stands next to the young man, as if uncertain of his intentions.

Ballomar, however, ignores Milo. "Your face," he says to Greta, almost in a whisper. "I have seen your face in my dreams. Since I was a child. I know you. But…who are you?"

Slowly, Greta's relaxes, her expression changing from confusion to wonder. "Are you Suevi? Were you once from Germania? Were you taken by the Huns as a slave?"

Ballomar smiles and nods. "Yes," he says. "I have lived among the Franks as a slave for as long as I remember. But I know where I came from."

Then he names the family's village on the Danube.

OVER THE NEXT HOUR, THE entire family gathers around the table in the villa's main room to hear Ballomar's tale. Greta's cousins, four of whom had recently become mothers as well, settle on stools with swaddled babes in their arms. The uncles and old cousins stand behind them, as Ballomar' tells of his life as a young slave to a Frankish king, one of several Suevi boys captured together almost twenty years before. As he explains, once he reached the age of majority, he was deeded to the king's son, who led a ragged militia of Roman confederates north of the Liger. As the Empire's army abandoned much of central Gaul, parties of a few dozen men at a time were sent west and south to scout out resistance to the Franks' expansion. His role, he explains somewhat sheepishly, isn't fighting but stitching up wounds, amputating gangrenous limbs, and at times, helping prepare meals for the men.

As they listen, Greta's eyes water, and when he finishes, she stands up and rounds the table to grab his hands.

"You are my son," she declares. Her cousins gasp in unison, their heads swiveling to catch each other's incredulous expressions. Nodding at Melia, Greta adds, "and my daughter's brother. You are the young boy who was taken from us by the Huns when Melia was still a baby in my arms."

Ballomar stiffens at her touch, but he doesn't pull his hands away.

Melia understands her mother's optimism and her reasoning: This new Ballomar's face is his father's—his eyes, full lips, and hair identical to his elder namesake. But Greta has been fooled before. Looking from his blue eyes to Greta's tearful ones, she shakes her head.

"Mother," she says. "You were certain that Ruggie was your son, too."

"Who?" asked the cousin standing closest behind Greta. "Who is Ruggie?"

"It doesn't matter," Melia says, waving the cousin's question away. "Mother, what makes you sure you are right this time? You know happened last time."

"What are you talking—" The woman tries to interrupt again, and this time, Greta swats the woman to silence.

"Ballomar," she says. "Do you have a scar on your left leg? Below the knee, running toward your ankle?"

"Yes." Ballomar looks surprised at the question. "I've always had it," he answers. "I don't know where it came from. How did you know?"

"Let me see it," Greta says.

Scrunching his brow, Ballomar looks up at Milo, as if for permission to bare his leg. Then, he pushes his stool back and pulls up a trouser leg.

Greta looks at the pink, puckered scar and nods. "I know how you got that. You tripped and fell in the village center, chased by one of the curs in the yard. A sharp stick sliced your leg to the bone. I was worried it would never heal. When you were taken from us by the Huns, it was still raw."

Melia groans and throws her hands in the air. "Many boys cut themselves playing. Mother, you must stop believing every Suevi named Ballomar is your son!"

Greta ignores her. "I have always worried about that wound," she says to Ballomar, her tears starting afresh. "I am so relieved that it healed."

Melia shakes her head and walks away from the gathering. If, indeed, this Ballomar is Greta's son, the healing of a leg wound would be the least miraculous thing. The real miracle is this improbable reunion.

As darkness descends on the day, the family settles down to supper and to hear the rest of Ballomar's stories, but Melia stands back, refusing to eat. By then, it seems everyone else is certain that Ballomar is her brother, but she resists. Ruggie was fooled by Greta's same fantasy. This time, she won't fall for her mother's wishful thinking; instead, it makes her angry.

As Greta and her cousins set wide bowls of stew on the table, Ballomar explains what the Franks, who are encamped just a few kilometers north, will do. They had stopped for a day or two to rest their horses and wait for the blizzard to pass, but they are headed toward the village. It would be best, Ballomar says, if the Suevi welcomes them as allies.

"What you don't know is how many of our tribe were killed by the Franks on the other side of the Rhine," one of the cousins interjects.

Melia growls from the perimeter of the dinner table, "And my father was one of them. How can we welcome them?"

Ballomar looks around at their faces, and Melia recognizes resignation in his eyes. It is the same look her mother gave her that morning on the Danube when the Burgundians came—that resistance is futile.

"You need to agree to be allies or their next visit will be most unpleasant," he says finally.

Milo snorts. "You mean they will slay us all."

"Yes. Maybe not this time. These men are only a few scouts. But by the time the soldiers start campaigning in the spring, they will know if you are friend or foe."

"But they attacked us," Melia argues. "Why would they befriend us now?"

"Enemies. Friends. In Gaul they're always changing," Ballomar says. "It depends on what the different chiefs want at different times. There are no reliable alliances. What's expedient is what is right."

Melia can see she isn't the only one struggling with the idea of befriending the very people who had killed their relatives. Milo and Greta keep their heads down, seemingly focused on their stew, but anguish creases their brows. They eat in silence and let the others pry Ballomar for details.

Later, as Greta and Melia clear the bowls from the table, Ballomar talks about the Franks' growing control of northern Gaul, and Melia wonders if he isn't more Frank than Suevi now.

"Why did you leave them and bring this danger to us?" she asks.

Ballomar answers quickly. "I have always known I was Suevi," he says. "I have always known where I came from. I have lived a decent life among the Franks, but I'm still a slave."

He glances down at the slave stamp just above his wrist. "I have wanted to leave them, but I had nowhere to go. When I heard of this Suevi settlement, I decided this was my only chance to find my people."

"But when they see you here, they will kill you, won't they?" Greta's eyes widen with fright. "Don't they kill slaves who escape?"

Ballomar nods, his smile replaced with a grimace. "They will kill me if they find me." He plans to stay only a night, and then move on, he says. Eventually, he will catch up with the Suevi who headed for Hispania.

"They won't miss me for a day or more. I've been with them so long, they won't think I would escape. Some have forgotten I'm not a Frank."

"Will they come here tomorrow?" Milo asks.

"I don't think so," Ballomar says. "The horses are spent and need a day's rest, and the blizzard will delay them."

"I hope you are right," Milo says.

"They will want something from you—meat, most likely." Ballomar says. "They might inspect your houses and demand a head of cattle or sheep. But then they'll be on their way."

"And they'll look for you," Greta says.

"Yes, but I'll be gone," Ballomar answers. "It's Melia who is in danger."

Melia starts, a tiny shriek escaping her pursed lips. "What do you mean?" She follows his eyes to the tattoo on her forearm.

"If they find me, they'll kill me," he says evenly, lifting his eyes to Melia's. "But if they see that stamp on your arm, they'll take you with them."

Greta catches her breath.

"Many slaves escaped during the migrations over the Rhine," Ballomar explains. "They don't expect to find much booty—not since the villas have been looted by Alans and Vandals. But they never stop looking for fugitives—either deserters from the army or slaves. Slaves bring easy coin north of the Liger."

"But my owners are dead," Melia argues. "No one will be there to pay for my return."

"No, but you would be a quick sale on the auction block in Lutetia." The even tone of his warning is auspicious. Melia grabs the edge of the table. Her head spins and a wave of nausea washes over her. It is the first time since they left Mogantiacum that she fears returning to slavery. Could she live through that again? And could she drag her son into that life?

No, she decides quickly. If she is captured, she'll leave her baby behind. The Franks will never know the baby Ballomar is hers. It would break her heart, but she'll do it.

She drops her forehead onto the heel of her free hand, and tears burn her eyelids. The conversation at the table continues without her; her mother arguing now that Ballomar should stay with them. He can't get far on foot before the Franks catch him. If Melia has to hide somewhere in the village, he can too.

Suddenly Melia feels old. Old and tired. Tired and hopeless. She pulls the baby to her chest, and, as she closes the door to the sleeping quarters behind her, it sounds like Greta was winning the argument. Ballomar is going to stay.

MELIA'S PLAN

Melia lies awake most of the night, her mind stuck on two things: the dead Matildis and her possible return to a master like Hermann.

Over the year since she left Mogantiacum with her mother and Milo, she's thought little about her slaveowner's wife. While Hermann still ghosts her nightmares, Matildis haunts her thoughts or her dreams only at first. Now that she faces the possibility of capture and a return to slavery, she gins up a new fear: that someone has found the body in the candle vat, and she will be sought as a murderer.

To Melia, it seems improbable that, in a world as lawless as the one they now know, anyone would consider it worth the effort to solve the mystery of a body in a pot of tallow—if they'd found it. If Melia were returned to Mogantiacum, however, it would be easy for authorities to conclude she had escaped—assuming there are any authorities left in that ravaged city. More likely, she'll be taken to Lutetia at the center of the Frankish confederate.

Melia pulls off her shift, slips under the rough wool, and shakes her head on her pillow in the dark. If the slave auction in Lutetia were an option, she'd prefer death. Leaving little Ballomar behind, being raped by another slovenly master, suffering the abuse and torture by another jealous wife—no, she prefers to die at the hands of the approaching Franks. Perhaps better than finding a place to hide from them would be gathering the temerity to walk into the point of a Frank's dagger.

The discussion in the main room continues well into the night, the words muddled by the thick stone walls. Perhaps they are debating ways to save her and Ballomar; perhaps they are just weighing the benefits of turning them both over to the Franks to certify their alliance.

Sitting up to feed the fussing baby Ballomar, Melia panics. She can't allow the men of the villa to decide her fate. Waiting for others to rescue her over the past three years failed her every time. "Look at us," she murmurs to the suckling babe. "You and I are in as much danger as ever."

Off and on through the night, she falls into shallow, dream-haunted half-sleep, filled with ghastly enactments of Hermann's nighttime visits. She prefers insomnia and fights to stay awake.

When the household begins to stir again—long before winter's belated daylight—she rises and pulls on her dress, her heart pounding in her chest. Are the Franks on their way? Is Ballomar mistaken, thinking they'll not hurry after him?

In the main room of the villa, the fire is already blazing, and Greta and Milo sit across from each other, staring at the steam rising off hot cups of broth. They look up and greet Melia with weak smiles. "Come sit with us," Greta says. It sounds more like a suggestion than a command. Is that deference a sign that she already imagines losing her daughter again?

But it was Milo who spoke first.

"We have decided where you, Ballomar, and Canuto can hide," he says neither his voice nor his face radiating confidence.

"Canuto?" she says.

"Yes, he's an escaped slave too."

Melia nods. She should have thought of the boy. She waits for Milo to continue.

"The cistern below this room here is both large and bi-leveled," he says. "We don't believe the Franks will know of such things. They are common here and in Aquitaine, but not in the north. If you stay down there, I think they'll never think to look under the floor."

Melia frowns. Will it be it that easy?

"Won't that give it away?" she asks, pointing to where the water pump stands over a concrete basin in the room.

It isn't there! A pile of firewood is stacked over the opening that led into the cavern. "Where did the pump go?"

"We pulled it down last night," Milo says, "so it couldn't betray you."

"But listen," Melia says. She hands baby Ballomar to her mother and grabs a poker from the hearth. Standing directly over the cistern she pounds the stone floor. "It's hollow. Don't you think they will hear that?"

"Yes, they would," Milo says. "After you go down, we'll pull this table over it."

"But they won't give up that easy! They'll pillage the villa and village, looking for Ballomar," Melia insists, returning to the table. Anxious, she sits back down and reaches for her mother's mug. Greta passes it to her, and Melia finally notices her red, wet eyes. Perhaps she doubts the men's plans, as well.

"Yes, they might." But, Milo explains, they had another plan. They will escort the Franks to the funeral pyre and the corpse of an old village man cremated just two days earlier. Earlier that morning they had put Ballomar's broach and his bear coat on the pyre and relighted it. They made sure a torn remnant of Ballomar's coat fell to the ground with his broach pinned to it.

"We'll tell them that we killed him, thinking he was a spy. They'll see that we have few men, and no battle weapons, and we'll slaughter a goat for their journey, and they'll leave us in peace."

"And if it doesn't work? If they find us, will anyone fight to keep us from them?"

"Yes, to the last man," Milo assures her.

Melia doesn't believe it. The men who were left behind when the young, belligerent ones split for Hispania are sick of fighting, and some of them are too old to lift much more than a rake. Milo's plan makes sense, but they have to be sure the Franks won't walk over this floor and sense the space below.

"What if they are already on their way?" Melia asks.

"Our scouts left last night and will return this morning," Milo says. "We will know shortly, but for now, you and Ballomar and Canuto will have to be ready to go down into the cistern. In the winter, it's nearly empty and you three can sit on the top level, which is dry."

Ballomar walks into the room, and stands warming himself at the fire pit. Melia turns away from him, hating him for bringing this danger. She can't see him as a fellow victim. Even if he is her brother, she feels no kinship.

"This is because of him," she mutters. "Thanks to—"

She senses Ballomar has crossed the room to stand behind her, but she continues anyway, louder now. "Perhaps Ballomar should give himself up and spare the rest of us punishment for his escape," she says. She ignores her mother's gasp. "You can tell them all the stories you want, but do they even speak our tongue?"

Milo shakes his head. "We don't have to talk to them to show them the pyre or to offer one of the goats. And Ballomar says that one of them does speak Suevi. I expect they will still take whatever appeals to them. But the less we resist them, the less they'll plunder or rape."

His last word makes Melia shudder.

"We can't defend ourselves if they are provoked," Milo continues. "We will give them what they will want—anything but you and Ballomar."

"Why not just Ballomar? They don't know I'm—" Melia starts, but she stops with her mother's slap across her face.

"You are both my children," her mother says, now angry. "I came across the Rhine for you. I lost my husband and my sister. I thought I had lost you and your brother. But now I have you both back, and I'm not going to give either of you away."

Melia lowers her eyes to the floor between her feet. When Ballomar puts his hand on her shoulder, she shakes it off. She rises and twists away from him. "I have to feed *my* Ballomar," she says. She pulls her baby from her mother's arms and strides back toward the bed chamber. At the doorway, she turns back. "We'll be lucky if we live long enough to see him walk."

"Yes—" her mother says weakly before Melia closes the door on her words.

Melia sits with the baby at her breast and reviews Milo's plan in her mind. He is right about one thing: There aren't many Suevi men of fighting age or weapons here. There's no reason for the Franks to attack them. But would they be fooled by the old corpse? She doubts it. She bends her head to kiss her suckling baby, and her tears drop onto his pink head. With her arms wrapped around him, she lets the tears gather and fall at will. Her vision blurs and the room turns watery. She sneezes. And sneezes again.

Then it hits her. Tears! Sneezing!

Melia knows how to induce them—not tears of sorrow, but

tears of pain, tears that would drive the Franks back, tears that would blind them. She can make it happen with fumigating candles—the kind she made in Mogantiacum to rid the fort of wasps, bedbugs, and fleas.

If the Franks give them time, she can make enough candles to chase them out of the villa! She has the sulfur that she brought from Mogantiacum—never knowing how useful it would turn out to be.

Melia jumps up and pulls her dress back over her breast. Little Ballomar protests the interruption in his meal, but she wraps him tightly and runs back into the main room.

"I know what to do!" she yells. "I know how to keep them out of here!"

Her mother and Milo look up, startled.

"I've got it! All I need is a little help and one day, and I promise you, no Frank will be able to search this house."

To everyone's relief, the scouts deliver the good news; whatever value the Franks see in Ballomar or how much they worry about his disappearance, they don't appear to be breaking camp yet.

Ballomar and Canuto—both with an incentive to help her— join Melia in the candle shop. Melia shows Canuto how to put the right measure of sulfur crystals in the bottom of a couple dozen votives and gets Ballomar to stoke the fire under the tallow vat. She cuts lengths of wicks, ties them to sticks that will hold them in place while the tallow hardens. The trick to making fumigating votives is to mix the sulfur and wax at just the right time—when the tallow is still soft enough to combine with the crystals, but not hot enough to release sulfur fumes into the air prematurely.

It is crowded and dangerous with three people in the shop, so as soon as Canuto has finished his task, Melia sends him back to the villa. Once he has the fire built and the flames steady, Ballomar picks up the big tallow ladle and stirs the fat. "Where did you learn this?" he asks.

Melia doesn't answer right away. She needs his help if they are to save themselves, but she struggles to tamp down her resentment for the danger he brought to her and the villa. Finally, she takes a deep breath and answers: "My master in Mogantiacum was a candlemaker. Until I became the candlemaker, that is. Then he became a worthless, drunken bastard."

"How did you become a slave?" Ballomar asks. "Were you a child, too, when you were taken?"

"No, it was only three years ago. I wasn't kidnapped. I was traded to the Burgundians for safe passage to Mogantiacum for the tribe. I was no child. And Hermann made sure of that."

"Hermann?"

"The bastard."

Ballomar looks away, embarrassed perhaps. Melia wonders if this is the first time he's ever been alone with a woman in his life. It is unlikely there are women in the scout camps. Even if she is his sister, she is as foreign to him as a Goth or Hun.

Still, it wouldn't be hard for him to imagine—to know—what a female slave's life is like. He has always been a slave, a captive since he was three, and that would be long enough to learn what slavery meant for women.

"I can't go back," she says quietly.

Ballomar turns to her, lowers his eyes, and nods. "If this works, neither of us will."

"But this won't be the last time the Franks come through our villa, will it? Won't we be in danger forever?"

"I don't know," Ballomar says. "I believe the Franks have their own problems."

"What problems?"

"Constant warfare. Chief against chief. One chiefdom against another—brothers against brothers. They will never be happy with what they have. They are always jealous of their brothers' wives. I've seen lands change hands from one chiefdom to another six and seven times, and they never tire of fighting."

"Then the Franks are no different from the Huns, the Goths, the Burgundians?"

"No different. Do you think the Suevi were?"

Melia considers his question. Tying the last of the wicks to the sticks above the votives, she turns and sits on her work stool. "I remember the village as a quiet place, don't you? We didn't want to leave."

"But the Suevi did."

"Yes, the Huns had become greedy and violent. There were many tears as we left, but no one stayed behind."

Melia directs Ballomar to stop feeding the fire. "We will let the tallow cool some, and then we will dip it into the votives. Keep stirring. I'll be back in a few minutes."

Melia wipes her hands on the rags she collects for her shop and leaves to feed little Ballomar. In the bright, sunny midday, her eyes sting from the sharp shards of light reflecting off the snow and carefully picks her way to the house, stepping in the deep footprints they had made in the drifts earlier that morning.

She returns to the shop as soon as the baby has his fill and falls to sleep. As Melia pushes open the door, it buts up against something heavy.

"Hey! Be careful!"

Melia freezes. She knows that voice. The man steps to the middle of the room and looks at her, his eyes dancing with menace, and her eyes confirms what her ears had heard.

Granulo!

He reaches around her and shoves the door closed.

"What are you doing here?" she forces the words through a tightening throat.

"You aren't pleased to see me?" he teases, melting snow dripping from his bush of a beard.

"I never wanted to see you again." Melia backs up to the door and looks over Granulo's shoulder. Ballomar stands, calmly stirring the tallow as she had asked.

"Oh, that's not what I told your brother here," Granulo says, turning slightly to nod at Ballomar. "I told him what close friends we have become over the past year."

"Friends?" Melia spits the word as she slips sideways toward Ballomar. "This is no friend of mine, brother. Do not trust him and don't believe a word he says."

Ballomar looks from her to Granulo, confused. He drops the ladle and wipes his hands on his jacket. "He said he was sent by the warriors of your tribe to check on you, Melia. Why don't you trust him?"

"I will not burn your ears with stories of what this man has done to me," Melia says, not taking her eyes off Granulo. Could he assault her right there, in front of Ballomar? Perhaps. He has no shame.

Ballomar frowns. "You should leave us to our work," he says to Granulo, catching on quickly and moving between him and Melia. Ballomar is nearly a head shorter than Granulo, but standing with his arms hanging loosely at his side, he appears powerful, in charge. His voice is her father's, commanding and sure.

"Go back to the house and announce your arrival," Ballomar says. "Perhaps Milo will find some way for you to prove some worth."

The change in Ballomar's posture has its intended impact, and Granulo smiles sheepishly. "Yes," he says. "I have much to talk with him about. I needn't waste my time here with the cooks." He snorts and swings the door open. It slams against the wall and gapes open. He takes a couple of steps outside, turns, and points at Melia. "We should get reacquainted later," he says. "I'll come looking for you. You can't hide from your friend Granulo."

Melia leaps forward, throws the door closed, and stands with her back against it, her chest heaving.

"I'm sorry," Ballomar says, picking up the ladle where he had dropped it and hooking it on the side of the vat. He walks to her. "I had no idea he wasn't what he said."

"He's a rapist and a liar. I'm sure he didn't tell you that."

Ballomar looks down. "Is he the father of your baby?"

Tears fill Melia's eyes as she shakes her head. "No, Ruggie was." She sees the confusion in her brother's eyes.

"And what happened to him?"

"Mother chased him away."

"Why?"

"Mother thought he was her son. That's why it is hard for me to accept that you are." Melia pushes herself up straight and wipes angrily at her tears. "We have to finish our work here, or I will not only be at the mercy of Granulo but all of the Franks as well. Let's get these candles made and take our place in the cistern."

"You have not felt safe for a long time, have you?"

Melia looks into Ballomar's eyes. Once again, it strikes her how much he looks like her father. She regrets having turned against him in the house. Perhaps he would be the one who will understand her better than any of the others.

"No," she says quietly, accepting the arms he holds out to her. "I have not. Maybe no woman ever does."

Melia and Ballomar work for another hour, pouring the cooling wax into the sulfur crystals, and making sure the wicks stay in place. Melia works in a daze, stunned by Granulo's reappearance. Even with her brother at her side—yes, she is beginning to accept him now—she feels more vulnerable than when she waited for Hermann to creep down the ladder in Mogantiacum.

Even if they manage to evade the Franks, will she be at the mercy of Granulo again? Perhaps no one can protect her from him. Perhaps he will prey on her the rest of her life.

THE FRANKS

Greta's heart pounds; even the veins behind her ears throb. She stands in the villa's main room next to the hearth, trying to stay calm, sipping a cup of fermented cider. Usually, she drinks intoxicating beverages sparingly, not liking the cloudy sensation that either cider or beer bring on. But now she needs it. She had lost both of her children, and she has found them both. Now she is terrified that they'll be taken from her again.

Greta hasn't prayed to Thor, Woden, or Frigga since the tribe settled in the villa. The Gallic villagers had converted decades before, and the local deacons had visited the villa many times, trying to convince the Arian Suevi to accept Catholic orthodoxy, reject their pagan gods, and be baptized. Greta and Milo resisted the pull, but now she wonders if she would feel better if she had the Christian God and his disciples on her side. Perhaps it is too late to ask their God to save her and her children, but if the villa succeeds in warding off the Franks, she will consider it.

Late in the afternoon, Ballomar and Melia bring the fumigating votives to the house, and Greta helps set them around the main room and the rooms where the families sleep. They set a dry stick of kindling in each room so they can light the candles quickly when the time comes. Then Melia and Ballomar pull the heavy stones off the top of the cistern, scraping them back onto the floor. Greta drops to her knees and sniffs at the dark cavern. It smells musty and moldy, but it would be bearable for a short time.

Her children—sister and brother—look comfortable with each other already, Greta notices. Perhaps the common experience of enslavement was the reason. They lack the awkwardness that usually grows between brothers and sisters once they reach the age when sex is both intriguing and scary.

Ballomar lets himself down onto the cistern's upper platform first, and Greta hands him a lighted candle—one of Melia's nearly smokeless tapers, heavy on the beeswax. "Check for rats and snakes," she calls down to him.

Greta and Melia wait for his answer. "There is nothing to fear here," he calls through the opening after a few moments. He reaches up for Melia. "Come on down."

Melia lowers herself into his arms, and Greta sees her reach for the candle and survey the cavern herself.

"He's right," she says. "A few beetles, but nothing else. We'll be safe here."

Relieved, Greta hands down three wool blankets, a tin of biscuits, a jug of cider, and a couple more candles. Lastly, she hands Ballomar a bucket for their waste and a tall stool.

"There are bugs on the water," Melia calls up to Greta.

"Better water bugs than the Franks," she responds, trying to sound cheerful. "Come back up now and eat some supper."

Ballomar climbs onto the stool and his head and torso pop up above the opening. With his palms on the floor, he hoists himself back up into the room. He makes it look easy, and Greta feels proud. He reaches down and helps Melia climb up. They leave the stones where they are, and Melia goes to the sleeping room to feed her baby.

"Where is Milo?" Ballomar asks Greta.

"He left with Granulo to warn the village and get one of the longhouses ready for us. We'll stay there while the votives burn," Greta says. She sees Ballomar's face cloud over with distaste. "What is wrong, son?" she asks.

"Granulo," Ballomar says. "He is not a good man, is he?"

"I don't know," Greta says. She thinks about the story Melia had told her months before, when she lost the water bucket. "Perhaps he isn't. I know that Melia doesn't like him, but I don't think she should be so particular. She should be married by now. There are not many men here in the village who haven't already taken a wife."

"He threatened to force himself on her," Ballomar says. "I heard him in the candle shop. She isn't safe with him here." His voice is suddenly angry.

Greta spins around to face him. How quickly he has taken Melia's side! "She's been running from him since we left the Rhine. Maybe if she accepted him, he would be kind to her."

"I believe she has a good reason to run from him."

"She isn't a virgin, Ballomar," Greta retorts. "She was lying with a man in Mogantiacum. Where do you think that baby of hers came from?"

Ballomar draws close and looks down at her, frowning, his eyes narrowed to slits, and Greta backs up. Why is he angry at her? He should understand. He should be more concerned about Melia's behavior, not about Granulo's intentions.

"I know what slave women endure, Mother," he says, his voice nearly a growl. "What Melia needs is your protection. I think you should not defend that man." Ballomar turns toward the door and pulls his bear skin off a hook. "I'm going to see Milo and find out what other trouble Granulo has in mind."

Milo and Ballomar return as darkness settles over the villa, and Greta is relieved that Granulo isn't with them. Even if she doesn't think he is a bad match for her daughter, she worries that he might notice the displaced floor stones, realize their plan, and betray them to the Franks. Already she can see that he and Ballomar do not care for each other.

"The village is ready," Milo reports. "You will go to the longhouse as soon as you light the votives. Clotild will feed little Ballomar while Melia is down below." Clotild delivered a child two days earlier who lived only a few hours, and her breasts are heavy with milk, compounding the young girl's sorrow.

"Melia is lucky for that," Greta says. "Where is Granulo?"

Greta sees Milo and Ballomar exchange a glance. "He's in the village. We ordered him to stay there tomorrow when the Franks arrive."

"Why do you say that? He's a good strong man. You may need him if the Franks are intent on violence."

"We must hope they aren't," Milo says. "Even with Granulo, we haven't the men to stand against them. And I don't trust his wild nature. He may well betray us."

Greta watches Melia, who sits on a stool with the baby in her arms. Her eyes are wide and red, and Greta sees her wince at the mention of Granulo's name. When her daughter told her of her rape and torture at the hands of her owner in Mogantiacum, Greta hadn't comforted her. Why didn't she? How difficult had Melia's life been as a slave? Greta never asked to hear any more than Melia told her that first night in Mogantiacum. She hadn't wanted to know more about the pain she had brought on her daughter in selling her into slavery.

She watches as tears fill Melia's eyes, and wonders what Melia fears most: a return to slavery or Granulo. Why has it taken Ballomar only one day to know Melia's pain when Greta hasn't acknowledged it for a year?

THE SCOUTS BRING NEWS MID-MORNING. The Franks are on their way, and they are travelling fast. The Suevi men and women gather in one of the longhouses, no one wanting to be alone when the Franks arrive. Greta and a cousin wait with Melia, Ballomar, and Canuto, ready to help them slip into the cistern at Milo's warning.

No one speaks. Greta can feel Melia's fear, and Ballomar's anxiety. He paces the room, circling the opening to the cistern. Caputo fidgets with his wooden horse, which he plans to take into the cistern with him. Greta sips cider.

Finally, a shout floats over the wall, and they hear Milo respond to the foreigners with a friendly hello. The small group inside the villa swings into action. Greta helps Canuto drop down into the cistern first. Melia stokes the coals in the firepit, and Ballomar places a tower of wood on top of them. Their hope is that big fire will increase the draft up through the roof and keep fumigating smoke from seeping down to them.

Melia sits on the edge of the cistern and jumps down. Greta hands her the candle and backs away. She and Ballomar push the stone cover mostly over the hole, and he squeezes through and drops to the ledge. Greta hands him a lighted tinder, and her cousin gives the stone a final push to close the opening. They pull the table over the cistern, arranging the stools around it.

Greta's hand shakes as she sticks a long tinder in the fire and waits for it to light. Shielding the flame with her palm, she lights her cousin's stick, and they walk back into the villa's inner rooms to light the votives. It will be just a couple of minutes before they start to release the sulfur; the women work fast.

In the sleeping room, the first two votives light quickly, but

Greta fumbles with the third and drops it. She leaves it on the floor and moves through the other rooms, transferring the flame from the first stick to the other kindling. Somehow, she grows calmer as she moves through the villa. Perhaps it is the cider. Perhaps it is the realization that it won't be long now until they know what happens.

Lighting the last of her votives, she remembers that the fumigation was Melia's idea. Pride swells in her chest. Her daughter is clever, and her son is strong. Her new son and grandson are healthy, and her new husband is a strong leader. She throws the last of her lighting stick in the firepit and waits for her cousin to finish. They sneeze as they pull the villa door closed behind them.

As Greta rushes through the snow to the longhouse, she sees Milo and the handful of elders out on the road, gesturing to a group of foreigners on horseback. The exchange is spirited, although it appears only one of the Franks speaks Suevi, the others shouting words for him to translate.

The cousin knocks on the longhouse door, and they wait for someone to lift the bar and let them in. She turns to watch the Franks dismount and Milo lead them back into the forest, heading toward the funeral pyre and the charred remains that are supposedly those of Ballomar.

The longhouse is weirdly quiet, even though it is packed to the walls with Suevi women and children. Only the soft sounds of the animals stirring below them color the silence. The women sit with babies and young children in their arms and laps, and the older children sit together near the fire, their eyes wide. Greta looks around and sees the unfortunate young mother is already feeding little Ballomar, a beatific smile on her face as she looks down at the suckling infant.

For a long time, they wait for news; the silence is excruciating. Did the Franks believe the story Milo told them about Ballomar?

Greta expects they will search the longhouses, as well as the villa. The women and children pose no threat, but the Franks won't have any sympathy for them either.

The longhouse door shakes as if struck by battering ram, not a fist, and the women and children jump. Greta looks around at them and nods, reassuringly. Even if she doesn't feel safe, she doesn't want the others to panic.

"Milo?" she calls at the door.

"Open," he answers. He sounds calm and sure. Greta lifts the bar over the door, and Milo steps in. Behind him stand several Franks, their long hair hanging down over their shoulders, spears in hand and hand axes hanging at their sides. The women behind her gasp. The children run to their mothers and bury the faces in their coats.

"We must let the men assure themselves that Ballomar is not here," Milo says softly. "You must stay calm and still, and you won't be harmed." Then he turns and lets the Franks stomp around him.

The women cringe as the men move through the crowd, searching faces. A few push back the sleeves of tunics with the tips of their swords. Greta realizes they are looking for slave stamps, just as Ballomar had predicted. They exchange few words in their unintelligible Frankish tongue.

Finally, the largest Frank—one with an intimidating set of elk horns on his head—heads back to the door. They are finished. Milo follows them out and Greta hears the men push through the cattle and goats underneath them. A goat's pained bleat signals the animal's quick demise.

Milo calls and knocks again on the door and Greta opens it. He leans in and whispers, "They are going to search the villa next. The candles are lighted?"

Greta nods, gaining confidence that things are progressing as planned. As long as Granulo stays away and doesn't initiate trouble, as long as the votives do their duty, the tribe might survive this visit with no loss but one goat. But now she wonders how many times they'll have to do this again. Will the Franks come and force Ballomar and Melia into the cistern over and over? She can't imagine they can fool the Franks with this subterfuge more than once.

Loud coughs and angry shouts rise over the villa's walls, and Greta peers out the door past Milo to see the Franks running out through the front gate, clutching at their throats.

"Didn't you tell them about the sulfur?" Greta whispers.

Milo smiles crookedly. "Yes, but they didn't believe me or they didn't understand. I scratched my head and told them we had lice and bedbugs. After that, one man stepped back from me, but they insisted on searching the villa."

"It looks like the votives worked."

"Yes, they won't believe anyone could hide in that smoke."

Greta is about to return to the warmth of the longhouse when she spies a lone figure walking from the direction of the village with a hand axe.

Granulo! She looks to Milo, who frowns as he spies the young man as well.

"I will go and stop him," Milo says. "Go inside and rebolt the door. Let's hope our young warrior doesn't betray us."

THE CISTERN

Down in the cistern, Ballomar lets Caputo sit on his lap. The youngster's lanky legs are nearly as long as a man's, but he is still a sprite of a boy. Melia wonders if he is remembering his enslavement and dreads being recaptured. He never speaks of that time, and she doesn't press for details. She reaches over to pat him on the knee.

As Ballomar settles with his back against the wall of the cistern and puts his arms around Caputo, Melia covers herself with a blanket to ward off the chill of the cistern and keep her teeth from chattering. Since they have decided on this hiding place, she has been planning to pray to both the gods of her villagers and the god of the Christians, but as a little of the fumes sink and hang just below the floor of the main room, she concentrates on breathing easily, and listens for footsteps on the stones above. If any of them cough, they will be discovered.

They wait in silence for many long minutes. Melia tries to

imagine where the Franks and her uncle are in each moment. Are they trudging through the drifts to the funeral pyre? Are the Franks inspecting the long houses, now, looking for women with slave stamps? Are they going to brave the fumigating haze and run through the villa?

"How did you escape?" Ballomar's whisper surprises her. Do they dare risk being overheard? Hearing nothing above them that indicates anyone has entered the villa, she answers.

"My owners died," she whispers. "We buried the wife in the candlewax. The husband died in the street, fighting. Or more likely, running from the fighting."

Ballomar nods in the dim light. "You have survived, and you are strong."

Melia shrugs. Is it true? Is she strong? What does strong mean? She cannot fend off the likes of Granulo. As a woman, she will never lead a raiding party or stand up against an armed attack. Her place had been at the back of the wagons for months. And now it is deep in the villa, helping care for the children, making a place for men to come home to.

As if he can read her mind, Ballomar continues. "There are many ways to be strong. I saw it in the slave women in Lutetia. Some were weak and debased, and they suffered more for their lack of resistance. Others had spirit like yours. They were abused, but they held their heads high and created what peace they could in their minds or in their homes. I could not imagine dredging up such sanguinity in the face of such degradation."

Melia considers his words. She held her head high in Mogantiacum despite her nightly abuse by Hermann, but once she returned to the road with her mother, she felt only shame. Why? She had nothing to be ashamed of, regardless of what Granulo thought.

"Thank you for those kind words," she whispers, finally. "I have not thought well of myself for some time. I hang my head and rarely speak up. Even my mother, who sold me into slavery herself, commands more respect than I have."

"Yes, I can see that," he answers. "It is time for you to shed your slave countenance. You have saved the three of us. No one else could have done this."

Melia peers through the candle-lit doom at Ballomar's face. He looks so much like her father. Was her father also so wise? She wishes she could remember him more as an adult and a leader than as the stoic father.

Suddenly, a door slams against the wall above them, and voices and heavy footfalls announce the arrival of the Franks. Melia feels her heart leap in her chest, and she holds her breath. Blood pounds in her ears, and she shakes uncontrollably.

She is not strong! She wants to scoot on her butt across the cistern shelf and huddle with Ballomar and Caputo, but fear freezes her in place. She focuses on the echoes of the Franks overhead. As she expects, they cough, and someone shouts in the language of Fritigil. Apparently, it is not an order to leave, as boots continue to pound on the stone floor above. She hears parchment rip, and she imagines the Franks are slashing at the window skins to clear the air.

Will they put out the candles and clear the air fast enough to allow them to search the villa? Melia looks up at the ceiling of the cistern, expecting at any moment to hear the table scrape along the floor and see a crack of light break through between dislodging stones. She lets out her breath, breathes in slowly, her chest stuttering.

The shouting and coughing continue, but it sounds as if fewer men are now inside now, and eventually, the footfalls above them retreat. They are leaving. Melia reaches her hand out to touch Ballomar's shoulder and feels him shudder with surprise.

As the men's hacking coughs recede, silence settles around and above them, Melia breathes normally again, even though her heart continues to pound. But still they have to wait. Who will come to open the cistern for them? Her uncle or the Franks?

"What did they say?" she asks Ballomar in a whisper. "Were they giving up their search?"

"I could not tell," Ballomar whispers.

"Are they gone?" Caputo says a little too loudly. Melia touches her fingers to her lips, and he nods. He understands. Trauma has made him a wise little man.

They wait another hour, which is as long as it will take for the house to clear of the fumes. And finally, the table above them scrapes along the floor, and Melia's heart skips again. The stones that seal them in move aside, and she looks up, blinking at the bright light of day.

"Melia? Ballomar?" asks her uncle, and Melia sobs with relief. "Are you guys okay down there?"

"We're alive," she answers. "Help us out of here."

Ballomar holds the stool still, and Melia helps Caputo step up. He is swallowed up by Milo's arms and disappears into the light. Melia climbs up on the stool and waits for her uncle's hand to pull her out. She stands shakily and watches Ballomar's head below catch the light. He throws the blankets and the candle up out of the hole and lifts the stool up for Milo to retrieve. Milo helps him climb out, and the three former slaves stand for a moment, letting their eyes adjust to the light. Melia opens her arms, and they cling to each other for a long minute. The front door is wide open, letting in winter's clear, cold air and blowing out the last of the candles' fumes. Greta walks in with little Ballomar, her face wet with tears of relief. Only then does Melia allow her own tears to gather and fall.

THE WAY MILO TELLS IT, Granulo had come close to sabotage. As he approached the Franks, he shouted Ballomar's name. Coughing and wiping their eyes, the scouts paid him no heed.

Perhaps his accent was too foreign. The man who carried the slain goat was the one who spoke Suevi, and before Granulo could make himself heard, that Frank had reached the horses back on the road, out of earshot. Milo and two other men threw the traitor to the ground. One held him down in the snow with a knee in his back and a knife to his throat, and Milo escorted the wheezing Franks back to their horses. They wasted no time before heading south.

In the end, Granulo had proven useful by showing the Franks that the Suevi had no problem mistreating their own. It might have helped them believe the story of Ballomar's demise.

Granulo is shackled and thrown into the barn below one of the longhouses to await the judgment of the elders. However, before the men can meet in the villa the next day to determine his punishment, the boy who feeds the cattle and goats finds him lying in a pool of blood, his head thrown back and his throat slit, his dead eyes staring blindly at the ceiling.

No one admits to the slaying—indeed, no one is accused—but Melia is sure she knows who wielded the knife. She never confronts her mother about it, and the question dies quickly among the villagers. No one is sorry to see the troublesome warrior gone, least of all Melia.

When the Franks return a month later from their survey of the Roman strongholds in the south, they stop only to take another goat before moving on. Perhaps their memory of choking on the fumes of sulfur is enough to spur them along. Other than the goat's meat, the villa holds little but bad memories for them.

As spring approaches and summer ripens, the new Suevi settlement surrounding the villa grows into a permanent village. The Suevi warriors who continued south into Aquitaine and Hispania never return either to settle down or to search for Granulo. The marriage between one of the original Gallic villagers and a Suevi widow begins a trend that will blur the lines between the Germani and the Gauls over the next decades.

The Roman church, meanwhile, fills the vacuum left by the departed Roman administration in governing the region, litigating disputes and collecting taxes that had once gone to Rome. And most of the Suevi get used to hearing if not speaking Gaul's vulgar Latin. Some like Melia and Canuto have heard it enough in Mogantiacum to pick it up quickly.

As the church's power grows, most of the Suevi convert to Catholicism, and the Bishop Martin arrives with a large entourage to consecrate a new basilica and install a priest. Shortly thereafter, a deaconess starts a small convent beside the church grounds.

More Germanii pour over the Rhine River into Gaul. Stilicho's field army is busy battling Constantine, the self-proclaimed emperor from Britannia intent on ascending the throne. Germani refugees stream through the village, unfettered by Roman legions. Most continue on to join the Suevi, Alans, and Vandals in Hispania, but a few stay and set down stakes.

The tension between Melia and her mother evaporates after Greta slits Granulo's throat, although Melia isn't sure why she had done it. Was it for nearly betraying her and Ballomar, or was it for attacking Melia back in the woods?

Ballomar tends livestock and develops a reputation for healing wounds and setting broken bones, skills he'd learned among the Franks. Melia's candle business grows and supplies more and more of the nearby villages. She procures tallow and beeswax from livestock and bee farmers near and far. Canuto becomes her assistant, and Ballomar delivers the raw goods. Their short time in the dark cistern together, although fairly uneventful, has bonded the three of them in the way that war does soldiers, and Melia finally starts to feel she has a home.

Still, she can't shake thoughts of Ruggie.

THE LETTER

One warm, rainy summer afternoon, taking a break from the stuffy candle shop, Melia straps little Ballomar onto her back and walks to the old village square. She wends her way through the merchant stalls and finds the small table under an eave at where the village scribe conducts his business.

"I need to send a letter to Castra Regina," she says in the local vulgar Latin, stepping out of the rain and throwing off her hood.

The old man looks up quizzically.

"From who?"

"Melia."

"To anyone in particular there?"

"Yes. To the brewery."

"How do you know there's a brewery there?"

Melia frowns. She hadn't expected the scribe to push back or be so difficult. She was paying him to do this.

"Someone told me," she answers.

The scribe sits back against the wall of the bakery and grins broadly. "Perhaps he was mistaken."

Melia throws her arms out at her sides, irritated at the scribe's tease. Perhaps he is bored, sitting there all day, waiting for a customer. But Melia isn't looking for entertainment. She wants service.

"I'm certain he wasn't mistaken," she says.

"How did you know him?"

Melia takes a deep breath and leans forward with her palms on his table. "What difference does it make how I know him? I will have paid you even if I am wrong about everything. How much will it cost?"

Still, the old scribe isn't in a hurry. He eyes her, as if evaluating her not as a customer, but as a woman to be bedded. A year before, she would have cringed under his inspection, but she is stronger now. Her poise has grown as her business has blossomed.

"Today?" Melia says, encouraging an answer. "Could we get on with this business now?"

The old man drawls and sits up. "How long will this letter be?"

"Short. 'Ruggie, my brother is here. You have a son.'"

The old man counts the words on his fingers and frowns. "That doesn't make sense, Melia." He stresses her name, assuming a new level of familiarity.

"Oh, it will to Ruggie," she says. "And tell him where we are."

"Maybe this Ruggie doesn't want to have a son."

Melia laughs. She has wondered the same thing. But finding out involves much less risk than nearly anything she's done in the months since she'd seen him last.

"I am not here to argue with you, my good man," she says. "This is simple. Can you write it or not?"

The scribe nods. "Don't be impatient, young woman. I like to help the pretty ones. Perhaps if this Ruggie doesn't answer, you will consider marrying me."

Melia rolls her eyes. "We will see." If he wants to tease, she can too. "Meanwhile, I guess I should learn to be a scribe myself, and I would never have to haggle with the likes of you."

The old man chuckles. "I do not think that is a woman's place. It requires years of learning. But, yes, I can write your letter, and it will not cost much." He names his price.

Melia reaches into the small purse hooked to her belt and counts out the coins. "Can you send it to Regina for me?"

The scribe, still unhurried, sits back again and strokes his beard. "I hear that the bishop is sending a young priest down the Danube in a few days on a mission to convert Arians. Perhaps he will agree to carry your letter. But I will need more coins to arrange it."

"How do you know he will still want you?" Greta asks that evening as she and Melia finish cleaning after supper.

"That's why I sent the letter. To find out."

"You may have wasted your coin."

"We will see," Melia says. She rinses their beer mugs out in the sink and sets them on the shelf.

"He may have married," Greta says. "A wife won't be very happy to know you are writing to him."

"If he has married, Mother, he will not tell her, and he will stay with her."

"And what if he comes and takes you away? Will you take Ballomar?"

"Of course. A boy should be raised with his mother and father."

"But young Milo will miss him."

Melia knows that is true. The boys have spent their first

several months together, and they are inseparable. They sleep in the same bed and crawl around together during the day, never losing sight of each other.

"Will you go away with him if he comes?"

Melia pauses and thinks for a moment.

"I think not," she concludes. "But I do not know how I'll feel when I see him. *If* I see him. I don't want to leave. I don't know what Ruggie will want either, but whatever happens, it will be up to me to decide where I live. I have work in this village, and I have a son and a brother here."

"Two brothers and a mother."

"Yes, a mother and a stepfather and two brothers. Cousins. Everyone here is precious to me." Saying that, Melia decides. "If Ruggie comes and wants to be with me and little Ballomar, he will have to stay. And the village could use a fine brewer like him."

"You talk like a man sometimes, Melia. If your attitude does not change when Ruggie comes—if Ruggie comes—he'll probably leave you again."

Melia spins around to her mother. How can she say that?

"You know, Ruggie would not have left for Regina without me if it had not been for you," Melia snaps.

Her mother grimaces and sits down at the table. "I am sorry," she says. "I am sorry for that. But I did not know. I did not know."

Melia looks past her mother to watch little Ballomar and Milo on the floor, playing with the stick and straw dolls the older Ballomar had made for them. She surprised herself that afternoon, making the decision to send the note to Ruggie and then making it happen so quickly.

She longs for Ruggie's arms. She needs his touch. His face dominates her pleasant dreams now; Hermann visits her nightmares only rarely.

Melia sits down across from her mother and reaches out for her hands.

"I know you did not know. There has been too much …" She stops. There had been too much of everything: running, slavery, rape, death. Her mother did not cause it all. She, too, has lost so much—a husband, a sister, her village.

And through it all, Melia knows, she herself has grown stronger, maybe now deserving Ballomar's words down in the cistern. In Mogantiacum, she thought her future depended on rescue. First by her mother. Then Ruggie. But in the end, she had rescued herself, her brother, and Caputo. Her escape wasn't from Mogantiacum or even from Granulo—it was from the way she had come to think of herself on the road to this village, as the weak, worthless whore Matildis told her she was.

But she isn't. She took what she learned from her enslavement and used it to make a life. She will stay in the village and make the most beautiful candles in all of Gaul. She will raise her young Ballomar to be happy and strong. She will learn to be a scribe, if only to show up those who think she cannot. She will be the one who would decide what her future will look like.

She will stay, yes, but it is now her choice. She needs no one's rescue.

THE ANSWER

Greta runs out into the villa courtyard to break up a fight between her son and her grandson. They have learned to walk only a couple of months before, but already, they run around with the courtyard curs, getting themselves into trouble. Young Milo is much bigger than his nephew and a bit of a bully, but little Ballomar refuses to be intimidated, and he fights back stubbornly. They will always be best friends, but for now, Greta intervenes often to keep them from hurting each other.

Returning to the kitchen, Greta sits down at the table and unfolds the letter the bishop's emissary delivered minutes before. She flattens the crinkles out on the table, the same table they brought from the candle shop where she found Melia in Mogantiacum. How long ago that seems! Has it been only two years?

Greta can't read, but when the courier read the letter to her, she made him repeat it until she had the words memorized. Now she moves her finger along the lines, pretending she recognizes the words as she recites them.

She can barely sit still as she waits for Melia to return from the village market so she can share the message.

Dearest Melia:

I have received your letter. I am leaving today to come to you, and soon I will embrace you and our son.

Ruggie

AUTHOR'S NOTE

On Christmas Eve, at the end of the year 406, during a particularly cold winter in late antiquity, my fictional Melia sent up a silent prayer that her mother would cross the Rhine River and change Melia's world. Her silent prayer was answered—the world did change overnight—but not just for Melia. Thousands—perhaps tens of thousands—of "barbarians" crossed the frozen Rhine days later, on New Year's Eve, and the Roman *limites* dissolved.

Some historians have painted that and similar events of the same period as catastrophic, as transforming Western civilization, and dooming the Roman Empire. Others, more recently, have argued that the crossing of the Rhine was only a minor event in a long process of decline and rebuilding—the gradual fall of Imperial Rome, the emergence of Germanic kingdoms from Gaul to the Balkans, the origin of modern Europe, and the birth of nations that now define the Western world.

Over the past few years, I devoured many versions of these events, trying to come to my own conclusion: Was the fall of Rome a cataclysmic, world-changing event as Edmond Gibbons portrayed it in *The Rise and Fall of the Roman Empire,* or was the decline of Rome much like other transitions in history resulting from climate change and population pressures that pushed people around the globe and brought disquieting political, cultural, and ethnic shifts?

I didn't need to decide for the purposes of telling Melia's story. Melia isn't aware of the significance of the migrations to history. As Lisa Scottoline, author of *Eternal,* noted in an interview, "You don't know you're entering a historical period when you are in one." In the context of a lifetime—the building block of historical fiction—no one can know whether the changes they see happening around them amount to a shift of tectonic proportions or not. And, to Melia, Ruggie, Greta, and others who populate my novel, it is similarly unknowable. All they know is what they experience.

To them, it was the end of their world as they knew it. To the soldiers in the military outpost of Mogantiacum (near modern Mainz), it was the end of the world as they knew it as well. To the provinces of Roman Gaul came waves of Germanic peoples. Some of the changes were gradual. Over the next century, the world as the Romans knew it did come to an end, as first a Gothic king became emperor, and eventually, the Empire was reduced to little more than Ravenna, Rome, and southern Italy while new kingdoms rose and fell in the provinces. Wealth was destroyed, classic Greek and Latin knowledge and philosophy were pushed underground or lost, and the Catholic Church stepped into and filled the political vacuum left by the fallen Empire.

The difficulty of writing about such transformations is that they can be seen only over an expanse of time longer than any one person's life. The end of the world as one person knows it can be a personal tragedy—the death of a husband or wife or child. Can that serve as a metaphor for a larger social or political evolution, or are our personal tragedies too common, too inevitable that they can't stand for anything other than the existential riddle of living within a tiny speck of time in the 600,000 years of human habitation?

THE INSPIRATION FOR THIS NOVEL came from a lecture by Purdue University professor of English and Medieval Studies, Dorsey Armstrong, in her course, "Turning Points in Medieval History." When Dr. Armstrong described a bitterly cold New Year's Eve in 406 when the Rhine River froze, allowing the starving and frustrated Germanic tribes to cross into the Roman Empire, I got goosebumps. I wish I could tell a story as well as she does.*

I can't imagine a high school student in a minimally effective school district in America who hasn't learned that "barbarians" sacked Rome and precipitated the fall of the Roman Empire. Yes, Barbarians! Vandals! Huns! Visigoths! If they went on to take ancient history classes in college, however, those well-educated students would have learned that "barbarians" is both a simplistic and derogatory construct. And they would have discovered that there were as many internal causes of the decline of the empire as there were external ones.

What I think still persists, even among those well-read, is the notion that the Germanic tribes "invaded" Gaul, Italia, Pannonia, Dacia, and Illyricum as armies of fanatic, barbaric warriors who sought to overthrow the empire. In writing *A Candlemaker's Woman*, I wanted to offer a counter-narrative to the story of the "barbarians" as an invasion.

The movement of the many different ethnic and culturally diverse populations over the Danube and the Rhine into the Empire in the third through sixth centuries is, perhaps, more fairly characterized as a "diaspora" not "invasion." Germanic and Gothic tribes were pushed west and south by people from the steppes of Western Asia, including the Huns, and by people from the lands south and east of the Black Sea, including the Saracens, themselves pushed outward by changing climates and war in their homelands. Powered by superior horsemanship—their huge mounts bred through centuries of nomadic and warring traditions—and the most sophisticated and advanced armor of the time, these people of the steppes forced the Suevi, Vandals and Alans to make brittle and fragile alliances with each other to undertake a desperate migration to find security and new lands for their villages and farms inside Gaul.

These "barbarians" were little interested in "conquering" the Roman Empire. They wanted to exist within it. Even Alaric—the Gothic King who sieged Rome in CE 410—sought not to defeat the Roman army, but to be awarded status in it. The empire had wealth, infrastructure, and cultural amenities that the farmers and their families envied. They wanted what migrating tribes before them had achieved—status as citizens. Since the middle of the third century, the Suevi, Vandals, and Alans knew that Franks, Alamanni, Burgundians, and Goths had been accepted into the empire as federates, often supplying the military manpower the Romans needed to organize and protect their borders. They wanted the same.

The tribes who crossed the frozen Rhine on Dec. 31, 406, were not just warriors, but also old men, women and children, traveling with oxen, sheep and goats, and crude wagons piled high with household goods and the moldboard plows they had developed for the heavy soils of the Germanic plains.

Rome's refusal to admit and settle these peoples peacefully changed—at least temporarily—the nature of leadership within the tribes. Rome wanted to negotiate with discrete equals, not with a tribal council. This forced the tribes to name kings—up to then, unusual for the less heirarchical Germani. It could be argued as well that Roman resistance radicalized and militarized the people, changing the nature of the Germanic villagers as the migrations progressed.

I owe this perspective to the historians who write and teach about late antiquity and the early Middle Ages, including Ian Wood, Peter Heather, Guy Halsell, John Drinkwater, Yitzak Hen, Kenneth W. Harl, Nancy Gauthier, Peter S. Wells, Chris Wickham, and Thomas F.X. Noble. Some of their books, articles and lectures I read in my research are listed in a short bibliography at the end of this book. I thank them all for their work, and to whatever extent my extrapolations from their writings and lectures are incorrect, it is my fault.

Fact and Fiction

From those writers and others, I have borrowed these historical facts for my story:

• Suevi, Alans, and Vandals crossed the frozen Rhine River at Mogantiacum on Dec. 31, 406.

• Stilicho pulled troops from the Rhine *limites* to bolster the defense of Italia, Pannonia, and Illyricum, the territories south of the Danube.

• Sassanid and Hunnic migrants from the steppes of Eastern and Central Asia pushed the "barbarians" before them.

• Constantine's ambition to march from Britannia to Italia to claim the title of Emperor added to Stilicho's military challenges.

• The Roman army relied on Germani recruits as military service became less popular among native and elite Romans.

• The Suevi, Vandals, and Alans moved into Iberia in the years following the Rhine crossing.

• The Franks attacked the Suevi east of the Rhine at Rome's behest. Vandals rescued the Suevi.

• Many Gallic Romans evacuated Gaul in response to and

ahead of the Germanic diaspora.

• Catholic Christianity grew more prevalent among formerly Arian Christian and pagan Germanic peoples after the migrations.

• The Franks increasingly controlled Northern Gaul and began exploratory missions into Aquitaine.

• Slavery was very common, representing at times and in places up to one-third of the population of the empire in early antiquity.

These elements are entirely from my imagination, but informed by research:

• All conversations and internal monologue of all characters.

• The characters Melia, Ruggie, Greta, Ballomar, Canuto, Milo and all other named Suevi; Dodi and Theo; and Hermann and Matildis, and their specific actions and activities.

• The route of Melia's family across Gaul, their settlement and their villa.

• The scouting party of Franks and their actions.

• The location and construction of the candlemaker's shop in Mogantiacum.

Other research from sources listed in the following bibliography helped me fashion the descriptions of candlemaking and beer brewing in late antiquity; common dress and hairstyles of Gallo-Romans, Suevi, Franks, and Alans; architecture and market activities in Mogantiacum; the cultural practices of Germanic tribes; and modes of migrant travel. I appreciate all the work non-fiction authors do that make historical fiction possible.

Modern Diaspora

If readers have misunderstood the mass migrations of late antiquity as invasions of culturally homogeneous and warlike "barbarians," they have a good excuse: they took place some fifteen centuries ago. But it doesn't take a particularly open mind or heart to see parallel stories in the movements of people from South and Central America and Mexico into the U.S. today, or the migrations of people from Middle Eastern war zones or dysfunctional North African nations into Western Europe.

Syrian refugees and Honduran migrants are not seeking to overthrow the European Union or the United States any more than Melia and her family sought to rule Gaul. The motivations of today's migrants are the same: they want safe places to raise their families, and they want an opportunity to work.

My own family—and probably yours—was no different. My Swiss great-grandparents came to the U.S. in the mid-to-late 1800s, my great-grandmother as an indentured servant, my great-grandfather as a farmer seeking a place to raise livestock. She died shortly after the birth of my grandfather, and great-grandfather left for Texas to reunite with fellow Swiss immigrants. Grandfather was raised by Iowa neighbors, and family lore held that he didn't speak English until he entered school. He reverted to French in his last years. My mother's family has been in the U.S. for centuries, coming here with the influx of Dutch and German citizens and, as most people were those days, as farmers. They settled in Pennsylvania, but when land became too precious there, my more immediate ancestors migrated to Iowa, again in search of opportunity.

If we look back far enough, we all walked out of Africa. Native Americans were likely northern Asians who migrated across the Bering Strait anytime between 25,000 and 5,000 years ago. They can claim the title "First Nation," as they did not displace an indigenous people, but their biological origin, going back to the beginning, was African as well. The Nazis' claim to much of Europe in WWII was based on an ersatz historical origin story blind to the reality that their ancient ancestors did not originate there, they migrated there. And they were not the first inhabitants of Germania, nor were they homogeneous, ethnically or culturally.

Mass migration is not new; it is human history. And it has never been easy. Before judging those who choose to move from one place to another, I hesitate, remembering that my birth in the United States was a matter of luck, not one of good judgment on my part or my parents'.

I grew up in Iowa. At times in my life, local snobs have snubbed me for not being a "native" of the states I have lived in as an adult—Colorado, Wisconsin, Illinois, Montana, Texas, Washington, or California. But I appreciate the freedom I've had to move from one state to another—to move for opportunity, or for love, or for a simple desire for a new environment.

*Professor Armstrong's lectures were also the inspiration for my first historical novel, *The Rebel Nun* (Blackstone Publishing, 2021), about a rebellion by nuns at a monastery in Gaul in the late sixth century.

—————————————————————

SOURCES

—————————————————————

Drinkwater, John and Hugh Elton, eds. *Fifth-Century Gaul: A Crisis of Identity?* (Cambridge, UK: Cambridge University Press, 1992), especially: "Barbarians in Gaul: the response of the poets," M. Roberts, pp 97-106 (on the nature of barbarian warriors); "Recovery: Social and Economic," an section introduction by the editors, pp. 107-109 (on economic and social changes); "Town and country in late antique Gaul: the example of Bordeaux," H. Sivan, pp. 132-143 (for descriptions of late antiquity villas and their resettlement and transformation); "The fifth-century villa: new life or death postponed," J. Percival, pp. 156-164 (on the survival and transformation of villas of antiquity); "Slavery, the Roman legacy," R. Samson, pp. 218-227 (on the prevalence and treatment of slaves); "Ethnicity, orthodoxy and community in Salvian of Marseilles," M. Maas, pp. 275-284 (on contemporary views of barbarians and Romans); "The Pirenne Thesis and fifth-century Gaul," R. Van Dam, pp. 321-334 (on the impact of the barbarians on the fall of the Roman Empire).

Ehrman, Bart D. *The Triumph of Christianity: How a Forbidden Religion Swept the World.* (New York: Simon and Schuster, 2018).

Gauthier, Nancy. "From the Ancient City to the Medieval Town: Continuity and Change in the Early Middle Ages," *The World of Gregory of Tours,* pp. 29-46.

Gregory of Tours, "Book IX," "Book X," *History of the Franks.* (San Bernadino, CA: First Rate Publishers, POD 2018, originally published 591), translation by Ernest Brehaut.

Guigot, M. Francois. *A Popular History of France,* republished on Createspace, Translation by Robert Black, 2016.

Halsall, Guy. Bar*barian Migrations and the Roman West, 376-568* (Cambridge, UK: Cambridge University Press, 2007).

Hen, Yitzhak, *Culture and Religion in Merovingian Gaul AD 481-751* (Leiden, The Netherlands: E.J. Brill, 1995).

Hochstetler, Donald. *A Conflict of Traditions: Women in Religion in the Early Middle Ages (500-840)* (Lanham, Maryland: University Press of America, 1992); pp 20-24; 134-139.

Lifshitz, Felice. *Religious Women in Early Carolingian Francia* (New York: Fordham University Press, 2014).

MacMullen, Ramsay. *Christianity and Paganism in the Fourth to Eighth Centuries* (New Haven, CN: Yale University Press, 1997)

Musset, Lucien, *The Germanic Invasions: The making of Europe 400-600 A.D.* (New York: Barnes and Noble Books, 1993), First American Edition.

Nelson, Max. *The Barbarian's Beverage: A History of Beer in Ancient Europe* (New York: Routledge, 2005).

Norris, Janice Racine. "Nuns and Other Religious: Women and Christianity in the Middle Ages," *Women in Medieval Western European Culture* (New York and London: Garland Publishing, 1999), ed. Linda E. Mitchell.

Wells, Peter S. *Barbarians to Angels: The Dark Ages Reconsidered* (New York: W.W. Norton and Company, 2008).

Wergeland, Agnes Mathilde. *Slavery in Germanic Society During the Middle Ages* (London: Classic Reprint Series, Forgotten Books, FB &c Ltd., 2018). Originally published by University of Chicago Press, 1916.

Whitney, Elspeth, "Witches, Saints, and Other "Others": Women and Deviance in Medieval Culture," *Women in Medieval Western European Culture*, Ch. 17, ed. Linda E. Mitchell, (New York and London: Garland Publishing, 1999).

Wickham, Chris. *The Inheritance of Rome: Illuminating the Dark Ages, 400-1000* (New York: Penguin Group, 2009).

Wood, Ian, *The Merovingian Kingdoms 450-751* (Routledge: London and New York, 2014).

THANKS

Writing this book was more of a solo effort than I would have liked. I left my writing community in California in the midst of the final drafts and felt adrift at first. I have now made new friends in Colorado, and I will enjoy their advice, empathy, and sympathy going forward.

I thank the Dorland Mountain Arts Colony for accepting my application for a month's residency in the quiet foothills near Temecula, CA. Most of this book's first drafts were written in near solitude there, as the pandemic kept me and the other residents from interacting. And I thank the Vashon Artists Residency in Washington state for supporting my efforts as I finished this manuscript and started another.

Thanks also to Janet Day, Nancy Holt, Smith Holt, Jodi Bowersox, Jeanette Minniti, Jean Jacobson, Ellen Fisher, Logan Steiner, Ginny Purvis-Smith, Margaret Moore, Sandra Dallas, and Griffin Brady for welcoming me to my new Colorado home with their support and encouragement. Thanks to Cargo for allowing me to visit, bring toys, and run around like her crazy sister labrador in her backyard.

And Ben. This could not have been written without your love. Thank you, thank you, thank you.

BOOK CLUB
DISCUSSION QUESTIONS

• Did this novel change your impressions or understanding of the barbarian invasions that coincided with the fall of the Roman Empire? If so, in what way?

• Do you see any parallels between the mass migrations of the fourth and fifth centuries and today's mass migrations in Europe and on the southern border of the U.S.?

• Much historical fiction about the fall of Rome and the barbarian invasions is told from the point of view of military leaders, kings, and legionnaires. What is gained from this new perspective: that of a young female slave and a family chased from their homelands?

• How did Rome's treatment of migrants change the behavior and intentions of those who crossed into Gaul? Could Rome's leaders have avoided plunder and bloodshed by choosing a different way to deal with the mass migrations?

• For most U.S. readers, the word "slavery" evokes the horror of slavery in the American South before the Civil War. Does the prevalence of slavery in the Roman Empire and the Middle Ages surprise you? Has it changed how you think about the history of slavery?

• In what ways were the laws pertaining to slavery in the Empire and the Middle Ages different from those in the early American South?

• Compare little Caputo's bondage with Melia's enslavement. In what ways were Melia's purchase by the candlemaker both more horrible and more serendipitous?

• Greta's relationship with her daughter goes through many stages in the novel. Why do you think Greta was unsympathetic to Melia after their reunion in Mogantiacum? Did you find yourself getting angry at Greta for it?

• Childbirth was a dangerous endeavor throughout history (and still is), and Fritigil's death was not unusual in antiquity and the Middle Ages. How has the experience of childbirth changed and not changed over the centuries?

• Melia's self-reliance and hopes for independence grow over the length of the novel. What lessons did she learn about herself and her destiny?

ABOUT THE AUTHOR

Marj Charlier is the author of contemporary women's and historical novels. Her novel *The Rebel Nun* (Blackstone, 2021) was named the best historical fiction and best fiction overall (Herb Tabac CIPA Choice Award) in 2023 by the Colorado Independent Publishers Association. She lives in Colorado Springs with her husband, the journalist Ben Miller.

www.ingramcontent.com/pod-product-compliance
Lightning Source LLC
Chambersburg PA
CBHW060652190726
48289CB00002B/379